Minus the Imple

It's simple, really...

A fictionalized true story
by Robert R. Chandler

Edited by Frances M. Reed and Robert R. Chandler

Minus the Imple - Twelfth Edition
© 2008 by Robert R. Chandler and Privileged Publishing

ISBN
978-0-6151-9772-2

Printed in the United States of America.

Prologue

My little Italian grandmother always made me feel special. In her broken English, she'd often tell me I had a good heart and a kind soul. I remember asking her what she meant by "a soul." She tried to describe, as best she could, her personal beliefs on the topic. She explained that each of us has a soul and that God makes every person complete by blessing him or her with a unique spirit. She said that people may look alike, as in the case of twins, but their souls are not the same. Their souls are the true essence of who they are.

She went on to explain that some people have evil in their souls, and their actions are a reflection of the evil that colors their spirit. Others are blessed with good souls, and they cannot help but be thoughtful and kind throughout their lives. In her mind, a person's soul was the most powerful force imaginable. I asked her how she knew she had a soul if she couldn't see it. She said she always knew she had a soul because she "felt" it and didn't have to "see" it. She tried to explain it to me by using the example of someone she once knew in Italy.

She told me the story of a young man she had met when they were in school together as teenagers. She said he was a strong, handsome boy with dark eyes, wavy black hair and a charming smile. She said that in all the years that she knew him, he always did good deeds. Even though his family was poor and his father was in jail for many years, this young boy was always happy and kind toward others, even strangers. His name was Antonio. She said she was first attracted to him when they were classmates, but that she had been "too young to have such feelings."

One day, this handsome young boy was in a terrible accident when a horse kicked him in the head. He nearly died because they had to take him to the only doctor in the region, which was in another town, and they lost a lot of time in transporting him. His life was spared, but when he returned home to be cared for by his mother, he was paralyzed from the neck down. Nana said there was a lot of weeping and that she herself cried and cried. She missed his big smile and his kind words in the classroom. She said she still felt the loss and could still picture him when he was healthy and young. She continued to tell me that she could never visit him when she was still a schoolgirl in Italy because his family did not allow many visitors.

Antonio and his family temporarily moved to a larger town so that he could be admitted to a hospital where he could be looked after by nurses. In her early twenties, Nana was sent to America with her aunt to make a new life for herself. She exchanged letters with her remaining family in Italy, and after several years they sent her enough money so that she could return for a visit. For a few days, she reconnected with her family and caught up on recent news. They told her that Antonio's family had moved back to town, after years away in the hospital. They also told her that he had asked about her and had expressed sadness that she had moved to America.

At the urging of her sister, Nana decided to pay a visit to the paralyzed young man. She mustered the courage to visit, and she put together a beautiful bouquet of fresh flowers. When she first saw Antonio, she said he was propped up in his bed. What she noticed first were his bright, beautiful smile and his strikingly dark brown eyes. The next thing she noticed was that the walls of his room were completely covered with dozens of colorful paintings and drawings.

When she commented on the artwork, Antonio told her that he had painted them all. He went on to tell her how he had worked at using a paintbrush held in his mouth. While away at the hospital, he developed his skill and he painted every day. He said that he had learned to accept that he would never run through the fields again, but he could still enjoy their beauty. By painting the things he was missing, he was able to keep them in his life. She said that a tear came to his eye only briefly, when she placed the vase of flowers on the nightstand next to his bed. His demeanor quickly changed, however, when she started to cry.

He said, "There is no cause for tears. I am happy, healthy and well fed! I could have died, but the doctor did a wonderful job and he saved my life. I am fortunate, and now I have learned to paint. I may not have become a painter had this not happened to me. So, please, don't cry. There is nothing to be sad about." She learned something that day. Although he was paralyzed and cheated out of so many things a young man dreams of, he was truly happy. He had discovered new things about himself and had found satisfaction in expressing himself through his art.

Nana said to me, "Bobby, this is what is meant by a person's soul. Antonio had a terrible accident, and he did not deserve this fate. But his soul was the same, all those years later, after the accident had changed his life. He still looked at me with those same beautiful eyes and smiled. He asked me many questions about America and promised he would one day come visit me there. His mother had arranged for a tutor from the school to work with him, to keep his mind sharp and to continue his education. He was still the same optimistic person he had always been. His soul was that of a strong and kind person, and he remained unchanged.

His body was no longer working, but his soul was undamaged. And it was his soul that kept him from being sad and from giving up hope. I felt very relieved and very proud of him after that day. He had his mother send me one of his paintings after I had returned to America. It was a small painting of the vase of flowers I had placed next to his bed. He had lovingly and carefully depicted each flower just as it looked that day. In the background of the painting he had added a little yellow butterfly. He did that because on the day I visited him I was wearing a hair pin that was adorned with a tiny yellow enamel butterfly."

*　*　*

One of my earliest and most powerful influences, Nana was always willing to tell me a story or just talk with me when she tucked me in at night. These bedtime chats were special moments during a few special years when my maternal grandmother lived with our family on our small farm in Pennsylvania. Her husband was hospitalized for the last years of his life, suffering from schizophrenia. Many of my memories of him took place in the mental ward of the veteran's hospital in Pittsburgh.

He was kindhearted and gentle, but at the end of each visit he would take me aside and plead with me to help get him released from the facility. He would say, "Bobby, get me out of here. These people are crazy. They talk to themselves all the time. Get me out of here, please. You have to do something to help me."

It broke my heart every time he asked for my help. And when I would ask my parents about it, they would always calmly reassure me that "Nunu" was where he had to be and that there was no other solution. When I was only about three years old, my grandfather actually lived with us for part of the summer. My parents told me he was prone to hallucinations and he would make comments about people "watching everything we did through the TV set." He also claimed that there were people on the roof of the house listening to all of our conversations.

I fondly remember Nana telling me a story that she had told many times at my insistence. She always smiled and obliged. "In Italian! In Italian!" I would plead. She gladly told the old folktale in Italian one more time, even though I didn't speak the language. I did understand it, however, due to the repetition of the same tale. Once in a while I stopped her to ask what a word meant, and she would always describe it in a very colorful fashion. She spoke English fairly well, but not fluently. So her typical communication style was a blending of the two languages, often in partial sentences composed of a little of one with the other. It seemed quite natural to me after all the conversations we had together.

I always listened intently as she wove a charming little story about a poor vendor trying to make a living in a small Italian village. The disheveled little man had no possessions to speak of other than the tattered clothes on his back. He lived a day-to-day existence, sleeping under the stars or in barns and other shelters when the weather forced him inside. During the mornings he would often stroll through village streets, trying to drum up some work for himself. Sometimes he would sing a little tune or juggle some fruit and passersby would toss a coin or two into his little black hat. He would shout from the streets to all within earshot, *"Qui mi vuole à padrone?"* ("Who will give me a job?"). On one particularly hot day, he was starving and feeling desperate. He hadn't eaten a decent meal in several days. One well-to-do lady in a nice home called down to him from her second-floor balcony. "What type of work can you do?" she inquired. Bluffing all the way, he told her that he would have to talk to her about his many services. She asked him to wait at the doorstep while she came downstairs to open the door. Thinking quickly, the poor little vendor grabbed a nearby wheelbarrow that someone had propped up against the stone wall next to the lady's house. It was empty except for one small flowering plant.

When the matron of the house arrived, the little peddler stood up as straight and tall as possible and put on his best winning smile. Dirty and unshaven, the thin little man hardly made an impressive introduction. The lady was dressed very nicely, draped in jewelry and reeking of perfume. The little peddler said, "Pleased to make your acquaintance," as she cautiously opened the front door. She looked him up and down and started to close the door, but the poor man reached out and held the door open. With a broad smile he said, "But wait! I have a special gift for you today!" The snobbish woman sneered and asked dryly, "What would that be, my neighbor's wheelbarrow? Hmmph! You smell bad and you look like a typical beggar to me!"

"No, no, my dear woman!" he quickly offered. "I was merely finishing my chores next door and was about to put the tools away. I apologize for my haste, but I wanted to catch you before you left your house. I have a special offer for you!" The gray-haired woman looked suspiciously at the little leathery-skinned man, but she didn't slam the door on him. Before she could ask, he said, "I am a fine chef by trade. I recently moved to this town and have made arrangements to open my own café. While I am waiting for the building to be constructed, I am doing odd jobs to feed my family. Would you have need of a cook? If so, I can prepare almost anything you dream of! And I can have it ready whenever you desire!"

The wealthy lady nearly dismissed any thoughts of this offer, but then she surprised the little peddler by saying, "You are fortunate indeed. Two very important guests are coming for dinner this evening, and I will not have time to prepare a full meal today because I must go to the next town to visit my sister. My guests are very discerning, and I do not want to disappoint them. If you can prepare a full meal by dusk, I will pay you two gold coins." She then described the complete menu, which included antipasto, salad, wine, a main course of pheasant, and two desserts. The peddler wrung his hands and rubbed the back of his neck, pondering the proposal. While he was a decent cook, he really wasn't a chef, and he had never prepared a large meal such as this. But he was famished and desperate. He gambled by responding, "Two gold coins are not enough payment to prepare such a large meal. If you pay me three coins, I will gladly prepare you the most wonderful meal you have ever tasted!"

In a bit of a bind, the lady agreed with the stipulation that he would be paid after the meal. "Beggars and thieves cannot be trusted," she sneered. "I will pay you the gold only if my guests are satisfied, and you will get nothing if they do not enjoy each bite." The poor man smiled broadly and thanked the rich lady for having faith in him. She gave him a small pouch containing enough money for the supplies he would need. As she adjusted her pearl bracelet, she gave him one final warning before she left. "You are forbidden from entering any rooms other than the dining room and the kitchen. Do you understand?" she condescendingly inquired. "Yes, yes. I agree completely!" the man reassured.

Stating that she would return in late afternoon, the woman abruptly left the house and closed the front door behind her. The poor peddler stood alone in her foyer wondering what he had gotten into. Clutching the coin purse in his dirty hand, he quickly exited the home and ran down the street toward the public market. In the market, he shrewdly haggled over every item's cost and managed to buy everything the lady wanted while pocketing the sizeable difference. He bought fresh vegetables, an array of fruit, three pheasants, flour, spices, two bottles of wine and everything else he needed. Struggling to tote it all, he returned to the house and put everything in the kitchen.

Realizing that time was tight, he plunged into the meal's preparation. He feverishly chopped, diced and sliced. He prepared three beautiful pheasants and set them on ice, ready to be cooked. Once he finished assembling the huge antipasto tray, he began work on the desserts. He remembered a simple recipe his mother had taught him, and he was able to recreate a lovely dessert of Mandarin oranges and apricots drenched in a thick glaze of sugar and rum. Finally, after a couple of hours of relentless effort, he was finished preparing everything.

As the afternoon waned, he finally dressed the pheasants and placed them in the oven; he was on target to serve dinner at just the right time. He had worked up a tremendous appetite with all the labor involved in making such a feast, but he was afraid to sample any of the food he had prepared. The lady had been so stern; he just knew she would be very angry if she suspected he had dared treat himself to any of her foods. He was so hungry, though. His stomach made such startlingly loud noises, he was afraid the neighbors would think an animal had been trapped inside the well-appointed home.

He quickly took inventory of the items he had purchased. The only thing he had not used was half a bag of flour. He didn't think the lady would mind if he used a little of it. Because he was sure he had at least an hour before her return, he decided to make a batch of *pizza fritte*, fried dough, to satisfy his growling stomach. Using only some leftover flour and some of the plentiful supply of oil, he made himself a basket of nice, hot *pizza fritte*. A poor man's feast, he quickly began to eat a hot morsel. To his starving body, this was as good as any food he had ever tasted.

Before he could finish swallowing even one bite, he heard an alarming sound in the street. The wealthy lady had returned early! She was exiting her carriage and talking to the driver. He could hear her angrily chastising him for not avoiding the bumps in the road along the way. Panicking, he immediately realized that she would see the boiling oil on the stove and knew she would be so angry that she wouldn't pay him his gold. He recalled her admonitions about the off-limits areas of the house but did the only thing he felt he could do. He grabbed the pot of hot oil from the stove and scampered upstairs with it. In a bit of a panic, he lifted the toilet seat and set the pot down in the bowl and closed the lid over it. He ran downstairs and quickly put the fried dough inside a bag and threw it into the pantry.

The little peddler quickly washed his hands and slicked his hair back to try to look as composed as possible. He heard the latch rattle, and, before he could reach the door to open it, the wealthy woman burst in. Still flustered from the disagreement with the carriage driver, she barely glanced at him. Instead, she made a beeline for the stairs. Gulping hard, he tried to stop her. "Please, madame. Wait!" he exclaimed. She glared over her shoulder at him and shouted, "Don't say a word! I am tired and sweaty, and I must freshen up before my guests arrive! You get in the kitchen where you belong, and get back to work!" Before he could utter another sound, she stormed up the wooden stairs. The next sound he heard was the slam of the bathroom door.

Crossing his tired, bony fingers, the little peddler prayed she was only in there to use the sink to splash some cool water on her bloated, sweaty face. The next noise he heard quickly dashed those hopes. "Ayyyyyyy!!!!!!!!" he heard bellowed from above. The bathroom door then flung open violently, and the next thing he knew, a half-dressed, red-bottomed blur flew past him and out the front door! He ran to follow, but the well-done woman was just a small silhouette, running down the street toward the lake.

For a moment, he was tempted to follow after her. But then he imagined what she would say, and he was certain she would call the police to have him arrested. He also realized that if the pheasants were left in the oven they could cause a fire, which would result in an even bigger disaster. It also dawned on him that he would never collect his gold coins for all his hard work. He quickly used the paper bags from the market to gather up the *pizza fritte*, one of the pheasants, some provolone cheese, a few choice pieces of fruit and a bottle of wine.

He placed everything else in the ice box or on the kitchen counter. Then, he swiftly exited the house and headed in the direction of the next town. Along the way, he stopped and found a quiet spot under a large mulberry tree. He feasted upon the pheasant and the fried dough. He slowly savored the wine and the cheese. Though his stomach protruded dramatically, he also ate a succulent apricot for his dessert. He was full and satisfied for the first time in recent memory. As he reflected on the comical image of the half-naked lady running madly down the street, he had to chuckle to himself. Though he felt badly about what happened, he could not feel too sorry for such a vile person. He slept well that night, under the stars. The very next morning he set out toward the next village, another small town in the Italian countryside. The empty-handed beggar's raspy voice could be heard echoing through the streets. *"Qui mi vuole à padrone?"*

As a very young boy, I always enjoyed this story. It was simple and silly and charming, but there was something to be learned, nonetheless. The poor beggar was equipped with nothing. He had no possessions aside from the clothes on his back. His talents were limited to a basic knowledge of cooking and cleaning. He was not tall or handsome or especially witty, but he was resourceful and honest. He was merely trying to survive in a harsh world, and he refused to resort to begging. Instead, he was willing to work for a meager reward. I instinctively liked his approach and realized that he represented ingenuity and inventiveness. In some ways, I guess I lived most of my life adhering to similar principles. Maybe this story, told to me by my grandmother when I was a small child, was influential in a profound way.

A dream remains just a dream
until you take the first brave step.

Only you can make it real.

Acknowledgements

*Thanks to my children
for being the reason*

*Thanks to Mom
for saying the words*

*Thanks to Dad
for providing the fire*

*Thanks to Nana
for demonstrating faith*

*Thanks to Barbara
for two priceless gifts*

*Thanks to friends
for endless life lessons*

*Thanks to lulu.com
for the vehicle*

*Thanks to "Annie"
for the euphoria*

*This story is dedicated to all
who have loved and lost.*

MINUS THE IMPLE

The Chapters

1

All Choked Up and Nowhere to Glow

The bed sheet was coarse and uncomfortable against the skin of my neck. After all, I was in a hospital, not a four-star hotel. It really didn't matter in this case as I was not concerned at all with comfort, just functionality. I was finally going for my last resort, the potential antidote for the intense emotional pain that was destroying me. The previous night, I had attempted to negotiate a slightly different solution with my roommate. A diminutive black man, the gentleman in the bed across the room had a voice that indicated he routinely gargled with glass shards. Even though twenty years have passed, I remember Carl very clearly, and in my mind I can still hear his rough baritone voice. A seemingly decent man with a wife and a couple of young kids at home, I'm certain he never envisioned himself in this dark, austere room, talking life and death with some jerk like me.

Despite the unsavory and unsettling circumstances of being "held prisoner" in a psych ward of a suburban hospital, we had managed to share a few laughs during the several weeks we roomed together. My new friend was an alright guy. A little rough around the edges, he struck me as having a kind heart and a sympathetic ear. Apparently, he found himself in this predicament because of ongoing problems with alcohol, which directly contributed to a history of beating his wife and scaring the living hell out of his kids. He was making an attempt to get some help, and had the right idea, making a last-ditch effort to preserve his marriage.

From what he told me, he felt this was the last chance to stop his headlong slide into divorce or prison, and he was "finally ready to give it a shot." I have no idea whether he checked himself in or if his family had brought him, but that didn't really matter much. Once you were in, you were pretty much committed in more ways than one. I felt guilty putting this nice guy on the spot, but I was at the end of my rope this particular night. I had not received even one visitor during the week I had been there. My aunt and uncle called me a few times; they were obviously concerned for me and my state of mind. Those few calls gave me no solace, though; they only made me feel guilty and ashamed.

My self-critical nature just exacerbated an already desperate situation. Filled with self-hatred and guilt, I wanted to be delivered from my pain. I remember asking Carl from across the dark room, "Do you own a handgun?" No answer at first. Then, a bewildered, "Why do you want to know?" was immediately followed by, "Come on, now! Don't be talkin' like that." Although annoyed, I remember thinking I could conceivably coerce him into helping me. I offered this part-time house painter a sum of cash if he would find a way to have his brother smuggle a handgun in to me the next day.

It turned out that Carl did indeed own a couple of handguns, and for a moment it appeared as though he was actually considering my poorly conceived scheme. Instead, he started to counsel me. He reminded me that I would never again see my children if I took my own life. He tried to remind me that they would always miss me if I were not there for them in the future. I was so far gone from the relentless emotional pain, it didn't matter what words he used. I was no longer thinking, just feeling, and all I could feel was pain.

I became angry and cursed him for not coming through for me the one time I asked him for anything. He was a man with his own set of demons, yet he understood the gravity of my circumstances. He understood that I was not bluffing and it was not a false cry for help on my part. Genuinely concerned, Carl tried in vain to get me to put the notion out of my mind, but I would have none of it. I was an open wound.

As I lay staring at the ceiling through teary eyes, I fantasized about Carl's brother smuggling a pistol into the hospital. In my imagination, I walked through the entire process of Carl leaving a worn and faded duffle bag beneath my bed. I had it all worked out in my mind. I would wait until the middle of the night, slip the weapon out of the bag and silently take it with me into the bathroom just down the hall. I would very efficiently and systematically put it to my temple and pull the trigger. I imagined what the shattering sound of the blast would indicate to the staff and the other patients, and I reveled in the thought that they would all jump out of their skins. Finally, the last laugh would be mine. I was angry at the world and everyone in it.

But it wasn't meant to end that way. Carl became seriously irritated at my constant badgering. He not only stopped talking to me, but he went and said something to the attending physician. I don't know if he told them everything, but he obviously put in a request for a new room assignment because the next day I was informed that he would soon be moving down to a different room. Annoyed at the prospect of dealing with another roommate, I decided I was not going to let that happen. I was sick and tired of having these people telling me what to do, and I was furious at Carl for letting me down. He had ceased talking to me, so I decided to hatch a new plan.

We were required to be in our beds by 11:00 PM. On this night I got into my bed around 10:00 PM and pretended to read a book. I don't remember what book it was, because I really wasn't reading anyway. It was merely an act to feign a sense of normalcy. Carl entered the room quietly just before 11:00, climbed into his bed and quickly fell asleep. He didn't bother saying "Goodnight," his usual routine. There was a palpable tension in the air between us ever since speaking about the gun.

3

Bitter and desperate for escape from my personal agony, I had concocted a plan I thought might actually work. Around 1:30 AM, I decided that the ward was sufficiently quiet. I knew they usually checked in on us a few times during the night, to take a head count. A member of the hospital staff had already poked his head inside our doorway around midnight, and I knew he and his friends often played cards during the early morning hours. This was the time to finally do something. I had mentally rehearsed each step of the plan in a cold-blooded and calculating manner.

After cautiously getting out of bed and tiptoeing over to Carl's side of the room, I leaned in and listened to his breathing pattern. Satisfied that he was no longer awake, I quietly walked back to the side of my bed and slowly removed the top sheet. As silently as possible, I folded the top blanket and placed it at the foot of the bed. I had been curious about the mechanisms on these hospital beds for the entire time I was locked in this ward. They were equipped with push-button controls that raised and lowered the beds to various heights, and I had noticed how silently they operated. A simple button press could change the level considerably. I calmly used the controls to lower the bed to its minimum height, praying there wouldn't be too much noise.

Carl remained motionless, snoring away all the while. Once the bed had reached its absolute lowest level, I carefully eased myself to a prone position on the floor beneath it. Taking the white bed sheet, I twisted it into a rope-like "rat tail" and tied one end securely to one of the legs of the frame. The metal carriage of the hospital bed was conceivably low enough to the floor for my plan to succeed. Lying on my back, beneath the bed, I wrapped the twisted sheet around my neck two times and then pulled it snugly against my throat. Having thought this out for a while, I felt it was essential that the sheet constrict my throat as tightly as possible. I was unsure whether it was tight enough, but I cinched it as best I could. Then, in the penultimate part of the plan's execution, I tied the remaining end of the sheet to the bed's metal frame, just beneath the mattress. I was being very careful to do all of this silently, and so far it was going according to plan. The last step was the most difficult: pressing the button.

I admit that I hesitated, but only for a moment. So intense was my self-loathing and emotional pain at that point, it was a decision I had already made. I wanted out, and this was the best idea I could come up with. Visions of my children entered my mind, but I quickly brushed them away. I double-checked the tension on the cotton noose that was snugly encircling my throat. Content that it was as tight as I could make it, I pressed the button. I was mainly worried about the sound, hoping it would not be loud enough to awaken my roommate.

I recall being relieved at how minor the noise turned out to be, despite the deathly silence of our room. I held down the button as the bed continued to rise. "Will it be powerful enough?" I wondered. "Will it be pulled taut enough to do the job?" As my windpipe became more and more constricted by the pressure created by the tightening noose, I became concerned it would not be sufficient to end my life. I firmly pressed the button as the bed frame traversed those last few inches. Now barely able to breathe, I began to panic that this was not going to do the job, so I repeatedly struck the side of my head with my fist, trying to render myself unconscious. Frustrated that this process was unsuccessful in completely cutting off my air supply, I hoped I could knock myself unconscious to improve the odds of reaching my ultimate goal. While painful, I was unsuccessful at that too, although the self-abusive exercise was having some effect.

I felt a tingling sensation throughout my face and head. My eyes began to burn, and I could feel only the slightest amount of air passing into my lungs. As badly as I wanted to stop breathing, I couldn't keep from instinctively drawing air in through the severely constricted passageway. In my mind I pleaded for

5

death. I wanted so badly to stop the emotional pain that this physical pain was easy to endure. At that moment, I begged God for relief. I cursed Him and dared Him to let me succeed in taking my own life. In my cynicism, I knew my wish would not be granted.

A vision of my young daughter, Violet, flashed in my mind at that very moment. She was scolding me by waving her raised index finger side to side. It was clear to me she was saying, "Don't you do it, Dad. I will never forgive you if you do this!" It was at this time that Minus made an appearance. I can't say I actually *saw* him as much as I *felt* his presence. There seemed to be a strange harmonic communication directed toward me from both Minus and Violet. Their unified "voice" pierced my soul, and convinced me to rethink my actions.

While my breathing had been relegated to a raspy, deliberate intake of air, I still had enough mental clarity to control my body. Resigned to failure, I slid my thumb down the hand-held controller to drop the bed frame and thereby release the tension on the homemade noose. Airflow to my lungs gradually increased as the carriage of the hospital bed gently lowered to its original level. Lying there on my back, I slowly began to take stock of my condition. It had been a few minutes of very limited air intake, and my arms and legs were burning and tingling. My face felt numb and my throat was dry and sore. I felt emotionally drained and disappointed, and was angry that guilt had caused me to fail. I felt resentment toward my daughter and I felt trapped, forced to live when I really wanted to escape from the pain of reality. And, as much as I had grown fond of him, I was angry that Minus had chosen this time to appear again.

Laying there on the cold floor beneath my hospital bed, I decided to forgive my daughter. She was just an innocent child, but I could only feel resentment toward Minus, who had no right to interfere. Still lying there, I was amazed that no one had heard what had just happened.

Carl lay in his bed, still asleep and snoring. None of the on-duty staff had been alerted, despite the outer door being propped open. I felt exhausted, depressed, lonely and afraid; certainly, I was afraid of what the future might bring. I had a pounding headache, and was drifting in and out of consciousness. I fought to remain awake as long as possible, lying flat on my back on the cold, unforgiving linoleum.

As I finally blacked out, a torrent of memories flooded my mind.

2

Chilly Con Carny

I grew up on a small farm in a very small town in Pennsylvania. Zelienople was a peaceful little place and my parents had moved there from Pittsburgh just before I was born. Both parents were of Italian descent. My dad had changed his last name to Chandler soon after he returned from the War, several years prior to my birth. His original last name was Cerchiara (Chuhr-KYAH-rah), and many people had a difficult time pronouncing it correctly. My father's previous employers put pressure on him to change his name because of his position in sales.

My mother was born in nearby Washington, Pennsylvania and had always been very fond of the area, so she never was willing to move very far away. Soon after my parents married in 1946, they purchased a 20-acre farm, complete with a chicken coop, a small orchard of cherry and apple trees, and a beautiful garden next to the dilapidated house. We had a solitary apricot tree and a beautiful, enormous mulberry tree, both directly behind the house. A long wooden fence bordered the front of the property, which my father had completely reconstructed with his own two hands. He eventually demolished the chicken coop and worked tirelessly to improve the aesthetics of every aspect of the property.

Born in 1955, I truly enjoyed the early years of my childhood there, and I learned a lot about making the most of whatever I had. I also developed a love of nature that I would not have otherwise had. I remember many beautiful mornings when the rising sun would peek over the tops of the cherry trees to the east of our house. The morning dew often sparkled like so many diamonds across the lush, green lawn between the gravel driveway and the great garden.

My dad had been quite an athlete when he was younger, especially during his high school years. He was a great baseball player on his varsity squad and was named team captain two years in a row. He also wrestled and was a sprinter on the track team, and he won many medals and awards. He kept most of the trophies and other symbols of his glory days in a steamer trunk up in our attic. Once in a while, after I begged him and pestered him enough, he would reluctantly come up the dry, rickety steps to open up the large black case. I would ask questions, while he would recount some of the moments he most cherished. Always humble, he never claimed to be "great" or "one of the best," but from all I gathered, he was not only very gifted athletically, but he was looked up to by most of his teammates.

One of his awards was particularly fascinating to me. It was a small gold medallion attached to a simple red ribbon, with the lone word Leadership inscribed upon it. When I first asked him about this small metal disc in the velvet-covered, hinged case, he just smiled a half-smile and said "This one means more than all the others put together." I wasn't sure at the time what he meant by this, but as years went by and we talked more about his athletic achievements, I grew to understand that this particular award was bestowed upon him at the end of his high school years, a unique award created in his honor. Subsequently given out annually to future star athletes at his school, it was established for my father, due to his leadership on and off the playing field. His teammates had gathered to design and plan this tribute to the one person they admired most.

I used to go up to the attic alone, open up the dusty trunk and take that small medal into my hands and just stare at it. Tilting it so it would catch the limited light and gleam just a little, I tried hard to imagine my father running the bases or breaking through the finish line tape. Once in awhile I got a chill down my spine because I could literally feel the wind blowing through my hair as I broke the tape with outstretched arms.

There were times when I wondered just how much of my father's athletic talent I had inherited. In grade school gym classes, I was generally more than competent in any sport we played. It was obvious that I had been blessed with above-average agility and balance but I just didn't have the desire to compete in organized team sports. Of course, I realized I was young, though, and hoped that one day I might feel the urge to test myself on the playing field. I think there was a bit of fear and trepidation because I felt in my heart that I could never match what my father accomplished as a scholastic athlete.

These thoughts entered my mind subconsciously, with relative frequency, any time I was engaged in physical activity. I started to develop my own sense of competitive drive in subtle ways. If my friends and I were skipping stones, I would keep at it relentlessly until my stone traveled further than anyone else's. When we would race each other, I felt like I just *had* to win. I usually did, maybe because I was a fast runner and maybe because it meant a little more to me than to the others. I didn't analyze it; I just wanted to do well in whatever I did. For me, it was always about getting the most fun out of every experience.

In early summer of 1965, I was your basic happy nine-year-old boy. With little to worry about, I basked in the glory of school-free days, riding bikes with friends and catching frogs. My dad worked a lighter schedule in the summer months, so I had him around more than usual, and I liked that. We went fishing in the nearby river, usually once or twice a week in June, July and August. Often, we would catch only a few small ones, but it wasn't so much about the fish.

On one particular Saturday morning, my friend Jay had shown up on his bicycle to join us. I was envious of him for having that beautiful bike. It was new and had hand brakes and one of those banana seats, and it was my favorite color: a loud, bright red. Jay was a good kid. His mom gave him a paper bag loaded with home-baked breakfast rolls. I think those rolls, so lovingly made by Jay's mother, were what launched my lifelong appreciation of cinnamon. Their aroma was intoxicating.

He knew right where to find us, and it wasn't all that odd for him to suddenly appear. Jay, who was in my class at school, reminded us of the upcoming Firemen's Carnival, which was always held in late June in our town. In those days in small towns like ours, the Firemen's Carnival was a big event to look forward to, especially for kids. Jay's dad was a volunteer fireman, and he always worked at these carnivals. I had only been to one of them before, but I couldn't remember much about it. It had been when my mother was still alive, so I was no more than four years old. My mother had been killed in a car accident the previous winter. She was pregnant at the time of the accident and the baby didn't survive either. My mom was driving to visit her sister Angela, who lived about 100 miles away. I only recall the somber expressions on everyone's faces, the black-clothed cluster of family and friends at the services, and the absence of my father's smile. I also remember not talking to anyone much for a very long time.

My father, being the strong man he was, tried to help me through it as best he could. He was devastated by the sudden loss of his wife and unborn child, but before too long he had poured himself into the dual roles of mother and father. I had his undivided attention and concern, and it helped me enormously. Within a year, I had adjusted to our loss, but, then, I was only a child. I had been emotionally close to both parents, but my memories are now limited to images of a smile, the phantom arm around my back, a fleeting memory of her perfume. In the wake of my mom's death, my dad and I pressed onward as best we could. I never caught him crying, even at the funeral. His eyes were moist and he was obviously shaken, but he still thoughtfully tended to the older family members and the smallest ones, too.

He was unable to really smile for the longest time, but he was the epitome of grace under pressure, and he helped the rest of us accept the reality of what had happened. I have one keepsake from my mother, one that I have never shown to anyone else other than my father. Shortly after Mom died, my father took me up to their bedroom and handed me a small box. It was a music box he had given her when they were dating, he told me. She had always cherished it and kept it on the small end table next to their bed. At first I thought he meant for me to keep the music box, but I instinctively knew that would be wrong for me to have; I felt he should keep that. He motioned for me to open the box, and then he softly put his hand on my head for a moment before he turned and walked downstairs.

When I opened that little white music box, I saw it: the fragile gold chain brought back a flood of memories. Vague and fleeting, the memories were real. Memories of my mom cradling me in her arms when my fever had reached 105 degrees one time; memories of her sitting on the edge of my little bed, telling me stories she made up on the spot; memories of her smile, her eyes, her gentle kisses on my eyelids. The tiny chain held a small, red crystal heart. She often wore the chain, and I vividly remember, as a very young child, asking her if I could hold the heart up to the sunlight. One morning I awoke very early, right around dawn, and silently made my way downstairs to the kitchen. My dad was still asleep, but I discovered that Mom was in the kitchen. I wondered what she was doing up so early because it was even earlier than her usual wake-up time. I sat on the lowest step, just watching her. I don't know why I didn't just run up to her and hug her legs like I usually did, but I just sat still and listened and watched her on this particular morning.

The sun had just peeked over the low rolling hills behind our house, and the sheer curtains covering the kitchen window were painted a golden hue. That same light, so magical and subtle, caressed the side of my mother's face, and it shrouded her head in a warm, peaceful glow.

As she turned to one side, I could hear her gently humming to herself, unaware of my presence. For just a moment, the tiny red crystal heart around her neck caught that same playful sunlight, and it provided me with an image to cherish for all time. I didn't know what made me turn and sneak my way back up to my room, but feelings of security and peace came over me, and I fell back into a sound sleep for a few more hours.

As I clasped that little gold chain with the red crystal heart, I cried for the first time in quite a while. I cried quietly because I didn't want to upset my dad, but I clutched that little necklace tightly and just let the tears flow. Once I gathered myself, I put the music box back in its proper place, and took the necklace and placed it in my own small box next to my bed.

Mom used to say, "Bobby, you're my little ray of light."

Jay asked if I could go with him to the carnival the following week. Immediately, I was torn between wanting to go with my father and wanting to go with my friends for the first time. The thought of taking off with my friends was so tempting because it was such a new concept. I was at the age where I still felt completely attached to my father, yet I wanted to feel grown up enough to be a little more independent. Before I could sort out my thoughts, my dad surprised me by saying, "It's okay with me." I told him I wanted to go with him, too, but he told me he was going to tag along with Aunt Elena and Uncle Pete. Jay went on to invite me to come over for a sleepover the night before the carnival, along with a couple of our other mutual friends. Dad agreed to the plan, and I was excited for this big social event on the horizon.

I had saved up some money from allowances and chores, and was prepared to have the time of my life that Saturday. It turned out to be a beautiful day in June, and that Saturday evening was gloriously warm. Jay's mother ushered us into the family station wagon around dinner time. We had insisted that we wanted to eat at the carnival, and she made us promise we would eat something like a hamburger or hot dog before we started in on the candy apples and other decadent treats. She gave us each a couple of dollars for food, saying something about us being "her responsibility for the day." We all gladly agreed and off we went. I wondered if I would be able to find my father in the burgeoning crowd.

Our little group was bubbling over with anticipation as we made our way up the dirt road that led to the grass parking area. Over to one side, we could see the Ferris wheel proudly towering over the rest of the other attractions. Car windows open, we could immediately smell all the signature aromas that help identify carnivals. The chicken barbecue seemed to go on endlessly, manned by a small army of firemen and other volunteers. The smoke blew sideways across the parking lot, extending a bold invitation to the hungry families pouring from their shabby little vehicles. Eyes wide open and mouths agape, we exited the car and just stared at the buzzing beehive that was the carnival. Jay's mother herded us toward the entrance. Once inside the makeshift rope barrier that identified the fairground's perimeter, the cacophony of music and chatter was undeniably invigorating. I hated being so small! It was nearly impossible to see much of anything unless we wove our way around all the "big people." We were allowed to separate from Jay's mother as long as we promised to stick together and watch out for each other. She was headed over to the barbecue pit to meet up with Jay's dad. Tommy, Jay, Andy and I all agreed we wanted to go on rides and play all the games. I just wanted to see it all!

To our nine-year-old eyes, this huge new world was seemingly endless in its magical possibilities. We encountered plenty of familiar faces, but we saw a lot of new ones, too. People came from quite a distance to enjoy the carnival, and therefore, we saw things we were not accustomed to seeing. Tattoos, in that day, were a sign of either one of two things: we would sometimes see them on veterans of the military, and the only others we might see sporting them were labeled "hoods" or other disparaging terms. At the carnival, we saw more tattoos than we had ever seen before, which was a little unsettling because it was so foreign to me.

Another aspect of the carnival that intimidated me was all the yelling from the "barkers." These were the men who were bellowing, "Step right up and win a prize," and things of that nature. In my mind, they had awesome news to share, but at the same time, it was a bit unnerving to hear all that boisterous behavior punctuating the quiet summer night. Some of the carnival workers looked kind of scary, besides. These people were not from our town. They traveled with the carnival, setting up and doing the same thing in many towns across the area, according to my dad. A few of them looked downright mean, barely able to fake a smile. They just kept on with their ranting sales pitches, immune to the naïve euphoria welling up in our tiny hearts.

As we made a few circuitous passes by the various attractions, one booth caught my eye. There were many games of skill and chance sprinkled throughout the grounds. Some appeared far too difficult for me to attempt. There were some games that seemed like they might be fun to try, but the prizes they offered didn't interest me. No, this one had what I wanted. I spotted a golden horse sitting on the top shelf of the prize rack in this particular booth. There it sat, glistening, giving off dazzling multicolored reflections from all the carnival lights. This bizarre golden horse with a clock molded into the area directly beneath its stomach had a heavy base, perfect for placing atop a mantle or shelf. I had just the place for it on my bedroom dresser, which was wide and plain looking. I thought it would be so wonderful to have this shiny, golden symbol of success and wealth adorning my bedroom dresser.

I boasted to my friends that I was going to win it, and they all laughed. New to this whole realm, I didn't realize the way these things worked. Jay informed me that you don't just win the top prizes by winning once. You had to win a small prize and then continue to win and trade your smaller prize for a bigger prize, and so on. It would take a lot of winning to work one's way up to one of these spectacular top prizes. The gold-plated horse clock was definitely the most impressive prize we had spotted within the entire carnival. It took on a Holy Grail status for me, and I was fixated upon it.

The game itself was simple. The player had to roll a heavy billiard ball up an elevated ramp and have the ball drop into one of several holes cut into the panel. Directly above the prizes on the shelves was a colorful simulated racetrack with three-dimensional horses lined up behind the starting gate on the far left side. Depending on which opening your ball dropped into, your horse would move a respective number of spaces forward. The center hole cut into the end of each elevated panel was worth the most spaces, of course. If your ball dropped into one of the gutters along the edge of each panel, your horse wouldn't move at all. So, if you missed, you had to wait for the ball to return to you, thereby losing valuable time. The first horse to cross the finish line was the one and only winner of each game, and the player could select a prize from the lower level only. That is, unless you had already won something. You could trade in one of the low-level prizes for a slightly better prize, and then you could continue to trade prizes until you won a truly worthwhile prize.

Usually, the lowest-level prizes consisted of things like whistles, ugly plastic combs or Chinese finger traps; stuff like that. The next-tiered prizes were generally cheap little toys like badly painted plastic dinosaurs, garishly dyed rabbit's feet keychains, and the like. Next, you could trade up for a very cheaply-made stuffed animal. Most of these were about the size of a child's fist and were not very well constructed. Up from there, you might be able to trade for a larger stuffed animal, a mirror with some liquor company's logo on it, or something like a pair of sunglasses that had been made in Japan. Slowly, you could build up to the point where you could trade for an oversize stuffed animal or one of the more unique items poised upon the highest shelf. I had my sights set on that horse clock and never really considered any of the other top prizes.

Armed with a small wad of dollar bills buried in my pocket, I squeezed between several curious onlookers and a couple of my pals to eagerly hand over my money to the man behind the tall counter. A heavyset, middle-aged man, the guy who ran this particular game perfectly matched the stereotype of the carnival worker. He had a disinterested look in his eyes and a permanent scowl on his unshaven, weathered, puffy face. Without as much as acknowledging me, he swiped the dollar out of my hand and quickly slammed my change on the edge of the counter in front of me. I could barely reach high enough to play, but there was a block of wood nearby, so I snatched it up and placed it under my feet. With eager anticipation, I grabbed the billiard ball and planned my strategy. I couldn't help but think to myself that this was not at all complicated.

"How hard is it to roll a ball into a hole?" I thought. There were many other players lined up to my left and right. My little group of friends crowded behind me, leaning in to watch. "Robby, come on. You're just wasting your money!" Jay chimed in. I told him to shut up as I refocused on the game. A bell sounded as the fat man with the grubby hands let out an uninspired, "And they're off!" The obnoxious noise caught me off guard and I got off to a bad start. I hesitated and took far too long to slide the first ball up the ramp and then had a hard time gauging the proper angle and power. My horse was a distant finisher, not coming anywhere close to challenging. A tall, thin man standing at the opposite end was the winner, and he traded his small stuffed parrot for a large teddy bear. He promptly gave the bear to his young daughter, held in his wife's arms behind him.

Annoyed with my friends yapping behind me, I shooed them away and refocused. I handed another quarter to the gruff man and got ready to play again. A strange wave of confidence began to well up inside me, a feeling I had not experienced before. Feeling calm and ready, focusing my attention on the end of the ramp, I could only see the center hole, ringed in red paint. I couldn't really even see the other holes clearly. I was no longer aware of the surrounding players or the annoying comments of Jay and Tommy, who were anxious to go on the rides.

As the bell sounded this time, I was so ready. Beating everyone else to the first roll, my ball found its mark in the center hole. I continued to tell myself to stay focused only on the target, and I never looked up at the race track and the little plastic ponies. Instead, I coldly fired ball after ball up that ramp and into one of the nine holes at the far end. Not all of them found the center hole, but I rarely missed advancing at least one forward block. I remember hearing the loud bell sound and hearing the fat man yell, "We have a winner!" before I raised my head to see that my horse had won. The joy of accomplishment far outweighed the tangible reward of the small plastic toy I selected. I really didn't care what I won from the bottom level of prizes; I was dead set on winning that top prize. My friends had stopped their whining for a moment to cheer when they saw my horse had won. I turned and told them to go on the rides without me. "I'm not leaving until I win my prize!" I announced with conviction, and they all just shrugged their shoulders and made off for the Ferris wheel.

I was relieved to be rid of their annoying distraction. There were a lot of people playing this particular game, none of whom I had seen before. Because the carnival attracted people from all over, that didn't surprise me. Out of the corner of my eye, I saw my dad, who was eating a hot pretzel and talking to one of the other men from work. I didn't know if he saw me or not, but I just wanted to keep playing. I figured I had enough money to play quite a few games, and if I won most every time, I felt I had enough to get that horse clock. As the next few games came and went, I felt powerful for the first time in my life. I felt unstoppable.

Focused as never before, I felt there was no way I could lose. It all seemed easy as I instinctively analyzed the game and identified the perfect angle and power to employ. I won two, three, and then four games in a row. Each time, the game was full, and I was the youngest competitor. The man running the game barely acknowledged me as he asked, "What prize d'ya want?" after successive winning races. I had quickly worked my way up to trading an ugly plastic football for a nice stuffed gorilla. For a moment, I was tempted to keep the gorilla but was still intent on winning that horse clock. It looked so much more valuable and impressive than any of the other prizes. I had to have it.

Over my shoulder, I noticed my dad had eased closer to me. He still didn't seem to actually see me, and I didn't acknowledge him because I wanted to remain focused on the game. I still had a few dollars in the front pocket of my worn blue jeans, so I handed another bill to the man behind the counter, and the next game began. After I won yet another game, I heard some muttering from a few of the other players. One man, in particular, who had lost to me on about three consecutive races, said something under his breath that made me uneasy. I didn't care much, though. I figured we all had the same chances to win, so he could beat me if he wanted to badly enough. I quickly pulled my focus back to the task at hand and won again, and then again, and again. After one victory, a lady standing behind me said something about me being "amazing." Another woman said I should let someone else win. For the first time, the sweaty man behind the counter directed his focus my way and actually made eye contact. It gave me an uncomfortable feeling.

He plucked the next quarter from my outstretched hand and said, "How about you let someone else have a chance, squirt!" I ignored him but had become aware of a growing mood of hostility around me. A few of the people who had lost on consecutive races just walked away. One guy said something derogatory about me, something like "little shit!" It disturbed me, to be sure, but I went right back to focusing on the end of that ramp and the red die-cut hole at its far end. Once again, the bell rang and I nailed it clean. I won easily, far and away dominating yet another race, and I felt the atmosphere grow thick with an ominous vibe.

The surly man with the sour face nonchalantly walked over to the end of my particular game unit and lifted up the hinged top. It was hinged down at the player's end, so it could be accessed and repaired from the other side. Stunned, I watched as the sour-faced man with the dirty hands pulled a pair of pliers from his back pocket. Without hesitation, he clamped onto a pair of wires inside the case and ripped them out. He said, "Somethin's wrong with the wiring in this machine. You gotta use a different one if you wanna play again." This time he didn't look at me when he spoke. He looked quite angry, and I admit I was intimidated.

Only a couple of wins away from my goal, and he rips the guts out of the game?! I was scared and angry, yet more determined than ever.

Just then, I felt a heavy hand on my right shoulder. I whirled around, nearly falling off the small block of wood upon which I had been standing. It was my father. After helping to stabilize me and prevent me from falling down, he whispered in my ear, "Don't let him bother you. You didn't do anything wrong." I thought to myself, "Hell. I didn't do anything wrong at all! Why would someone do that to me?" It was my first taste of the harsh reality of doing business. This Neanderthal behind the counter was just trying to keep more people playing, and it was bad for business for one little kid to be dominating his enterprise on this warm summer night. While it certainly felt like a personal attack, I realized even at that tender age, that this was all about "business." I didn't really give a rat's ass. I wanted that horse clock. My dad helped move the wooden block one unit to the right, and I hopped up and handed another quarter to my nemesis. With my father standing behind me, I stopped for a second to absorb my surroundings. A nice woman nearby said, "Don't let him bother you, honey. You go on and win the next race." A little boy said something to his mother like, "That kid's unbeatable!" My father said, in a low, serious tone, "Son, you have every right to play the game and no one better interfere again. Go after what you want."

The stocky jerk behind the counter avoided making eye contact with any of us. It was probably a good thing he didn't because I saw a look in my father's eyes that was truly frightening. It was one of the few times I had ever seen the expression, but I came to term it his "death look." His eyes conveyed an intensity I thought was very much out of character. If you didn't know him for the kind, gentle man he really was, you would have recoiled in fear from him when he looked at you with that expression. It only showed up a handful of times that I was aware of, and I'm sure it was involuntary. I knew he was such a fair-minded person that this cheating carnival worker was pushing all the wrong buttons. My dad hated cheaters and anyone who was cruel toward children. The fat man behind the counter was definitely asking for it on this night. He avoided eye contact with my father, and I actually felt relieved.

I focused my concentration and felt supremely confident in my ability to keep winning. One game, two games, and then three wins in a row. Finally, with spiteful purpose, the mean man handed me my horse clock. As he did so, he leaned down next to my ear and said, "I don't wanna see you at my booth again, awright?" I felt my father's hand, now resting on my shoulder again, tense up. He waited until I walked a few steps away, clutching my great reward, before he leaned toward the disgusting ogre and said something to him. I never asked what he said. As my father caught up to me, I realized that the man had never taken my big stuffed bear in exchange for the clock. My dad said, "Don't worry. He told me you can keep the bear."

A few months after the carnival, everyone was talking about attending the annual fair at the grange. We lived in farming country, and back then rural communities often had gathering places known as granges. I'm not exactly sure what their day-to-day purpose was, something to do with farmers' meetings and stuff, but every year they held this huge annual event. Most of the families in the area would go and eat a big picnic-style buffet and take part in an auction featuring all kinds of things, from furniture to appliances to actual livestock. It was like a miniature state fair, and it was practically in our backyard.

On a crisp, cool September evening, Dad and I got cleaned up and put on our good jeans and climbed into his pickup truck. Aunt Elena and Uncle Pete were going to join us at the grange later. They were finishing making up a huge pot of chili and were putting it into several smaller containers to bring it to the fair. They were going to contribute their chili to the picnic dinner. When we arrived, people were milling around the parking lot, which had been set up with rows of tables holding all sorts of items. One table was covered with costume jewelry, and it looked like a pirate had just dumped out his treasure chest. The sun reflected off the sharp edges of the gemstones embedded in the gold and silver chains and their settings. It was a spectacular sight to behold. An array of fragrances twisted their way through the cool air, hitting everyone at different intervals depending upon the breeze.

I got a big blast of cotton candy scent and tugged hard on my father's sleeve. He knew immediately what I was after and just slipped a dollar into my right hand. Without missing a beat, I ran up to that cotton candy booth and thrust my crumpled-up bill toward a freckle-faced teenage girl. I recognized her from the school hallways but didn't know her name. She had a mouth full of braces and orange-colored hair. She handed me a great big pink swirl of sugary goodness, and off I ran to catch up with Dad. He was near the entrance, talking with my teacher and another lady.

When he introduced me, I learned this other lady was my teacher's sister. She had come from Jamestown to spend the weekend and, specifically, to come to the grange on this night. She said she liked to dance, and the grange's annual fair always had some good local musicians playing. The building itself was immense; there was a huge room that made a perfect dance hall. My father was an excellent square dancer. I thought it was all pretty boring, to tell the truth, but I noticed my father was smiling broadly as he was listening to this woman talk about her life in Jamestown. I imagined he would ask her to dance later on in the evening. Getting terribly antsy, I asked if I could go inside to find some of my friends from school.

Released from the boredom of adult pleasantries, I scrambled inside, seeking familiar faces. Right away, I spotted three of my pals from school: Tommy, Angelo and Jay. They were roughhousing and trying to mess up each other's hair. Tommy was wearing a red necktie, and looked like he was dressed for church. He had to look his best because he was in the school choir and they were scheduled to perform the National Anthem to officially kick off the festivities.

I had been looking forward to playing some games and laughing with my friends. I had hoped that Sharon Massey would be there. She was the prettiest girl in my class, and I used to fall asleep fantasizing about kissing her. I never told any of my friends this, but it was a recurring dream I had for a couple of years. I barely knew her or anything about her, though, so I had really hoped she would be at the fair with her family. Another girl in my class, Martha Underwood, was here, and she ran over to our little cluster, arms flailing wildly. "Robby!" she shouted, "Where have you been?"

Martha was sort of my first "girlfriend," at least to the extent a person can be your girlfriend in the third grade. She and I were a lot alike, and we never seemed to get into arguments. Her family was poor, and she never had nice clothes or many toys, but she was a good friend and her parents were always nice to me. Martha was an only child, so they encouraged me to come over and play with her often. She and I were pals, just like any of my male friends, but we would sometimes hold hands and talk about subjects that boys don't typically speak of among other boys. We would pretend we were married and talk about the house we wanted to build and our children and our busy jobs, as if it were all real. I guess it was a fun way of imagining our futures, and it was an exercise in getting accustomed to the notion that we would not be kids forever.

She was excited about the games that the grange had planned for any interested kids, and was gushing as she told us about the first, second and third place ribbons and medals that would be awarded. She announced that she was going to win a whole armful of medals. Of course, Angelo, Tommy and Jay all chirped that they would be the ones to take home all the prizes. I knew what a fast runner Martha was, so I told them they better not brag too much in advance. They all scoffed and told her to go play with her dolls. Martha started to cry, but I put my arm on her shoulder and told her that they were just a bunch of sissies, and that made her laugh again.

I don't know what came over me, but as I looked over at Angelo, I got a strange feeling. It was the first time I can recall that I felt there was something at stake beyond the simple challenge of winning some silly games. He looked me in the eye, and I felt as if a message had been received. I felt something well up inside me, a competitive fire that was ignited for the first time in my life. He said, "I plan on winning my share. You can all fight for the red ribbons." Blue ribbons were tied to the first-place awards, while red ribbons signified second place. The third-place prizes had white ribbons, and the medals were smaller than the others. I didn't want those; I thought they looked stupid.

My dad had eased over in our direction, still talking with various people he knew from town. He looked so young to me on this night. His eyes sparkled as he rested his hand on the back of my neck and gave it a light squeeze. I recall him saying, "Robby, are you planning on bringing home a medal tonight?" For some reason, when he asked that, I felt as though a switch had been flipped in my mind. I had always just enjoyed the act of doing something. I used to "race" my friends in the playground, but I never really cared much who finished first. It was always enough for me to just play and have fun. Maybe I was thinking about the numerous athletic accolades my father had earned all those years ago. I remember thinking, "I wonder if I could win if I really put my mind to it." This was the first time I ever even considered what it meant to really compete, and it was a spark that would be rekindled again and again throughout my life.

The games were set up in another huge, open area inside the grange building. There were roped-off areas, chairs set up in specific configurations, and an obstacle course, using red cones to delineate the prescribed path. Another table, with all the medals neatly arranged upon it, also had chairs set up for the four judges. Our gym teacher, Mr. Holley, was one judge, and the other judges were also teachers from my school. My dad had noticed my sneaker was untied, and he quickly knelt down and retied it. As he looked up at me, he said, "Have fun, Robby. I'll be watching from the other side."

He patted me on the back and then headed over to an area where some of the parents had gathered to sit and watch while they enjoyed their soda or beer. Angelo's father came over and whispered something into his ear before joining my father and the others. Tommy ran over to the sign-up table, and the rest of us quickly pursued him. We wrote down our names, took a numbered piece of paper on a string, and draped it over our necks. I don't remember my number, but I do remember feeling a distinct sense of anticipation about the challenges. There were an awful lot of kids competing in these games of skill, and there were a lot of parents prepared to cheer wildly from across the way.

My memories of the individual events are vague. All I remember is that, once you had your number, you could enter all or some of the games. I never gave a second thought to it and just assumed I would participate in all of them. And, so, I did. By the end of the events, I had won almost every blue ribbon available. It really never dawned on me that I was winning almost every event until they were all over. As I looked back on it in the coming days, I was aware that the cheers from the group of parents gradually became less and less enthusiastic. I later realized that the mood in the building had slowly changed from celebratory to what might be described as somber. In the events where I failed to win first place, I won second place. It didn't really register with me at the time because the events were all strung together without a break and the awards were not handed out until the end of the final event. When I finally made my way over to the judges' table to collect my awards, I was actually embarrassed as they handed me blue ribbon after blue ribbon.

There was a lot of pride and excitement building up inside me as they kept announcing my name as winner of such-and-such event. I looked over to my father, and he had the strangest expression on his face. When I sat down next to him, a huge bundle of medals in my lap, at first he said nothing. I saw that he appeared happy, but there was also an obvious look of concern on his face. He said something like, "What a night, Robby!" But then I remember him speaking almost apologetically to some of

26

the other adults. I had mixed emotions as people made polite comments to me.

Looking over at Martha, I noticed she was sobbing and being consoled by her mother. Angelo said nothing to me as he walked by with Jay, heading for the lemonade stand. Tommy came over and asked if he could look at my medals. He held them up in one hand and just seemed mesmerized by the sheer number of them. I felt a new and unusual feeling of power, almost one of superiority. Something else was also weighing on me, an odd feeling of fear. I would wait until we left the grange before talking to my father about it.

The rest of our time at the fair was a blur to me. I was sweaty and tired from all the running and jumping around, and just wanted to go to sleep. After we feasted on roasted chicken and salt potatoes, we made our way toward the parking lot. On the way out, I recall looking back and seeing a lot of odd expressions on the faces of friends and acquaintances. It was as though they were angry, but I was confused as to why that would be the case. Maybe I was imagining it. I was so tired that I quickly stopped worrying about it and looked forward to my nice warm bed. My dad said a quick farewell to the lady from Jamestown, and we hopped up into the truck.

I took special care to cradle the ribbons and medals in my arms as I got comfortable in the passenger seat. The grange was still filled with people as we eased down the driveway and made our way home. Less than a mile or so away from the scene, I had to tell my father something that had been gnawing at me. He started to tell me how proud he was of my success in the games when I interrupted. "I heard a weird voice tonight," I announced. "What's that?" he wondered aloud. "Someone said something to me in the middle of the race tonight." I went on to describe how I heard a strange voice speak to me in the middle of the 30-yard dash, which I had ultimately won. The whispering voice said, "Show them all..." It struck me as so odd how I heard this voice in the middle of the race, which took all of a few seconds to complete. It was as if the entire universe had slowed down, and this voice in my head was my only focus. My father said I was simply excited about the games and was "dead-set on winning." He told me it was just my inner voice reminding me to give my best effort, nothing more. Maybe he was right. After all, he knew a lot about competing and winning.

He went on to explain that many athletes talk to themselves before and during competition. He said it was just a natural thing to do. He tousled my hair and said, "You sure had a night to remember!" And we both smiled as we looked back upon the past few hours.

I realized how much I enjoyed winning, and couldn't imagine why some people seemed satisfied with second place.

3

Take This Broken Wing

As I look back, I realize I can't imagine having lived my life without "Minus." I know I can't really remember much of anything before I first laid eyes on my lifelong companion. I was just eleven years old in mid-December of 1966, when Mrs. Simonetti's car plowed into me as I launched off that makeshift ramp atop my new skateboard. I'd been having a great time in the paved parking area adjacent to our apartment. Her car couldn't have been going more than five miles an hour, but my tiny body didn't offer much resistance. *Wham!* I went flying one way, my skateboard the other as my tiny body crashed to the asphalt. My head violently bounced off the unforgiving surface, and my arm slammed against the pavement beneath me. I can't say I consciously tried to break my fall, but I may have instinctively attempted to protect my back and head by throwing my left arm behind me. I wound up with an arm that was broken in two places and a severe concussion.

It was as though I was somehow flying or floating above my own body. I could see my father kneeling beside me and covering me with his coat. He had his arm behind my head, and it was covered with blood. I saw Mrs. Simonetti in her ugly brown car, just sitting there with her mouth hanging open. She looked like a figure you might see in a wax museum. That's when I first saw Minus. There he was, hovering next to my crumpled little body. I still remember that odd blue color and the unearthly glow surrounding him. That first glimpse was weird and cool and scary all at once. But then, suddenly, I was dropping out of the sky and I fell right down on top of my own

29

body. Then, everything went dark. The next thing I knew, I was waking up in the hospital room.

My father was sitting in the chair next to me when I first opened my eyes again. He looked awful: unshaven and tired. It was the first time he ever looked old to me. When he saw my eyelids flutter he jumped to his feet. "Robby!" he exclaimed as he grabbed me by the shoulders. I remember saying, "You don't have to yell, Dad," and he started to laugh and cry at the same time. Then, I fell asleep again for another two days. The doctors later explained that I had a "severe concussion." When all was said and done, I had lost about a week's worth of days to that head injury. I remember that moment in the hospital, then nothing else until I got home.

It was the day before Christmas when they finally let me go home. My dad said I was "a phantom" those first few weeks. I wasn't sure what he meant, but I was definitely out of it, sleeping about 14 hours a day. I would sleep all day and wake up at night a lot. We lived in a cramped two-bedroom apartment on the second floor. The building only housed six apartments, none of which were very large or very modern, but it was clean, relatively quiet and safe. After my mom died, my dad had sold our little farm and we moved into this place.

My father once explained to me that my mother was a "troubled" person who drank a lot more than she should have and paid a terrible price for it. She and her unborn baby were killed in a car accident that she caused. She had been drinking one night and decided to run to the store despite her condition. My dad had fallen asleep on the sofa, exhausted from a long day at work, and he had no idea she had grabbed his keys off the kitchen counter and hopped in the car. He was awakened by a phone call from the police telling him of the accident. He never told me much more than that, so I'm really not sure of all the details. It doesn't even matter much now. I just wish it had never happened.

30

I still remember being held and sung to by my mother. She made me feel safe. Had I been older the night the accident happened, maybe I could have kept her from driving.

Our new home was located right next door to my dad's brother and his wife, who owned a small two-story house with a nice backyard. Often, because my father worked so many hours, I would stay with them. They've always seemed like an extra set of parents because they really cared about me and always treated me as if I were their own son. Aunt Elena and Uncle Pete gave me a little black-and-white TV set for Christmas, so I would wake up late at night and usually watch some old movie until I fell asleep again. During my recovery period, it was all I could do to stay awake for even a few consecutive hours.

The second time I saw Minus was the day after Christmas. It's still nearly impossible to accurately describe him, all these years later. I woke up in the middle of the night again, and my little TV set was still on. It was so late that all that was on was static. I sat up on the side of the bed and leaned to turn the TV set off, when I saw him out of the corner of my eye. My arm was just frozen in place, barely touching the on/off knob. I couldn't move a muscle. First I thought I was seeing things, so I blinked my eyes very quickly, and then I realized it was real. There, at the foot of my bed, was a blue glow of a pleasant hue I had never seen before, just hovering in mid-air.

Mouth agape, I just stared as this nebulous form that seemed to be taking shape right before my unbelieving eyes. At first, an ambiguous mist-like form, the colorful glow slowly seemed to transform itself into the shape of a little person. Well, not a person like we're all familiar with, but let's say a small person-like being. I wet my bed for the first time in a very long time. I couldn't talk. I couldn't move. This little glowing mass appeared to be smiling at me, and for some reason, I wasn't really scared. Shocked, to be certain, but not scared.

It began to move, ever so slowly, from the foot of my bed, around toward me. And I was still locked in that frozen trying-to-turn-off-the-television, peeing-my-own-bed position. "What a revolting development," it said! "Huh?!" was all I could muster. Then, the blue glow laughed: maybe not a laugh like yours or mine, but there was no mistaking it was a laugh. And then I laughed. I felt at peace, despite having an arm that was held together with some screws, a dull headache, and a urine-soaked pair of pajamas.

"Did you just talk?" I asked. "Well, yes, unless a side effect of your concussion is that you're now able to throw your voice," it wryly smirked. "Holy shit!" was my best effort after that remark. I think I probably said "Holy shit!" about ten times before it stopped me by shutting off the television. Oh, it didn't reach over and turn the knob like you'd expect. Instead, a very electrical-looking light-blue arc jumped from this little being directly toward the television set. And it turned off instantly! There was no sound, no sparks, yet it turned off the TV in an instant. Again, my mouth just hung open.

Figuring I was dreaming, I actually pinched myself, just as I'd once seen Bugs Bunny do in an old cartoon. He pinched himself so hard he screamed out in pain and shot way up into the air! Well, I sure as hell felt the self-inflicted pinch. And though it hurt I could only eke out a feeble little, "Ouch." Realizing I wasn't dreaming, I wondered if I was experiencing some sort of medical side effect. Saying something like, "My head hurts. Goodnight, cartoon man," I flopped down in my pee-soaked bed. When my dad woke me the next morning, he noticed the bed smelled nasty. Because he was still pampering me, he calmly helped me into the shower and changed the bed linens without saying a word.

I tried to describe this peculiar event to my father after I got dressed, but I didn't quite know how. When I thought back to the night before, I really wasn't sure if I actually saw the little creature or not. I described it to him as best I could, but Dad told me it was probably something I ate that made me have a bad dream. I wasn't sure, but I felt it was something altogether different. By breakfast time, I wanted to put thoughts of the glowing little blue "thing" out of my mind, so I tried to convince myself it was all just a dream. That morning, Aunt Elena made dinosaur-shaped pancakes for me. I still can't figure out why dinosaur-shaped pancakes taste better than regular round ones, but they sure do. Come to think of it, they didn't really look all that much like dinosaurs. Aunt Elena could usually make a pretty real looking brontosaurus, but the other ones looked a lot more like cows or pigs than dinosaurs. Aunt Elena and Uncle Pete couldn't have children of their own, but I'm not sure why. It's not my business to know, anyway, but I think Aunt Elena was sometimes very sad about that.

I didn't know what to think about the strange experience of the previous night, but as my father used to say, "If you don't know what to make of something, don't make something of it."

4

Star Glider Meets Amazing Boy

Not long after the weird incident involving the little glow, the cast on my arm was removed and I was told I could do everything I used to do, except skateboarding. Dad wouldn't let me use it for a while, but I didn't care all that much anyway. Mrs. Simonetti died in her apartment the day I came home from having the last scheduled X-rays done. About a week later, we moved into her upstairs apartment, which had a nice view of the canal and the park.

Mrs. Simonetti's apartment smelled like old newspapers and mothballs, so we scrubbed the walls and painted everything. My dad let me pick any color I wanted for my room, so I picked purple. I just wanted to have it be special. It was actually a very cool color when it was all finished. Before too long, we got new neighbors downstairs. It was a girl, a few years younger than me, and her mother. My dad informed me that the girl's father had suddenly moved away one night, and they never heard from him again. The little girl's name was Annie Zaine, which I immediately thought was a fun name to say. Annie Zaine from Zelienople. She had beautiful moss-green eyes and the most striking mane of long, black hair. It was black as coal, shiny and perfect. It didn't take very long for me to develop a crush on her, but I was only going on 12 and was mostly interested in baseball cards, catching frogs and playing "Secret Agent" with my friends Jay and Tommy.

One evening, when I was going downstairs to head outdoors to play, I ran into Annie and her mother, who were carrying in their groceries. Mrs. Zaine said, "Robby, when are you going to come

34

over for cookies? Annie has invited you several times but tells me you always say you're too busy. How can someone be too busy to enjoy some fresh-baked cookies and milk?" Annie had never once invited me, so I was a bit stunned. "Um, how about Saturday?" was what came out of my mouth. Mrs. Zaine just smiled and nodded. Annie looked up at her mother with a thanks-for-nothing look. Annie's mom had been born in Czechoslovakia and had a thick accent, which used to make me happy for some reason.

My dad walked me to their apartment door that next Saturday, and Annie and I had an awkward beginning to what would become a special relationship. Her mom made me feel at home, but Annie was so quiet and still, it made me uncomfortable. She hardly said a word for hours on end. We just watched cartoons on television and gorged ourselves on potato chips and soda. I wondered why she hardly talked, but it was still fun to hang out in a different place for a change.

Despite her being a girl, Annie and I became inseparable over the next few months. She gradually opened up a little more and told me a little about her father and admitted that she missed him. I guess he just suddenly left when Annie was about seven years old. He never said a word, just disappeared one night. He took his car, a suitcase full of clothes, his checkbook and not much else. Annie said he was probably tired of working two jobs all the time and needed a break. I felt bad for her because she actually believed he'd eventually return.

Annie's older brother, Daniel, seemed to rarely stay indoors for very long. He was a few years older than her, and was always out playing with his friends whenever I came around. He was sort of hyperactive, but Annie seemed to get along well with him. Annie never seemed to have much spending money for candy or anything fun. I received a small allowance for doing my chores, and once we became the best of friends I often bought two of everything at the corner store so I could share with her. Annie once promised, "One day, I'll have a whole candy store delivered to you, just to say 'thanks'!"

Her favorite candies were those little flying saucers made out of some kind of wafer that would dissolve in your mouth. Inside the wafer saucers were tiny, multicolored spheres of pure sugar. The only place that sold the little flying saucer candies was the *Foods From Around the World* store, not far from our apartments. It was an amazing store in an old wooden building located close to the Interstate. The sweet old couple who owned the place greeted us warmly every time we stopped in. They sold exotic and unusual edibles, like kangaroo tail soup and ostrich eggs, to travelers heading to and from Pittsburgh. But we were mostly fascinated by the staggering array of incredible candies they stocked. Many were sold for only a penny each, so we'd often enter the store with a handful of coins and emerge with a bag brimming with delicious, hard-to-find goodies.

Annie would sometimes declare that one day she would pilot her own space ship and fly right through Saturn's rings. She said she would take me along and let me scoop the colored gems from the rings. Once, I started to argue that the rings weren't really made of gems, and she stopped me by asking, "How many times have *you* been there?" It made me think about talking before I had my facts straight, and then it got me to wondering if there might actually be billions of little colorful gems orbiting Saturn. Annie always had a way of being sweet, yet tough. She also had the unique ability to encourage me to truly open my imagination.

That summer we must have seen each other nearly every day for hours upon hours. Our imaginations never seemed to run dry. We played all types of make-believe games, and Annie was always great at coming up with the concepts and ground rules. My contribution was usually construction of simple props and adding in some colorful details. We'd often laugh so hard it would hurt. Once I swear I cracked a rib! Annie was always laughing at the things I said. She called me "Amazing Boy" because, as she said, "It's amazing how you make me laugh all the time!" When the two of us played Super Heroes, she was always "Star Glider," and I was "Amazing Boy." Even though I always felt that her nickname was cooler than mine, I didn't mind because I was convinced she was far cooler than me anyway.

Once I went over to Annie's apartment for cookies on a rainy, windy, nasty day. You could smell the chocolate chip cookies throughout the building. Annie greeted me at the door and promptly told me to remove my sneakers, asking me, "Were you raised in a barn?" It was obvious she got that from her mom, who was always saying stuff like that, and then smiling a gigantic smile and winking. While I can't recall all of the details of that afternoon, I remember sitting on the sofa with Annie and watching a movie on their little black-and-white TV.

Annie sat on the opposite end of the sofa, and her little feet, clad in fuzzy pink socks, were tucked underneath her. She was surrounded by oversize pillows and looked like a little china doll to me. We were innocently eating chocolate chip cookies and enjoying the cartoons when it happened again. I clearly recall looking over at Annie and admiring her striking jet-black hair. Her pretty, green eyes were partly obscured by her bangs, and that made her seem a bit mysterious. For the first time in my young life, I guess I was just enraptured by another human being. I didn't quite know what to do with this strange surge of unfamiliar emotions. Well, something happened when she turned her head ever so slightly and looked me right in the eyes. A flood of new and uncomfortable emotions welled up inside me, and I was unprepared to deal with them. Before I could even think, it felt like a river of energy coursed up my spine, unlike anything I had ever felt previously. Then, suddenly, I involuntarily blurted out, "One day I'm going to ask you to marry me." Stunned at my bizarre declaration, Annie bolted and ran to her mother's side in their tiny little kitchen.

She never saw the blue glow jump from my chest toward her as she flew down the hall. But I did.

Annie's mom was always incredibly nice to me, and she never really seemed to get upset. If something irritated her, she would usually take a moment to think before speaking in calm, soothing tones. She became my image of the perfect mother. She emerged from the hallway with a knowing smile and approached me with a tall glass of ice-cold milk. She didn't utter a word as she calmly set the glass on the table in front of me and leaned over to put a gentle kiss on the top of my head. I felt safe and loved and, more importantly, I felt accepted.

I heard the muffled sounds of soft conversation between Annie and her mom going on in the kitchen as I grabbed another cookie and started licking the melted chocolate morsels. Shortly thereafter, Annie bounded in and plopped down on the sofa next to me. "If you are completely done saying weird things, you can stay and have dinner with us." I nodded nervously and immediately began wondering what they were going to serve.

There was no more "saying weird things" for a very long time.

5

Minus Zero

My dad worked very hard, and throughout most of my childhood, he held two jobs. I never understood how he did it and was amazed that he almost never complained. He had his first heart attack on one of the coldest days I had ever experienced. On a frigid Thursday evening in February of 1967, I remember being sure school would be cancelled the next day because the pipes always froze in the old brick school building when the temperature dropped below 20 degrees. The ice-encrusted thermometer attached to our back window indicated it was zero degrees, and the wind was picking up, causing the power lines attached to the house to creak ominously as they swayed back and forth.

Of course, I had to run down to Annie's apartment to tell her, "It's nothing degrees! Nothing!" She wrinkled up her nose and retorted, "You nut! It isn't 'nothing.' That sounds silly. What are you talking about?" I replied smugly, "It is *zero* degrees on the thermometer. So it is 'nothing' outside!" She instantly pivoted and ran to her mother screaming, "Mom! It's nothing out! Nothing degrees is way too cold!"

We didn't have school the next morning, after all. Our ugly old AM radio proclaimed the good news, and my dad told me I could sleep a little later than normal. I did sleep a little more than on a school day, but when I smelled the bacon frying I jumped out of bed and blazed a trail to the kitchen. Dad was whipping up a big breakfast, something he generally saved for Sunday mornings. The smell of the bacon was just too much for me to ignore. He looked over at me and chuckled.

39

"I knew it. Works every time!" I just smiled as he handed me a luscious piece of hot, crispy bacon. He motioned for me to sit at our tiny kitchen table, already prepared for a nice, big breakfast. I asked why he was making our Sunday breakfast on Friday. He said, "It's a special three-day weekend, right? You and I both have today off, so let's have big breakfasts on all three days!" Of course, I agreed enthusiastically. He proceeded to explain, as he served me scrambled eggs, bacon and toast, that he had the entire day off due to the weather. His daytime job was at the high school, where he was a guidance counselor. His night job was at a small warehouse in town, where he helped with the accounting.

The high school was closed, and he always had every other Friday off from his other job, so for once we had the whole weekend to do what we wanted to do. We decided, as we polished off the last of our breakfast, that we would go bowling if the lanes were open. Turns out they were open in the afternoon, so we headed out to brave the frigid conditions. The car didn't want to start right away, but after a few tries it finally turned over. He patted the dashboard in loving fashion and we headed off to the local lanes. Annie and her mom were both under the weather with the flu, and I'd been advised to stay away for a few days. I was excited to have the day off school and, more importantly, to be going bowling with my dad. The roads leading to the bowling alley were slippery, and the temperature was frightfully cold. The car's heater didn't do much to warm us at all. The roads were slick and messy from the previous day's snowfall, but it was a reasonably short drive and we were both enjoying our freedom, so the conditions didn't dampen our spirits at all. Upon arriving safely, we eagerly got out of the car.

When my dad fell to the pavement, I figured he had slipped on the ice. Heaven knows it was a logical assumption. I had to hold on to the car as I got out, for fear I would slip and crack my head open. "Dad, are you okay?!" I yelled. When there was no response, I knew something was wrong. I slid around the back of the car, nearly falling down twice along the way. As I rounded the trunk, I saw my father crouching down on one knee in the icy parking lot, looking at me with a worried expression unlike any I had ever seen. "Don't worry! I'm fine," he rasped. I knew he was not fine. "What is it? What happened?" I pleaded. His right hand was covering his heart, and his face was contorted in pain. Still, he found the will to gently place his left hand on my arm as I knelt by his side. "Robby, it must have been all that bacon I ate!" I couldn't muster a smile; I was too scared. When my father asked, "Do you think you can go get help?" I started running before the last word escaped his mouth. How I ran as fast as I did, over that ice-coated parking lot, I'll never know. But I flew toward the front doors of the bowling alley. Time seemed as frozen as the cruel arctic air that had our world in its clutches. I was as frightened as I had ever been, worried that my father might have had a heart attack. I felt powerful in some weird way, too, as I ran as fast I had had ever run, hurdling a bike rack as I finally approached the doors of the run-down establishment.

Out of the corner of my eye, I saw a blue glow, like liquid light, seemingly moving alongside me as I bounded up the steps and threw open the glass door. Screaming, "Help!" as I entered, I nearly caused the proprietor to have a heart attack of his own. Next thing I really remember, we were riding in the ambulance, heading for Brentwood Hospital over the icy roads of our drab little town. I knew Dad would be alright because something inside told me so. It was incredibly peculiar to me that I felt so sure of that, and I was not nearly as scared as I thought I should be. This was my father's first heart attack. It was also the third time I saw Minus.

The trip to the hospital was all a blur, in many ways. As one paramedic took my father's blood pressure and another hooked him up to an IV, the ambulance seemed to be rocketing down the road, and it was quite a bumpy ride. The lights were flashing atop the speeding tin can, and they were reflecting off the icy road and the snow-covered countryside. When a bizarre glow encircled my father's head, I was taken aback. The blue-tinged light seemed to orbit his head, and then it appeared to jump directly from him to the chest of the attending paramedic. Almost immediately, I watched as this odd-colored light seemed to fly directly up and out through the roof of the ambulance. This all happened incredibly fast. So fast I had to rub my eyes and wonder if my mind was just playing tricks on me. No one else reacted; no one mentioned anything about what I had just seen. So I said nothing. At that point, all I cared about was getting my father to that hospital as fast as possible, but the image stayed in my mind long after that night.

Everything was very peaceful when we got to the hospital. A small town, it was a relatively quiet place all the time. On this night, it was almost like we had our own exclusive private hospital. We got there in record time, and the two paramedics wheeled my father into the hospital quickly. There was an overhang that prevented snow and ice from developing near the hospital entrance, so they were able to very quickly zip him in through the main doors. In close pursuit, I ran right alongside as they wheeled him into an examination room. I didn't really understand all the tests and what they were doing. All I remember is my father looking over at me and giving me a thumbs-up signal as three different people hovered over him. He never wanted me to worry, and he almost never gave me cause to. Even on this night, I felt confident he would be just fine.

Over the next several days, I saw my father for only a few minutes each day. I stayed with my aunt and uncle, and they only brought me to the hospital for about 20 minutes a day. They had their own busy schedules to deal with, and Uncle Pete was not feeling particularly well himself that week. But seeing my father smiling and joking with the staff made me feel sure he would be coming home really soon, and he did, that next weekend.

He was released that Saturday morning, and we picked him up around noon. He said he was "famished" and offered to treat us all to lunch. Even though Aunt Elena protested, he got his way saying, "I never felt better. That's the most rest I've had in ten years!" Dad put his arm around my shoulder and squeezed me tight. I started to forget how worried I was for him. I started to fantasize about the coming spring and going fishing with him again. Those days would indeed arrive, quicker than I imagined, and many fish would be caught and released, and many corny jokes would be shared along the way.

The heart attack had been described as mild, and the doctors had said they felt Dad would be able to resume normal activities fairly quickly. He returned to work and actually insisted he felt better than he had before the attack. I never knew how much of that talk was for my benefit because he was surely capable of putting on a brave front for those people who cared about him most. Over the ensuing months, I kind of forgot about the whole hospital visit and instead focused on my little world of school, friends and pursuing my dreams.

But strange memories sometimes haunted me in my sleep. I had dreams about the little blue being, and sometimes during waking moments, it entered my conscious thoughts. With no way to comprehend the meaning of it, there was a nagging feeling of incompleteness. There were other times during my childhood when I tried so hard to understand these fleeting moments, these mysterious incidents. I would try to talk to the little blue light, thinking it resided within me. I imagined there was something or someone locked inside my mind, and I wondered how to reach it. I would pose questions to this entity, usually as I lay in bed trying to fall asleep. What are you? What are you doing here? What is it that you want? Are you me? Am I just imagining you?

I was afraid to talk about the little flashes of light with anyone, and had almost put the thought of the little glowing creature out of my mind. I figured that my imagination had been playing

43

tricks on me, and chalked it up to my accident and the possibility that I was experiencing lingering effects of the concussion. But these incidents had not stopped, and I experienced a troubling feeling that there was someone or something dwelling inside my mind. There were times it merely puzzled me and times of outright frustration. As I progressed through my pre-teen years, I kept physically active, as it was the most effective distraction from the growing concerns I began to have.

I had never really been afraid of the unexplained phenomena, but I was very afraid of losing my father.

6

Never Can Say Goodbye

Our little town had an organization called Pee Wee Baseball. One day during the spring of 1967, my dad surprised me with a new baseball glove. Actually, it was the first one I would own. He presented it to me in a very matter-of-fact manner, one night after dinner. I was working on my math homework, and he suddenly came up behind me at the kitchen table and set the glove down next to my tattered notebook. I looked at it, then up to him, and he just smiled a wry smile. He said he wasn't sure if I was interested, but he offered to teach me what he knew if I wanted to try. I'd played baseball with friends once in a while but never really knew much about the game and its rules. We didn't have a local team nearby, so I had never been to a real professional game in person. Watching it on television was a bit boring to me, so I only had a basic knowledge of it. At least I was sincerely interested in trying to become a better player, and I knew my father would be a good teacher. So I thanked him and agreed to give it a try.

Over the following months, he taught me a lot more than I ever imagined there was to learn. He also told me much more than I had ever known about his experiences playing baseball during his early 20s. He was a real good player in his high school days, and was offered an athletic scholarship at Buffalo State College. His parents had wanted him to become a dentist or a doctor, but he told me he never had any intention of doing that. He did go to college, but he focused on baseball and track, where he excelled at speed events like the 50-yard and 100-yard dashes. I imagine I inherited my running ability from him because I was always one of the fastest runners in school. I loved running, just for the joy of feeling the wind against my face and through my hair. I loved those split seconds when both feet were off the ground and I felt like I could take flight. My dad must have felt that same way when he was younger. He could still run well, but I imagine he had been twice as fast in college. He played shortstop most of the time and was named Team Captain at the start of his junior year. He sometimes pitched, too, and he told me that he really wanted to be on the mound more regularly, but chronic shoulder weakness made it impossible for him to log a lot of innings. So, he focused on playing middle infield. He said he could have been a big home-run hitter but he concentrated on hitting the ball "where nobody was" and prided himself on driving in runs. When I asked him how many homers he had hit in college, he just smiled and said, "Only the ones that mattered."

So I decided, after hearing some more stories of my father's exploits on the diamond, that I wanted to learn to be a pitcher. I was always good at throwing stuff: rocks, snowballs, just about anything that fit in the palm of my right hand. So I figured it might be possible for me to be good at this. Dad and I decided that we would go out to breakfast every Saturday morning and then head to the nearby park to practice. I was a little concerned that this meant less time for fishing, but he assured me we would make time for both. I wanted to please him as much as I was sincerely curious about learning everything about the game of baseball.

The first Saturday of our training was a washout. It rained so hard that morning I thought the paint would melt off our house. The neighbors down the road had their backyard flood so badly they had an enormous pond of their own for a month. I was pretty bummed out, but we decided to work on my model car instead. I had received a plastic model car kit for the previous Christmas, and I had never gotten around to building it. So we ate breakfast at home, and then we opened up the box containing the '57 Chevy. The instructions were hard to follow, but my father patiently read them to me and watched as I began to assemble the chassis. I often wonder if he ever truly realized how much his involvement meant to me. I think he did, but I still wonder about it.

Once we were able to begin our baseball workouts in earnest, it was great fun. The park was often our exclusive playground on Saturday mornings or early afternoons. Open and sprawling, it was equipped with an old baseball diamond that still had a semblance of definition to the baselines, as well as an old chain link backstop. That was a real blessing as it would have been a lot harder on my father if he had to chase all my errant throws beyond that point. It was rough going at first, especially when he tried to get me to throw harder. I was fine when I just soft-tossed the ball to him as he squatted behind the plate. But when he prodded me with, "Put your weight into it," I was all over the place. The poor man must have lost ten pounds that summer chasing all my wild pitches. He never once complained or expressed any disappointment, though. Instead, he always said something like, "You're getting it now," or, "By next year, you'll be mowing down those batters!" I wasn't so sure, but I loved being out there with my father on those long, sunny afternoons. The breeze almost always came in from the northwest and kept things pleasant until those nasty, sticky days of July and August. Even then, we just came out early in the morning on most Saturdays, and we guzzled water like it was going out of style.

My dad taught me a lot that summer. He taught me the rules of the game and about pitching, in particular. I had previously thought that pitching was all about throwing as hard as possible and was under the impression that every pitcher just threw in a straight line to the catcher. I didn't realize the catcher's importance to the pitcher or the fact that there were situations that greatly affected the pitcher's mental approach. Little by little, my father tried to give me a greater understanding of the game's nuances.

The larger-than-life exploits of Babe Ruth fascinated me, and I was particularly impressed to learn he had been such a phenomenal pitcher. To casual fans he was a larger-than-life legend, perpetrator of mammoth home runs and terrorizer of pitchers. When I read about the pitching records he had amassed, I was confused. I asked my father if this was indeed the same Babe Ruth that people often talked about as a home run hitter, and he said it was. He imparted what he knew, having been a big fan of Babe Ruth as a young child. He also said something that stuck with me all my life. He said, "Robby, greatness is greatness, and it knows no limits. People who possess inner strength push themselves to be the best and can often do almost anything well. It's all about the voice inside. Listen to what your inner voice tells you, and always believe in yourself." At eleven, I was a bit shaky on what he was talking about. I got the basic idea, but it would be a long time before I grew to truly understand.

I quickly became an avid student of baseball history and scoured bookstores and libraries for anything about baseball, especially books on the fundamentals of pitching and hitting. I was also fascinated with stories about professional ballplayers, and Roberto Clemente was my favorite player. There was something special about him; he was a larger-than-life presence who was very proud and confident, yet never arrogant. On the rare occasions when the Pittsburgh Pirates appeared on television, I marveled at Clemente's abilities. My dad admired the way he played, too, and he would sometimes watch the games with me and point out how Clemente could throw with superhuman accuracy from his position in right field.

Having been born in Pittsburgh, Dad had remained a loyal Pirates fan his entire life. I guess I was mimicking him, but it felt quite natural to do so. On my twelfth birthday, that October, my father surprised me with a scrapbook of Roberto Clemente press clippings, photos and interviews from various newspapers. He had been working on the collection the entire summer. It was a great birthday present, one I'll never forget. It's now yellowed and weathered, but it's still beautiful to me. I added to it little by little, since it had lots of room for more content, right up until Roberto Clemente's death. Then, admittedly heartbroken, I locked the scrapbook away in a brown suitcase for many years. It was not until twenty years later that I would open the book again. Roberto died in a plane crash, personally accompanying a mercy mission to Nicaragua, after a devastating earthquake. It happened on December 31, 1972. Upon hearing the news on the radio, I wept and just held my head in my hands at the kitchen table. It would be the worst New Year's Eve and the saddest holiday season I ever experienced.

As for my Pee Wee League experience, it was scheduled to begin the following spring. Open registration took place on a Saturday at the end of March in 1968. My father gave me the money I needed to sign up, and away I raced on my bicycle. The field was only a couple of miles from our apartment. I wanted to go sign up by myself, not wanting the other kids to think I always needed my dad to help me. When I got there, I was surprised to see so many kids and their parents. At first, I regretted not letting my father come along, but I knew he was there in spirit. I remember them dividing us up based on some criteria of age and experience, but we mainly got placed on teams based on our birthdates.

I was assigned to a team called "the Reds," which included about four teammates who I knew well from school. The town we lived in was so small that I recognized almost every kid in the league. Over time, I got to know just about all of them pretty well. The team's manager was the father of my friend, Jerry, who was very small and skinny. He looked like he was eight years old, despite being a month older than me, but he was a funny kid with a ridiculous permanent smile and deep dimples. I always called him "Smiley" because that's all he ever did. He was one of those easy-going never-a-problem types, generally quiet and agreeable.

49

His dad, "Coach Brock," was just about the same way. He was about as mellow as you can be and always seemed to be happy just to be alive. After he familiarized himself with the players, he asked if any of our fathers would want to help him out with coaching and practices. Of course, I knew my dad would want to do this and I couldn't wait to pedal home to ask him. He would surely want to be one of the coaches!

I found him in the driveway, peering under the hood of his old, beat-up car. He was whistling the way he always did whenever he was tinkering with something. Whether he was making dinner or repairing a damaged window screen, he always whistled some old favorite tune. He often pretended to not hear me approach, and then he'd feign surprise at my arrival. True to form, he acted stunned at my appearance as I basically flew off my still-moving bike. "Robby! Fancy seein' you here!" he exclaimed, a big grin stretching across his oil-decorated face. I blurted out all the details of the baseball league in typical staccato style, overwhelming him with words and expressive gestures. He never could resist my enthusiasm because our DNA was lousy with the same passionate stuff.

Once I took a breath, he held up his hand to signal me to calm down. "When does the season start?" was his only question. He didn't ask about the number of practices we would need to attend, although I knew it was a concern. He never suggested it might be in any way inconvenient or a hardship for him. He just placed his one clean hand on my shoulder and said, "You'll need a new pair of baseball cleats, so we'll have to see what they have in town." I should have expected this typical show of support, but, for some reason, it stopped me in my tracks and I was speechless. He gently squeezed my shoulder and told me he'd take me to the sporting goods store right after dinner.

I ran to wash up and immediately began to imagine the type of shoes I might get and what position I would try out for. I had always idolized the great hitters of the era but really wanted to try my hand at pitching. I thought it would be great to be the person with all that responsibility, to be able to control the game as a solitary figure on the mound. A loner by nature, everything about it appealed to me.

To show appreciation for his supportive attitude, I wanted to do something nice for my dad, so I hurriedly set the kitchen table. Selfishly, I figured if I sped up the process of eating dinner, we'd get to the hobby shop that much faster. I realize now that those brief moments when I was placing the dishes and silverware at our respective places at our wobbly little kitchen table were the last purely carefree and happy moments of my life.

As I finished setting the table, I was excited and happy, looking forward to the impending visit to the store to pick out my new cleats. I ran upstairs to my bedroom and grabbed my piggy bank off the nightstand. I brought it down to the kitchen table, yanked the plug from its belly and began digging for the wadded-up bills inside. I just knew I had at least enough to cover half the cost of the new shoes. Counting my coins as I slid each one across the table, I suddenly heard the sound of rain splattering against the screen on the kitchen door. I had noted the grey clouds approaching earlier but didn't expect rain so soon. It came up rather quickly, and the sky had darkened considerably while I was preoccupied with my counting. I had expected to hear the slam of the car hood, followed by heavy footsteps on the wooden porch. I had also expected to hear my father asking me to close the windows upstairs. Figuring I would be the good boy to repay my dad's generous promise, I bolted upstairs and closed the window in my room. I closed the window in the bathroom and then slid across the hardwood floor into my father's bedroom to close the two windows there. I could see the wind was blowing some rain into the room and was relieved that I acted so quickly, without being asked. My dad used to say to me, "You'll know you're growing up when you start doing things without being asked."

I can't remember now if I ever did close those windows in his room. Peering out onto the driveway, I saw my father lying on the ground, face up next to the car. It was so odd; he looked as if he had been gently placed there. Feet together, his legs were stretched out straight. It didn't matter that I practically flew down the stairs, nor did it matter that two of our neighbors were already running across our yard toward him when I skidded on my knees across the gravel driveway and clutched his shoulders. He was already dead.

The neighbors had already called the ambulance, which arrived seconds after I was gently pulled away from my father's lifeless body. The police had also arrived, and Officer Wilkes guided me to his squad car. He kept asking me if I was okay. I don't think I ever really responded, not audibly anyway. I was obviously in shock; I was not able to cry or speak. The squad car followed the ambulance to the hospital, wending our way down rain-soaked roads to that place I never wanted to see again. It was raining very hard, and the sound was almost deafening on the metal roof of the squad car. The siren was off, but the lights atop the car were rotating, casting alternating red and blue reflections onto the shiny asphalt roads.

I knew he was dead by the way the officer was talking to me, by the way the ambulance was leisurely proceeding. No sirens meant no false hope. I felt oddly at peace. It must have been shock, but I wasn't crying, too stunned at the way my entire life had just changed. It was annoying how the policeman continuously asked me, "Are you okay? Are you sure you're okay?" When we arrived at the hospital, I couldn't see where the ambulance had gone. Officer Wilkes had radioed ahead, and an orderly came out to meet us at the front door. The young man, wearing a blue hospital outfit, opened the door to the squad car and gently helped me get out. I had no idea what was going on but thought it was just what happens during these moments. I imagined it was routine for the hospital to treat family members like this. There was something else happening, I would soon find out.

The orderly slowly walked me to a small, sterile examination room and told me he would wait with me until a doctor arrived. He sat me down on the examination table and asked me if I wanted to lie down. I shook my head no, and he shined a small flashlight into my eyes. He peered into each eye and asked me if anything hurt, but I still couldn't speak. I was getting perturbed at these repeated questions. It wasn't until he started to dab a wet cloth on my knees that I noticed the blood flowing from them. I never felt any pain, but I had sliced up both knees very badly when I skidded across the gravel driveway to my father's side. Blood was saturating my socks, and I had begun to feel light-headed. Seeing the blood started to bring me back to reality, but I felt no pain. It was as if I were in a dream.

But my father was dead. I knew it.

The doctor entered just as the orderly was finishing bandaging my knees. He had sprayed the wounds with a stinging disinfectant, but I didn't even flinch. I was numb in every way. The orderly whispered something into the doctor's ear, and then he left the room. He handed the doctor a clipboard, and before he left, looked back at me with a very concerned expression. The doctor, whose name I never knew, began asking me the strangest questions. He asked me if I understood what had happened to my father, and I nodded affirmatively. Though he urged me to speak, I still couldn't muster any sound. He asked if I realized that my father's heart attack had been fatal, and asked me if I knew what fatal meant. Once again, I nodded. Then, he informed me that he was very concerned about my condition. He asked me to lie down on the examination table, and he carefully examined me from head to toe. He had a deep, soothing voice, and he was successful at making me feel safe and secure. I fell asleep while he was still conducting the exam.

When I awoke, I found myself in the same hospital room I had been in after my skateboard accident. "Was it all a dream?" I wondered. I had actually become convinced that it was only a dream and that my father was still alive. Then, the door opened and a nurse poked her head in. She gently called to the doctor, who came into the room alone. He asked me how I was feeling, and I still couldn't make myself speak. He proceeded to tell me why the hospital staff had been so concerned about me.

According to the two neighbors who had apparently run over to attend to my father moments before I saw what was happening, something very bizarre had occurred concerning me. They had reported to the police and the ambulance driver that they observed a strange phenomenon when I came bolting down the stairs to my father's side. "A blue light," the doctor said. "Do you recall a bright blue light?" I had no idea to what he was referring. He proceeded to inform me that the neighbors had expressed concern about my well-being. They claimed they saw me burst through the screen door on our porch "completely engulfed in a bright blue ball of light." They said the light surrounded me as I slid on my knees across the driveway to my father's side. They described it as an eerie blue color that crackled and moved around me. They thought I had somehow been electrocuted, what with the wet ground and the fact that the three light bulbs lining the stairway in our house had all burst. They had informed the ambulance driver that I may have been injured during the incident.

They went on to explain that the light seemed to disappear once I arrived at my father's side but that my eyes appeared to be "odd looking" after that time. The doctor asked me if I remembered any of this or if I was aware of an electrical shock or anything of that nature. I didn't offer much help because I had no recollection of anything of the sort. During the two days I was hospitalized, they conducted all sorts of tests on me, everything from blood pressure tests to checking my eyesight and reflexes, to drawing blood samples. I had my urine tested, my temperature taken, and an EKG administered. I felt fine physically but was still in shock that I had lost my father, my best friend.

Annie and her mother came to see me on the evening of the first day. It was an unusually warm day in April. A nurse gently knocked on my door once and said, "You have a visitor," and then Annie skittishly entered the room. Her cheeks displayed tear tracks, and she was still sobbing gently as she approached. She didn't say a word at first; she just pulled something from behind her back and delicately placed it next to me as I sat on the edge of the hospital bed, legs dangling. It was Buddy, my stuffed toy bear, the one I still slept with. Aside from my dad, only Annie knew how attached I was to Buddy, and she had gone into my room to retrieve him. She knew he would bring me some comfort, and he did. I was upset at seeing her looking so sad, and I couldn't stand to look at her with those tears streaming down her face. She didn't often cry. I refused to cry on this day, wanting to put up a strong front because I figured my father would have expected me to be strong.

Annie couldn't look at me either, at first. Staring down at the floor, she just put her little hand on my hand and stood there. It was a surreal moment. I didn't notice her mother standing in the doorway for the longest time. Silhouetted against the harsh light in the corridor, she was motionless, just observing us. She had sunglasses on and was clutching something in her arms. Once Annie had inched over to the cushioned chair next to the bed, her mother approached me. She kissed my forehead and said, "I'm so sorry, Robby." She slowly unveiled what she had been holding. It was a framed photograph of my father and me. She had captured a moment at the park one day when my father had put his arm around my shoulder. We had just finished eating an enormous picnic lunch that Annie's mother had prepared. There was something magical in both our expressions, and I was looking up at him, wearing a huge smile on my face. He was smiling, too, obviously enjoying a memorable Sunday afternoon.

In the photo, my father appeared healthy, tan and very handsome. There was a special gleam in his eyes that I was accustomed to seeing over the years. It was a wonderful photograph because it captured one of the most carefree moments we had ever shared. It wasn't until many years later that I noticed the faintly visible presence of a hazy blue glow behind my head in the photo. Originally, it just appeared to be part of the multi-colored background of sky and trees.

Memories fade and details get confused over time, but that photograph will always occupy a special place on my wall.

7

Tough Things Come in Small Packages

Annie and I had been friends for a good portion of our childhood years, but as we got a bit older, things became awkward at times. Blame it on puberty. She and her mother moved to an apartment building across town, a week before Independence Day that year. But at least once a week, we would ride our bikes to a park halfway between our homes just to hang out and talk. Even though I sometimes thought of her as a sister, I began to feel a strange new set of emotions whenever she sat close to me.

She took me by surprise one hot and muggy August afternoon at the park by asking, "How old do you think people should be before they can date?" "Umm…I don't know," was my brilliant reply. We just left that question hanging in the air, suspended, perhaps, by the promise and fear we both shared. Annie was consistent in one notable way: she was always willing to express her feelings with me. I think she trusted me to accept her, no matter what she told me. We left that tantalizing question alone, but its impact lingers to this day. I say that because when I close my eyes and go back there in time, I can still hear her sweet, innocent voice asking it again. Annie soon went on to attend the local junior high school, and our paths diverged.

As it turned out, I never did play any organized baseball. Uncle Pete urged me to play and promised to be there for me, in my father's place, but I wouldn't hear of it. If my dad couldn't be there with me, I wanted nothing of it. I was probably a bit rude to my uncle, but I was angry and pledged to never play baseball again. Looking back, it was probably a typical reaction, to associate baseball in some way with the death of my dad. I just didn't want to stand on that pitcher's mound and search for my father's eyes in the stands.

My father's passing left me an orphan. For the first time in my life, I experienced depression and a feeling of abandonment. He had always been there with me, for me, around me. His absence was as powerful as his presence had always been. There was little debate over my next move. At fourteen years old, I was alone and scared. The best solution was to move in with Aunt Elena and Uncle Pete, who welcomed me wholeheartedly. Because they had no children and lived next door to us, it was actually a very easy transition for all of us. I was relatively low maintenance as kids go, and the three of us had always been very compatible anyway. Unbeknownst to me, my father had talked about this with his brother over the years, and Uncle Pete told me he had assured my dad that they would never let anything happen to me if he passed away. Soon after my father's first heart attack, they had apparently talked things over and came to an agreement about my future.

Aunt Elena was always very kind to me. Her light blonde hair was usually braided and arranged in a long ponytail. Of average build, she generally blended in with a crowd, in part because she was shy and reserved in public. She had pretty blue eyes, her best feature by far. Aunt Elena was a peaceful woman who sincerely enjoyed the simplest things in life. A real whiz at sewing and quilting, she did some consignment work for various customers all over town. She was the type of person who could sit in one place for hours upon hours, working on a very complicated piece of embroidery. It amazed me how she wouldn't drink or eat anything for long periods of time, her gentle smile fixed on her freckled face while lost in her work. Uncle Pete was also a fairly quiet sort. Stockier and a little taller than my dad, he was always puttering around the house, and was quite adept at fixing almost anything. And he was fearless in trying to do it himself, no matter the project. He owned a fine collection of tools that my dad had always envied.

It was a rough end of summer. For the first few nights following my father's death, I slept alone in our apartment. My aunt and uncle would check in on me, and I hung out at their house for part of each day, but I slept in my own bed for a while. I was brooding and moping after we moved my meager belongings into my aunt and uncle's house. We threw away everything we didn't need, but we kept some priceless items that reminded me of my father and mother. There was a decent little extra bedroom in the back of the first floor, and they had painted it and put in a nice new bed for me. I cried myself to sleep the first night in my new room, with the mixed emotions of dealing with the shock of losing my father and realizing how fortunate I was to have such wonderful people willing to take care of me. For whatever reason, it didn't really bother me to leave that old apartment behind. Without my father, there was nothing to miss.

One day in August, Uncle Pete sat me down and informed me that my father had asked him to take care of my high school education. I didn't know what he meant at first. He explained that my dad had saved up some money for the purpose of sending me to a private school for my high school education, because he had not wanted me to attend the local school in the village. He felt the level of education was subpar, and he wanted me to better prepare myself for college. To me, this was all news. I had never really thought much about it and had always assumed I would go to school with all my friends. When I learned that the school they had enrolled me in was in downtown Pittsburgh, I was more than a little hesitant. When I asked how I would get to and from the school, Uncle Pete told me that arrangements had already been made with another family whose son would be entering the same school this September. They were happy to have another student riding with them so their son would have someone his age to talk to during the commute. I didn't really know the kid, but when they told me his name I remembered seeing him around school. His name was Jeff Fraver, and his parents had a lot of money. His father was president of a small manufacturing business located in

59

downtown Pittsburgh. His mother was a very nice lady, and it had apparently been her idea to offer me transportation to and from school. His dad had to drive into the city to work anyway, and Jeff was much happier having someone his age along for the ride.

Summer ended far too soon for my taste, and the beginning of a new chapter in my life was suddenly upon me. Uncle Pete had taken me to the mall and properly outfitted me with some new clothes in preparation for the first day. As Mr. Fraver's Olds Ninety-eight slowly approached the school for the first time, I recall thinking, "This isn't going to be easy." The Jesuit Academy was a completely foreign world to me at first. Intimidated by its size and fast pace, I was also a member of the minority for the first time in my life. This was a Catholic school, and my family was Protestant. I was also from a poor family, raised on a farm, while most of the boys at this all-male high school were from the city or suburbs and members of fairly affluent families. In time, I came to learn that there were a handful of boys here on special scholarships, most of who lived in tough inner-city neighborhoods. They represented the minority within the minority, as they were African-Americans in a very lily-white school.

I had entered as an eighth grader, while Jeff was a freshman, so we never saw much of each other during the day. As time passed, I went through a lot of changes. At first I was scared, frustrated and angry. Picked on by many of the other boys, it was a minor miracle I made it through the first year without quitting. They called me "farmer" and made fun of my clothes. Since the school had a strict dress code that required us to wear a blazer and necktie every day, I had trouble adjusting to that, too. I only owned three pairs of pants and a handful of shirts, and only had two blazers that I wore on alternate days.

In time, my sense of humor and cleverness kept me out of fights and, gradually, I was accepted and became part of the scenery in this sea of about 850 young men. The second year was a lot better than the first. I had become close with one of the young teachers, a priest in training named Martin Clooney. Everyone called him Marty and he was probably the most popular teacher in the school. He was different than anyone I had ever met, and seemed so very un-priest-like. He taught Latin, which I always struggled to comprehend, but he was a great person to share ideas with and he seemed to genuinely enjoy my sense of humor. It made me feel more accepted to have a member of the faculty treat me as a friend. Because my guidance counselor had suggested I take an accelerated course of study, I had to take three years of Latin. A mediocre student when unmotivated, I struggled through the rigorous courses but was accumulating credits, even in summer school. Jeff had to repeat a few classes over the summers, so my transportation always remained intact.

The school's lone art teacher, Ms. Linehan, an attractive, young ex-nun (my friends and I used to say she was "just too hot for God") encouraged me to consider applying my artistic talents much more than I had been. She saw something in my work in class, and she encouraged me to think about a career in art or architecture. I shrugged it off for a while, but when I kept receiving rave reviews for my class assignments, I decided I really felt at peace when I drew or painted. In the early part of my sophomore year, I got involved in the Poster Club, which she moderated. We used poster paint to create wildly colorful, oversize banners for school sporting events. We also helped student government candidates make their campaign posters. It was a lot of fun after school on most days. Because Jeff's father didn't pick us up until around 5:30 every day, we had lots of time to kill. Jeff kept busy with the school band, having played trumpet for years and years prior to high school.

A loner by nature, I had collected a few good friends and was never part of any of the established cliques in school. I started to understand and accept the fact that I had nothing to get by on except my wits and my humor. At 5'5" and about 120 pounds,

I was a very inviting target for the bigger kids and bullies. In an all-boy environment, fights, of course, are not uncommon. Usually of the push-down-the-stairs variety or the shove-across-the-room-so-your-books-go-flying type, these skirmishes were usually more about inflicting a dose of humiliation than dealing out any serious physical injury.

I had become quite adept at avoiding altercations. Using my charisma, I was almost always able to make a quick comment that would freeze a would-be adversary in his tracks. I learned that I could actually make the menacer laugh, and that would break his testosterone-driven mindset and defuse the tension. Over time, these guys were either afraid I would use words to embarrass them in public, or they actually grew to like me for my sense of humor and perceived coolness under fire. I fooled most everyone over time, but it was often solely for the sake of self-preservation.

One day, though, things got much more out of hand than usual. I was in my third year, and I had formed a tiny circle of friends and had gotten to know most of the teachers and staff. Still something of a loner, I had at least become fully integrated into the culture of the school. One early morning, a group of students had clustered in front of the door to the classroom where we were taking French 2. The teacher, a tiny Frenchman who was not very popular with the students, was running late. About twenty of us were waiting near the room at the end of the hallway when an awkward, freckle-faced kid named Gorman passed by and bumped into me hard. Gorman wasn't very popular and was average in just about every conceivable way. He grunted a half-hearted apology, and I playfully patted his left cheek and said, "No problem, Gor-MAN!"

The truth of the matter is I didn't mean anything by it. It was just my smart-ass style at that point in my life, trying to be playfully funny. I had no previous issues with Gorman and wasn't upset or angry with him in any way. But that clearly wasn't how *he* saw things. I had just turned to adjust my books under my arm, and then it struck me. His fist, I mean. *Wham!* In the blink of an eye, he blindsided me when I started to turn away and landed a vicious blow to the bridge of my nose. I looked down at the front of my new white shirt and saw a huge splatter of my own blood.

The transformation was instantaneous. I felt the blood rushing from my torso to my head, and my eyes locked onto Gorman's. In a flash, I lunged at him and, with both arms, I violently shoved him against the classroom's closed door. The noise of him crashing into the wooden door made everyone nearby whip their heads around to see what had happened. His eyes opened wide, and he had a look on his face I had never before seen. This was uncharted turf for both of us. I felt like he had victimized me, and my instincts completely drove my reaction. He never hit me again after that first blindside blow. I, however, punched him repeatedly, and then I rammed into his slight frame so hard that we both fell to the floor. I had no control over my anger and was sitting atop his prone body and punching him in the chest as he frantically tried to cover his face in self-defense. With my left hand, I pulled his arms down away from his face and was struck by the glint of blue-hued light reflected in his silvery braces. I balled up my right fist and reached back, intent on nailing him in the nose. I wanted to give him a souvenir to match the one he had given me. At that moment of anger and frenzy, my hand was suddenly trapped in midair. I turned to look up behind me, and, in a surreal moment, I saw our annoying little French teacher, Mr. Roche, clasping my fist in his two bony hands.

All of about 5'4" tall, he had a slight build and was more than a little effeminate; he was the brunt of many jokes around school. In another bizarre moment, I heard all of my fellow students, who had formed a semi-circle around us, chanting, "Hit him! Hit him!" They actually wanted me to belt the French teacher! And, in the heat of the moment, I nearly did. Covered in my own blood and straddling a terrified classmate, I had never felt more powerful. The thought of pulverizing this prissy little teacher was extremely appealing at the time. Then, reason kicked in and counteracted my Hulk-like fury. Detention. Expulsion. I thought better of it, and, to a chorus of disappointed moans from my bloodthirsty peers, I allowed Mr. Roche to extract me from the chest of my classmate. He told me to go clean up in the men's room, and he took Gorman down the hall to the nurse's office.

As I stood in front of the sink in the dark bathroom, splashing cold water on my bloodied face, I saw something that truly frightened me. The first thing I noticed as I raised my head up to look in the mirror was my swollen nose and the blood still trickling from my nostrils. The very next thing I noticed, however, was the strange blue aura enveloping my hands. A little freaked out, I frantically tried to wash it away under the gushing cold water. It started to fade away, and I began to calm a little. But, then, I caught a glimpse of something strange in the mirror. There seemed to be something or someone directly behind me. I whipped around as droplets of reddened water flew from my face and hair. A vague form was suspended in air behind me. It was familiar in that it reminded me of the little blue lights I had seen before, but this was disturbingly different in its size and intensity. Ambiguous in shape, it was a milky blue-white, glowing mass suspended in midair, undulating and floating about three feet off the floor. Within a second or two, it lost intensity and began to disappear. I instinctively reached out to attempt to touch it, but my hand just passed through it. I leaned my back against the sink, mouth agape.

The water, overflowing the sink, splashed around my feet and soaked the bottom of my trousers. At that moment, the diminutive French teacher entered the bathroom and startled me. "Mr. Chandler! I need you to return to the classroom, please!" he insisted. I was stunned by what I had just seen. So much so, that our little fracas was already a near-forgotten incident. I was actually afraid, worried that I was having hallucinations or had experienced a seizure. Once the French class was over, I was instructed to report to the nurse's office, and I had no option but to oblige.

The school nurse was a humorless and uninteresting middle-aged woman with thinning, gray hair. I had rarely ever seen her, let alone spent any time in her presence. She had a stern look of disapproval on her face when she greeted me. With my disheveled and dirty appearance, I completely understood. I plopped my blood-stained books on the table near the entrance to the examination room and sat down at her request. She did a cursory exam of my nose and declared that it was indeed broken, but she said it would heal on its own because it was not displaced. She cleaned up all the dried blood I had missed on my face and put a small bandage on the bridge of my nose, all routine stuff in a day in the life of a school nurse. As she was just finishing up with my repairs, a knock came at the door.

In walked my adversary: Gorman. He sheepishly entered, his dark blue blazer still rumpled. Bloodstains decorated the front of his yellow shirt and his naturally curly reddish-brown hair was all messed up. He looked like some pathetic car wreck survivor. Mr. Roche had escorted him, and he walked in directly behind Gorman. Roche then quickly motioned to the nurse to join him in the hall for a chat and left me alone in the room with Gorman. After I assured him I was sorry I had reacted as I had, he admitted he was sorry he hit me first. He said something about being sick and tired of being the butt of everyone's jokes. I guess it didn't matter who he took it out on; I was just in the wrong place, patting the wrong cheek at the wrong time.

He finally looked up, tearing his reddened eyes away from the white tiled floor for a moment. He had a peculiar expression of concern and fear on his face as he asked, "What the hell was that thing, by the way?" I admit I knew exactly what he meant when he said it. "I don't fucking know!" was the best I could offer. At that moment I felt exposed and threatened for some reason

I couldn't quite understand at the time. It was as if someone saw you sneaking a look at your sister's diary or something.

I had been in denial about the strange blue blur that had haunted me since my early childhood. I had been curious about it, of course, but as days and weeks passed and it failed to happen again, I stored it away in my subconscious. This event had been significantly different from past experiences. I realized, as I sat there pondering the blood beneath the fingernails on my right hand, that I both *felt* it and saw it this time. And I was very worried that others saw it, too. Gorman said, "Man, do you even know what that was? Everyone's talking about it, but they have no idea what the hell happened. I don't really give a shit about you slamming me to the floor, but when I saw that halo over your head, I just fuckin' spazzed!"

At that point, Mr. Roche reentered the room and told Gorman to follow the nurse down the hall. He looked back at me with a very concerned expression as Gorman dutifully obeyed. Mr. Roche was certainly not one of my favorite people; he just rubbed me the wrong way. It was partly because I had never been around such a prissy man and, partly because I really hated the way he taught French. He just seemed to recite and repeat, recite and repeat. God, it was a crappy way to teach. He wore some type of disgusting oil in his hair, too, which smelled like flowers. The deep horizontal lines on his forehead were all scrunched together as he slowly approached me. I had a hunch what was coming but was not completely prepared for what he actually said.

"Mr. Chandler," he began in a near-whisper, "We have a problem to deal with." I had been looking down at my shoes until he said that. I noticed I had somehow ripped the toe of my shoe on something, and the lace on my right shoe was untied. There were several tiny bloodstains on my white sock. Snapping out of the damage assessment, I snapped my head up to look right into my teacher's beady eyes. I'd never before seen him look so serious. He went on to say, "Some of the other students are upset, and I've had to ask Father Graziano to settle them down. He's with the class right now, but you and I need to talk before I can return you to the classroom." I was somewhat surprised at what I viewed as a bit of an overreaction to our little fight. Even though it was my first personal involvement with fisticuffs at the academy, it was far from unprecedented.

Earlier that fall, one of the greatest boxing matches ever waged in blazers and ties happened right in front of the office of the school's disciplinarian. Our resident Mafioso hood, Anthony Como, squared off against our scariest inner-city thug, Ronnie Horne in a battle for the ages. Ronnie was the most menacing looking and toughest kid in the school. His skin was as black as coal, so he was impossible to miss in the usual sea of white faces. Stocky, built like a tank, he clearly displayed a tendency for bad intentions. I almost never saw him smile, unless he was having fun at the expense of someone else.

Anthony, who would only be addressed as "A.C.," was often the talk of the school, in part because he dressed better than anyone else and in part because of persistent rumors that his father was a mafia boss. I had never read about his family in the newspaper or anything, but A.C. sure looked the part, and few ever doubted there was some truth to the rumors. His curly dark blonde hair was cropped short and his scraggly looking moustache was barely visible on his angular face. He was a wiry little guy, much slighter of build than Ronnie, but A.C. was athletically gifted and possessed a sinister mean streak that kept other guys at bay. Let's just say there was a lot of street credit and respect for these two larger-than-life characters, mainly because it was commonly accepted that they would hurt anyone who crossed them.

On this particular day a year removed, it all happened during the break between classes in the early afternoon. Right after lunch I heard a loud commotion as I walked past the chapel, which was housed in a large room near the center of the school. The noise was coming from directly in front of the vice principal's office. A circle of students had begun to form around two figures I couldn't initially make out. As I shoved my way closer and squeezed between two kids, I saw that it was none other than A.C. and Ronnie Horne duking it out. This was like Frazier vs. Ali! Not some run-of-the-mill scrap, this was as big as a high school fight got! I couldn't help but fall right into the bloodthirsty mindset of the expanding crowd of onlookers.

As I quickly scanned the circle of humanity, I spotted a couple of teachers, one of them a priest. Father Graziano was standing between two freshmen, his hands up on their shoulders. "Why would he let this go on?" I wondered. I was more amazed by the fact that teachers and staff of the school were not only allowing this to happen, but they were enjoying it! I must admit it was quite a spectacle. A.C. shocked me with how skilled at boxing he had become. It was obvious that he had been training. Snapping off loud, whistling jabs to Ronnie's head, he resembled a Golden Gloves participant. He moved nimbly, exhibiting the footwork of a trained and polished fighter. And Ronnie was as Ronnie always was: menacing snarl, lifeless eyes. He bobbed and weaved, but he forced the action and looked very much like someone who could kill an opponent with one solid punch. A.C. was very slick, and he respected Ronnie's strength, so he moved fast, circling and slipping punches. A series of lightning-quick jabs *pop-pop-popped* against Ronnie's shiny, dark cheek. A small cut appeared instantly under his left eye, and although Ronnie barely even flinched, that exchange finally got Father Graziano to take action.

The hardened little priest burst from the swell of cheering onlookers and wrapped his arms around A.C. from behind. These three people were all small in stature, but I learned once and for all that "it isn't the size of the dog in the fight…" on that day. If you had seen these two kids fight, you would definitely realize just how foolhardy it was to cross either one of them. Trust me. And Father Graziano, who had been an amateur boxer in his youth, was no one to mess with. About 45 years old, he stood no taller than about 5'7". But when he looked into you with his dark, piercing eyes, you just knew it was in your best interest to shut up and look down. He was the most intimidating person in the school, despite being one of the smallest adults. He had a firm grasp of A.C., and the look on Ronnie's face was priceless. He wore an expression that said a thousand things, yet he never uttered a word. I saw anger, fear, disappointment and resignation all flash over his face within a split second: angry at whatever it was that A.C. did to provoke this fight, afraid that he would be punished harshly (as this was not his first offense), disappointed that he didn't get to hurt A.C. and resigned to the fact that the priests always got the last word at the academy. That was the one inescapable truth.

A.C. wound up getting suspended for a week, but his father somehow managed to get that reduced to two days. Ronnie didn't get suspended at all, for reasons I can't guess, but he did get detention for a week. I saw him picking up trash outside every afternoon after classes. In the days and weeks immediately following the "fight of the year," I witnessed these two pass each other in the halls many times, and they never looked at one another, let alone get into another altercation. About a month or so after the fight, one Monday morning, A.C. showed up for school with two black eyes and a broken nose, evidenced by white tape across the bridge. Strangely, he looked as though he had aged about ten years, too.

No one seemed to know what had happened, but the persistent rumor was that he and Ronnie had set up a rematch somewhere in the city. According to one kid who was a friend of A.C.'s, Ronnie had shown up to the designated location with a knife hidden inside his sneaker, while A.C. had stashed a set of brass knuckles in his own pocket. From what people said, it was a fight that turned very serious once A.C. had his nose busted. Ronnie had taped his right hand and had lined the tape with a lead strip. A.C. had not used the brass knuckles until after he had his nose rearranged, but then he got pissed and went for it.

The fight was brutal, and, finally, Ronnie resorted to the hidden blade he had brought. I have no idea what of this was true and what wasn't, but the most common story I heard was that once he saw the knife, A.C. pulled out a pistol. I was not surprised to hear he had a gun because he sometimes made remarks about target shooting and things like that. And I knew he had the money to get just about anything he wanted. But, bringing a gun to a fight in the city, for a high school kid at one of the nicer Catholic schools in the state? This had become a little more serious than the typical schoolyard rivalry. According to the whispers in the cafeteria, A.C. had definitely not been just joking around or trying to intimidate. He was dead serious as he pointed the gun at Ronnie's head. The story goes that Ronnie was frozen in his tracks and he and A.C. stood there in the dark street, two kids caught in a bizarre standoff.

From everything I heard, Ronnie made an offer to A.C. of some kind, and A.C. ultimately accepted it and put the gun away. They went their separate ways late that night, and that was the end of the story. Now, A.C. showed up for school looking like this, and Ronnie Horne was nowhere to be found. He didn't report to school that week and never did return. Speculation was rampant over the following weeks and months, and, to this day, I have no idea what truly happened. Some say Ron had offered to leave the academy if A.C. agreed to put the gun away. Others say they heard Ronnie was killed in a gang fight the very next day. I overheard one of Ronnie's friends say, "Ron got paid off and he headed for Jersey." I don't know who to believe, but it still intrigues me. A common rumor is that, on that night, Ronnie asked A.C. to let him go and offered to provide A.C. with some type of illegal drugs. Apparently, Ronnie was into all types of recreational 'activities', including pot, LSD and acid. A.C. agreed and specified the time and place for a drop the next morning. As the story goes, Ron agreed to the terms because he was afraid of A.C.'s powerful father and his alleged ties to the mob. He knew he was in over his head, and he knew A.C. was a ruthless kid with a very bad temper. He knew A.C. could afford to buy whatever he wanted, but he was convinced that A.C. wanted to acquire some quantity of drugs and guns from Ronnie because the transaction would be nearly impossible to trace.

The story goes that Ronnie never showed up after all, and that enraged A.C. to the point that he wanted revenge. Now, some say Ron moved to Trenton, New Jersey because he had relatives there, but others claim Ron hid out at his older brother's home downtown, to stay out of sight until the whole thing blew over. They say he was abducted by a trio of men wearing some type of masks, plucked from the basement of his brother's house. What happened to him after that? No one really knows. Maybe Ron is alive and well and living in the Garden State. All I know for sure is that Ronnie never returned to school, and no one ever made a statement to the general student body concerning his absence.

As Mr. Roche paused to take a deep breath, I was trying to imagine what he was going to say next. Was his main concern the way I lost my temper and went a little crazy in attacking Gorman? Was he aware that I had almost hit *him*? Or did he possibly see the strange blue glow, too? He proceeded to tell me he was very concerned about the other students who had witnessed the fight. Not because they were exposed to the violence, but because of their reactions. He told me that there were a number of students who were emotionally shaken up.

Then, he informed me that some guys were talking about "the weird burst of blue light" and "the glowing halo" they saw over my head. He said they were asking questions he couldn't answer. I felt embarrassed and exposed, for some reason. Mr. Roche went on to say that he wanted to hear my side of the story. I described how it had been a misunderstanding, that I didn't mean to upset Gorman, but he shouldn't have hit me when I wasn't looking. I apologized for swearing (I remember calling him a *son of a bitch* as well as a few other colorful words) and for punching Gorman in the mouth, but he was after something else. "Boys will be boys, Mr. Chandler," he said dryly. "I want to know what you think of the other thing: this odd light some of the boys are talking about." I didn't know what to say. "I don't really know anything about that," I sheepishly mumbled. He took a deep breath and said, "I think *something* unusual happened. Otherwise, how can you explain the reactions of the other boys?"

I wasn't lying. Of course I realized that this bizarre phenomenon had resurfaced from years ago, but I had no clue what it was. Nor did I have any understanding of whether it was following me or attached to me or if there was some external source that was causing it. I knew I didn't control when it appeared, but I also knew I wasn't afraid of it or overly concerned about it happening again. But I was curious, of course. "Did *you* see it?" I asked the uneasy teacher. "No. I didn't see this thing some of the boys are talking about," he replied. He paused, and then he looked at me sympathetically and asked, "What did *you* see, Robert?" I had to think hard about what I really remembered, and I tried to recall details of some of the incidents of the past as well as this day. I reflected on the vague memory of "the little blue man" I saw when I was recovering from my accident. I remembered the brief flash of light that chased Annie down the hall that day. And I recalled the blue bursts of light that "chased me" down the stairs on the day my father passed away. What was happening to me? On this day, I had seen a mist of weird light around my head when I looked into the mirror in the boys' gloomy restroom.

I was beginning to feel a deeper concern about this than ever before. I asked Mr. Roche why all this was important. I admitted to seeing some odd lights in the past, but, for some reason, I lied and said I didn't see anything like that today. He said that he would talk to the other students and get them to calm down. Father Graziano was doing some of that as we spoke, but Mr.

Roche said he wanted to talk things over with the boys who seemed upset. He said the nurse would come back to check my vital signs and that I should rest here until the school contacted my uncle and aunt. I just remember wanting to take a hot shower and get some sleep.

That afternoon I felt confused and exhausted. When I exited the nurse's office, I couldn't help but feel conspicuous. It was late morning, so I had lunch period to deal with. The usual group of guys at my usual table were already there, halfway finished with their meals. I skipped food and sat at the far end of one side of the table. My friend Andy Graves was there, and he immediately moved to sit next to me. "Whoa, Rob! You really kicked the shit outta ol' Gor-go! It was awesome! He was white as a ghost! Man, you really nailed him good a couple times!" I held my hand up to shut his stream-of-consciousness rambling, and calmly asked, "What about the other guys? What are they saying?" I asked.

He started up again, "Awww, man. They're probably scared of you now, most of 'em. I mean, that fat ass, Pulaski, he looked all pale and shit when you stood up with all that blood dripping from your nose! I never saw that loudmouth look so sick! He sat at his desk with his face in his hands all during French class. And what the hell happened to Roche? The little twerp looked like he saw a ghost or something. After he was in the nurse's office checking on you, he came back and looked like crap. He told us you were okay but not coming back to class, and then he said that anyone who wanted to talk about what happened should either see him after class or talk to one of the priests or to Graziano. Then, he just told us to read the next section in the stupid workbook, and he never said a word after that."

"Did he say anything else about me? About the halo or anything?" I asked. Andy looked a bit confused and said, "Not really. Why?" I sharply added, "Because of what some of the guys were saying!" "Oh, a couple of guys were saying they saw a flash of light or something, but I don't know what their problem was. I didn't see anything other than you beating the crap out of the kid! It was awesome, Rob!" Andy was a starting linebacker/defensive back on the football team, and he had a highly developed appreciation for violence at times. He seemed to be enjoying the situation so much, I just let it go.

I was relieved that very few students had apparently seen or thought they saw anything unusual. I was so confused about all that was happening; I just wanted to get past this day and onto the next. A student who I never had really spoken to stopped next to me for a second as I was organizing my notebooks at the lunch table. His name was Randy Torgelson, and he was a huge track and field star who was well known for the school records he'd established in shot put and discus, stuff that was completely foreign to my friends and me. No one ever seemed to hang out with Randy. He was even more of a loner than I was, and I don't think I had ever heard him speak to anyone in the years he was at the school. He paused next to where I sat, and I was impressed by his massive presence. He was easily 6'3" tall, and his shoulders were as wide as he was tall. He must have tipped the scales at over 260 pounds. His corduroy jacket made a soft *voooping* noise as he slowly approached. Looking straight ahead, not at my tiny form at belt-level sitting adjacent to him, he suddenly stopped, holding his tray in his right hand out in front of his gigantic body. With his left hand, he patted my left shoulder once.

It felt like someone had dropped a lead-weighted pancake on me. I didn't know what to do, so I just sat there. He only paused for a second and then slowly ambled to the exit and was gone. Pete was standing next to me and, for once, he had nothing to say. We both just looked at the exit door, through which Randy had just passed. The door swung shut and made a loud slam. After a minute or two passed, Andy just turned to me and said, "Christ! You have a new pal, I guess. What the fuck?"

In the days that immediately followed the incident, I never heard much of anything about the halo, or whatever Mr. Roche claimed some kids had complained about. I began to think it was mainly Roche who saw it as he was the only one who described it in any detail. I began to wonder if it might have had something to do with the fact that he grabbed my fist in the heat of the fight. I thought it could have been our brief physical connection that was the stimulus for him seeing something tangible. For whatever reason, that made some sense to me.

Maybe Mr. Roche saw it and was imagining that everyone else had to have seen it too. Maybe he wanted to reassure himself that he wasn't crazy, so it was possible he made it up or actually believed that the rest of the witnesses to the fight saw the same thing he did. I knew it was real, but I also knew I didn't want everyone to think I was a freak, so I was relieved when the weeks passed and nothing more was said. The only change was that I received a lot more respect following the fight.

Guys who had previously given me a hard time were strangely quiet. Friends were a bit more eager to talk to me and take my side in arguments. Only a handful of classmates had actually witnessed the fight, but word quickly spread around the school. I felt both uneasy and happy about it at the same time. Because I wanted to be the same kid who was largely invisible to most everyone else, it was uncomfortable to think people were talking about me behind my back. Gorman was seemingly unfazed by what had happened. A loner who had always existed outside all the cliques, he continued to blend in with the surroundings. I think he was resigned to being inconsequential to the masses. We spoke a few times, and there was no lingering tension between us, because I think he realized he had overreacted and that my instincts got the best of me. The only thing was that he and others were a bit surprised by the ferocity I showed. In the world of schoolboys, that type of demonstration earned some respect, and I was fine with that.

Sailing through the holiday season, I put that incident out of my mind and was enjoying getting more involved with my artwork. That Christmas, my aunt gave me a tremendous art kit filled with acrylic paints, colored pencils and a couple of instructional books. She had assembled the contents herself, putting the components together in a wooden box that Uncle Pete made in his workshop. My initials were burned into the front corner, in small type. I quickly developed a fascination with painting, and for the first time I considered that I might want to make a career of art. In that era, there was a burgeoning growth in the advertising field, with the media frequently alluding to the glamour and influence of the Madison Avenue advertising firms.

That winter I started asking a lot of questions of my art teacher, my guidance counselor and anyone else who might know something about careers in the art field. My art teacher was very encouraging, and she told me she thought I should start applying myself more if I was serious about an art career. She was a very talented painter, but she always said her work was not commercial. She displayed her paintings in tiny art galleries and at summer festivals and said she was satisfied with that. I knew I would never be happy if that was the highest limit I could reach, so I started to get more serious and drew and painted for hours on end. I didn't neglect my homework or stop seeing friends after school, but I spent the late evening and early morning hours trying to become better.

It was not out of the ordinary for me to stay up until the wee hours of the morning working on a painting. I had always enjoyed copying panels from my favorite comic books, like Spider-Man and Captain America and The Fantastic Four when I was younger, but now I wanted to start to develop my own style. That was going to be more difficult. I decided that one way to accelerate my education was to try to create photo-realistic paintings from pictures I would tear out of magazines. A huge fan of professional football, I decided to copy action shots from magazines like Sports Illustrated. Over time and with much practice, I learned I could duplicate almost any photo and make a painting that closely resembled the original. My technique was a bit unpolished, but with every painting I completed I felt I had learned some useful lessons.

I hadn't yet developed a signature style, but was determined to develop my technical skills, and I proved to myself I could draw almost anything. The first several paintings were small in scale, but they drew praise from classmates and from Ms. Linehan. She helped me to identify the skills I needed to improve, and I listened intently. Because she was my advisor in Poster Club, we had some extra opportunities to talk about my work, and she was generous with her time and advice. I once asked her if she thought it was possible for me to make a career in art. She assured me I was talented enough to do whatever I wanted, but she warned me about one thing. She said, "You have to stop hiding your ability under a basket. Be proud and be willing to show off a little. You tend to keep your talent to yourself. If you want to succeed, you need to make sure everyone sees what you can really do." Her words confused me at the time, but I took it in, and it made me feel I could do it, even if she was the only one who believed in me.

In the early spring, I had entered a school art contest and won it. It was a period in which I was experimenting with creating fantasy images, as the psychedelic era and pop art were upon us. The winning piece was a watercolor/pen and ink rendition of a trio of harpies surrounded by wildly-colored op-art patterns. You would think I was on magic mushrooms or something. Regardless, I won a $50 gift certificate for the best art supply store in the city. It burned a hole in my wallet until I had a chance to sponge a ride there one Saturday morning. I bought canvases, more acrylic paints and several new brushes. I felt like I was on my way to really becoming an artist.

In May, I received a phone call that took me by surprise.

77

8

I Can't Recall the Movie

On a beautiful May evening, the phone in the kitchen rang as I was rushing to my room, intent on starting work on a new painting. No one else was home yet. Aunt Elena had actually been out of town for the previous two days, visiting a friend who had been ill. Uncle Pete rarely got home before six on most nights. He had left a note on the refrigerator telling me he would not be home until after 7:30, due to a school board meeting. I answered the phone, expecting it to be my aunt or uncle on the other end. Instead, it was Annie.

"We're moving," was all she said. I immediately felt sick to my stomach. "What do you mean?" I asked. Annie was obviously sobbing while she explained that her mother was remarrying. I had been vaguely aware that her mother was in a relationship with a man who Annie had briefly mentioned, but I had no idea she was planning on marrying him. She told me they were moving to Atlanta at the end of the month. Her mother's future husband had just been transferred, and he had already relocated. It had all happened so fast. Annie was pretty upset, especially for her. She usually took things in stride. I did my best to reassure her that she'd make new friends and would fit in wherever she went, but she didn't want to hear it. She said, "I'm sorry," and hung up on me. I tried calling her back, but she didn't answer.

I was unhappy about her moving, but was so caught up in all that was going on in my life, it didn't affect me like it affected her. When Uncle Pete came home that night, I told him about Annie's news. He said he had already known about it since running into Annie's mother in town that afternoon. When he said he was sorry, I just shrugged it off like it didn't bother me at all. I was deeply focused on my latest painting, and had always figured we would eventually have to go our separate ways. So I turned all my attention to drawing and painting. It served as a way to take my mind off Annie, and it worked well enough, until a few weeks later when Annie called again. It was a Friday evening, and, once again, I was pouring my energy into one of my projects. This time I was finishing a portrait of my father, using a favorite photo as reference. The photograph was black and white, but I was painting the portrait in color.

Annie sounded quite upbeat, even though she reminded me that she and her mother were nearly packed and set to move the following week. She said she wanted to see me before the move and that she wanted to give me something. I suggested we ride our bikes and meet up at the park. We called it the "Rocket Park" because it had a fleet of metal rocket ships that kids could sit on. They had springs at their bases, and a child could rock back and forth on them. They looked all beat up, but a kid with a vivid imagination would never care about that. We used to act out our little Star Glider and Amazing Boy adventures there, years ago. "No, no!" she exclaimed. Instead, she insisted on going to see a movie with me.

"Like a date?" I asked. She quickly replied, "No, I just want to see this movie, and I want to see you again before we move. So let's go tomorrow night, okay? My mom said she can drop us off and pick us up afterward." I thought about it and felt it was possibly the last time I would ever see Annie, so I agreed. Annie made the arrangements with her mother. I had saved up some money, so I planned on paying for the movie tickets and refreshments. The next evening, Annie and her mother showed up in their old station wagon and off we went. Something felt different to me. Annie was wearing a tailored black skirt and a dressy-looking white blouse. She looked so much more grown-up than she ever had. I was dressed in my usual style, as in not much style at all.

Annie smelled good, but I was just not accustomed to this version of the little girl I had known for so long. She asked me if I was excited to see the movie, and I gave a half-hearted affirmative response. It was all odd to me. Her mom was driving and trying to make chit-chat with the two of us sitting in the back seat. We all knew each other too well for this awkwardness to seem normal. We watched the station wagon pull away, standing on the sidewalk in front of the small theater, just stuck in place. Finally, Annie grabbed my arm and led me to the box office. I tried to buy the tickets, but she stopped me and said her mother wanted to treat us. So she paid for the tickets.

Annie didn't want any snacks, but we stopped at the concession stand anyway. I liked the smell of the hot popcorn and enjoyed that unmistakable rhythmic popping noise. I bought two small sodas and we headed in. For the life of me, I can't remember what movie was playing. The whole evening was a surreal experience. Here we were, two longtime friends, and suddenly, everything felt weird. I remember sweating and wondering why, and then I realized that Annie was looking at this night as something special, something meaningful beyond two pals going to see a movie. Our emotions were tangled up like leftover angel hair pasta. I didn't know how to feel. She was obviously upset about moving away but trying hard to put on a happy face.

I was a little detached and resigned to the fact that our childhood was in the rear view mirror, and I was intent on going forward as fast as I could. At the same time, I really didn't like the idea of Annie moving so far away. I also felt the urge to do something romantic, for her sake as much as mine. In my heart, I knew she wanted me to take her hand and hold it throughout the movie, but I just couldn't summon the courage to do it. I wanted to, but I think I was afraid to send that message. Knowing she was at the brink of moving away, I also thought it would just be torture to become something more serious to each other and then have to miss her every day. So there we sat, watching a movie neither of us cared about, wanting to make the leap but not quite ready for it. In some ways, it was the most uncomfortable two hours of my young life.

As we slowly shuffled out into the lobby, we didn't speak a word to each other. It was all wrong in my mind. Why was it so impossible to just be who we had always been? We walked out into the warm, sweet-smelling night, just two kids drowning in our adolescent confusion. Annie asked if we could walk a bit since her mother wouldn't be there for a while. I agreed, hoping the evening air would change the tone and break the tension. We commented on passers-by and made conversation, and things started to feel like old times again. That is, until Annie turned and grasped my wrists. She just stopped suddenly and put her toes up against mine. I was taken aback because, for Annie, this was highly unusual behavior. She was never a very aggressive person, at least not around me. She had always followed my lead and was a lot of fun, but she was generally shy and reserved by nature. I guess I brought out her other sides.

While her hands were tightly wrapped around my wrists and she was gazing into my eyes, a wave of powerful emotions coursed through me. I suddenly felt flushed and feverish. I saw in her expression something I had never seen before. For reasons I was unable to fully comprehend, I felt threatened and flattered all at once. I felt a rush of adrenaline and unfamiliar emotions and I wanted so badly to kiss her, but just couldn't. Scared and uncomfortable, I asked, "Hey, what gives?" like a damn fool. She didn't flinch. Instead, she held on tight and closed her eyes. I didn't know what to do, so I closed my eyes, too. She must have wanted to kill me. I was still a little boy in my mind and my heart. She was clearly moving toward a new realization for herself. Did I like her? Of course. Did I love her? Yes, I did in my own way. But I was nowhere near ready for anything beyond playing board games, fishing, riding bikes and losing myself in all those make-believe stories we shared.

Looking down at her tiny hands clasping my wrists, I saw the slightest hint of a blue, mist-like aura emanating from my forearms. I felt as though I was about to explode from all the unleashed passion and the conflict in my mind. Damn it, I really cared about Annie and suddenly I felt like a loser. I felt like she was growing up and leaving me behind, in more ways than one. I didn't want her to see the freakish aura or to see me sweating like I was, so I did my best to break the tension. I distracted myself by opening my eyes wide and looking at the traffic passing by. It helped me get my mind back on reality, and the emotions I was feeling began to subside. I pictured Annie and her mother and her new stepfather driving away from the town we both grew up in. It made me feel angry, and that distracted me from the burning desire to kiss her.

She eventually relaxed her shoulders and loosened her grasp on me. I felt her entire body slump, even though I was not in contact with her any longer. I said, "I'm sorry." She opened her eyes and said nothing. She just turned and started slowly walking back to the theater. Her mom's car was just approaching, and I think we were both relieved to see her. We hopped into the back seat as if nothing had happened, and she looked out the window on her side of the car while I did the same. The colorful lights of the city had a relaxing hypnotic effect on me. Annie seemed both relieved and disappointed, and I felt she was done with me, in a way. That night, when I got into bed, I realized there would be no turning back. No more Star Glider, no more Annie. I felt convinced the world was a cruel place, and I decided I needed to harden my heart. I didn't see Annie on the days leading to her move. We talked on the phone one night, but it was all just bullshit and politeness.

Goodbye, Annie.

9

As I Look Back, Everything's So Sketchy

My final year of high school was marked by equal amounts of scholastic mediocrity and artistic achievements. I had begun to focus on painting portraits and was able to get some occasional commissioned work. I didn't charge very much for a full-scale portrait, selling a couple of them for about $25 each. But I wanted and needed all the experience I could get, determined to build a collection of actual portrait work in my growing portfolio. I even convinced a couple of local stores to display some of my paintings, including a nearby Sherwin-Williams hardware store, owned by a kind old man who was a member of a local artists' guild. He offered watercolor painting lessons on the side, and he allowed local artists to display and sell their work in his store. Although it seemed like an odd place for artists to show their paintings, with time it made more sense. They did sell art supplies at the store and had set aside a respectful little area for a makeshift gallery.

Exhibiting artists established the prices on their own work, and the store owner only took ten percent of the sale price. He made it clear that the commission money allowed the little gallery to continue, since it was valuable real estate within the store. I appreciated the opportunity to have so many people see my paintings, and I began to paint subjects I was certain would sell. In time, the paintings sold fairly quickly. They were priced at a level most could tolerate, and I had carefully strategized the right subject matter. In fact, I sold every painting I ever displayed in that store. The one mistake I made was in not photographing all the paintings. I didn't own a good camera during that time, which was unfortunate. Now I have no record of any of the paintings I sold, and I regret that oversight.

I was never confident I would be able to go to college, but Uncle Pete sat me down one day early in my junior year, and he made a good case for it. He said I would regret it if I didn't go to college, and told me that my father had definitely wanted me to go. He complimented me on the work I had put into becoming a better artist but suggested I consider a different vocational direction in college. He thought I should consider becoming a lawyer or businessman. I cringed at the thought of those careers and told him in so many words that I was sure I wanted to be an artist the rest of my life and couldn't imagine anything different. He just wanted me to realize how unlikely it would be to have a career in art and wanted me to agree to consider something different, even if it simply meant I would minor in something else. I verbally agreed with him, but I had no intention of that.

I kind of wanted to stay close to home, but I applied to several colleges outside of the area, including the University of Hawaii. It was a lark, but they accepted me! I had also applied to a couple of California schools. I don't remember if they accepted me, but I was always intent on going to Rochester Institute of Technology in Upstate New York. They offered a lot of high-tech disciplines, like engineering and the sciences, but they had a great reputation in the visual arts too. The school had good programs in graphic arts, printing, and especially in photography. The home of Eastman Kodak, it made sense that Rochester would have a college strong in photography and printing. Their fine arts program was small, but I figured that would give me the opportunity to shine rather than be lost in the shuffle at one of the huge California schools. Once RIT accepted me, I had no desire to consider other destinations.

Aunt Elena and Uncle Pete supported my decision and pledged to help me out as much as possible with finances. When the time came, they were instrumental in helping me identify and apply for grants and scholarships. I was able to borrow enough money to supplement the grants we acquired. My family could only contribute $500 to get me started in my first year. After that, I was on my own. But I was on my way.

Because of my accelerated academic schedule, I was able to graduate from high school in June of 1972, at the end of my junior year. Although I was only 16 years old, I felt very ready to move on. The graduation ceremony meant little to me, other than the sense of relief that I was finally free to focus on my dream. Not long after graduation I decided to spend the following year working and saving money before making the transition to college. I felt I was just too young to rush to college. My aunt and uncle supported the decision, so I worked on building my portfolio in preparation for my college application. I also got a job in a new 7-11 store that had just opened nearby. That didn't last long, as I cut off the tip of my right index finger with the rotary meat slicer. The tip was reattached, but my aunt insisted I leave that job and I just continued to paint and draw throughout the lengthy recovery period. I spent the next six months or so taking watercolor painting classes and working part-time at the Sherwin-Williams store as a clerk, aside from picking up some sporadic freelance projects. I realized I needed to earn more money for college.

During the summer of 1973, I got a job at a local microfilm company. Answering an ad in the paper for summer help, I applied and was hired on the spot. The job was simple enough: operating a vertical camera and making archival images of old newspapers, hospital records and other decrepit documents. All I had to do was position the documents under the lens and click the button. It paid minimum wage, but it was my first real job. During the course of the summer leading up to college, I was aware that I had not had any recent incidents with strange blue lights or glowing auras or halos. I had not heard from Annie in months, and although we still exchanged letters once in a while, gradually the periods between became longer and longer. She was attending high school in an Atlanta suburb, and I imagined she was on the receiving end of a lot of attention from upper class boys. Eventually, I got used to not hearing from her.

I had never dated in high school. It was an all-male school, for one thing, and, although some of my classmates dated girls from other schools, I just felt it was impossible for me. Without a car or a job I never had the means, nor did I meet many eligible girls my age. Instead, my life revolved around friends, sports and artwork, which took up all my spare time. Of course, I fantasized about girls I would see at the mall or on television and in movies, but I wanted to stay focused on my current passion, which was drawing and painting. Looking back, I think it was the right thing to do, for the most part.

At my new job, there was only one other person close to my age. He was a tall, scrawny guy with long, stringy blonde hair. Not very bright, he didn't have much to say, and I kind of avoided him. Instead, I hung out with the small group of thirty-somethings, who made up the majority of the small, close-knit staff. The owners were two former semi-professional football players who seemed to have bought the company for lack of any strong vocational direction of their own. The rest of the staff was pretty friendly toward me. They generally liked me, and, despite the age gap, they often included me in social gatherings after work.

We worked the late shift – 4:00 PM to midnight – and even though I was underage they took me along with them once in a while when they went out for drinks after work. It was odd that no one ever asked me for ID or any proof of age. The local bar we went to would serve me beer or ginger ale with whiskey, whatever I ordered. I used to drink Whiskey Sours at first, since I was new to the whole concept of poisoning one's brain and body. The thought of a Whiskey Sour now makes me want to puke, but at the time, I thought I was so cool.

I was attracted to one coworker. Her father was actually the daytime supervisor, and I liked him. The crusty old man's name was Charlie, and he always called me "Bobby Boy." He was an old navy veteran with a huge blue anchor tattooed on his right forearm, buried in hair. He looked a little like a gorilla. Luckily, his daughter didn't resemble the old man. She was a sweet girl, kind of average looking, and I think she was about twenty years old. Her name was Marsha. She was mildly flirtatious with me, and at times, I secretly fantasized about making out with her in the storage room. But I knew she considered me too young. Twenty-year-old women are rarely interested in awkward teenagers, which I fully understood. Still, it was fun to be flirted with.

The microfilm camera I operated was mounted on a tall, vertical stand. To remove and load film or to take down the frame count readings from the camera, the operator needed to turn a crank to lower the camera from its operating height well above the tabletop. We sat for hours (or stood on occasion), and when the camera had run out of film or if our shift was over, we had to lower the camera and record the frame count in a journal.

One particular evening, some of the crew wanted to go out for drinks after work, and I was extra excited to go because Marsha was going to join in and she almost never went out with us. My coworker Sean was rushing me to finish up a few minutes early. "Smoke on the Water" was blaring out of the tiny radio perched upon the file cabinet in the corner of the room. The supervisor had already taken off for the night, so we felt we could duck out early too. He was squawking in my ear from across the room we shared, telling me, "Take down the goddamn frame count already! Let's get outta here!" I was anxious to go, too, but knew I absolutely had to record the frames accurately because it would be verified by the supervisor in the morning. I jokingly said, "I know the frame count without looking," just trying to be funny and annoying. "I'm writing it down," I said as I wrote down the number 2,731. Annoyed with me for delaying his chance to consume alcohol, Sean threw his hands up in disgust and turned off the light over his workspace. At that moment, Marsha poked her head into the room and asked if we were ready.

Sean said something about me being "a dickhead," and she laughed. She said I still needed to take an actual frame count, and she walked over to my table. I told her I had just written down some fake numbers, and she smiled and shook her head. She was very agile and light on her feet, tipping the scales at just over 100 pounds. She had perfected this little trick of stepping on the boxes piled next to the table, then up onto the table itself to take a frame count reading in a flash. Before I could think, she bounded up onto the table and stuck her face up to the side of the camera. "Two, seven, three, one. Let's go!" she stated in a playful robotic voice. I started to erase my "fake" number, and then stopped myself when I realized what she had said. I asked her to repeat it, even though she had turned her face away from the camera and was ready to jump down.

She asked what the problem was as I just stood staring at the record book. She jumped down and peered across my body to see what I had entered. "You just wrote that down after I gave you the numbers, right?" she asked. I told her, "No," and explained that I had just guessed at the count when Sean was nagging me. I just wanted to mess with him and get him to shut up. How on Earth I guessed a four-digit number precisely like that was bizarre, to say the least! Marsha was a bit spooked by it. She insisted that I was kidding around and believed I had actually written it down only after she read the numbers off. But that wasn't true.

Sean vouched for my story at the bar later, but he and everyone else forgot it as quickly as the next soothing sip of beer entered their gullets. I couldn't quite shake the uneasy feeling it created within me. Only I knew that I *knew* those numbers were correct when I wrote them down. I actually "saw" the numbers floating

88

in the air in front of me, at least in my mind. But it was so real and so tangible I felt as though I could actually reach out and grab the numbers with my hand. It was as if they were little glowing Alpha-Bits cereal pieces floating in midair.

One other day, I had shown up for work about thirty minutes early. I rode my bike to and from work, which was a little more than three miles from home. I got there in record time and had entered the small break room to get a drink of water when I heard a muffled shriek from behind the building. I hurried out the back door to the bleak little area where people often smoked and ate lunch. There were several large garbage bins there, in an open area covered in rough gravel. I saw Marsha standing alone near the trash enclosure, with a horrified expression on her face. She called over to me when she saw me fling the steel door open.

I asked what the heck was happening, and she pointed toward the ground. When I ran up alongside her I immediately saw what had caught her eye. There, wriggling on the jagged gravel surface was a newborn baby bird. About a yard from the helpless, naked bird was a hideous scruffy-looking rat, steadily inching its way toward its would-be victim. I instinctively tried to assess the situation. There was no obvious place this bird could have come from. There were no trees anywhere in sight, and no evidence of any nests along the gutter spanning the length of the industrial building.

There were a couple of other rats in the area adjacent to the trash bins. We would frequently see rats when we spent time out there, but they usually scurried into the shadows as soon as one of us stepped close to them. I considered trying to scare the rats away, but then I couldn't imagine what we would do with the bird. I'd always been told that if humans handle a young bird its mother would refuse to take it back and would never care for it again. Maybe that was an old wives' tale, but I had no other information to draw upon.

All I could think was this poor little creature was going to be eaten alive by the ravenous, disgusting rats. I acted on instinct because I felt there was no time to ponder it further. I told Marsha, "Go back inside!" but she just stood there. I grabbed a large rock, about the size of a lunch box, lifted it over my head and brought it crashing down on the tiny bird. It was crushed instantly. A wave of emotions struck me. I felt guilty for killing a helpless creature in such a brutal fashion. Yet, at the same time, I felt like a savior. I was sure I had spared the little bird a very agonizing torture. Then, I wondered why I felt I had the right to "play God." If I had just ignored the situation and let nature take its course, would that not have been the best option? I could have spared myself the memory of what I had done. I should have been selfish and walked away. The end result was that the bird was brutally destroyed, the rats lived on, and I was saddled with guilty memories and the ugly images.

Marsha looked stunned and sad. She said nothing as she slowly turned and went toward the door. I said something like, "I'm sorry," but she didn't react. She just disappeared into the ugly metal building. I stood there for a while, staring at the rock I had just used as my executioner's axe. Below it laid the crushed bones and delicate translucent skin of a creature that just got cheated out of everything life had to offer, and I was the agent that made the decision for God. I was disgusted with myself at that moment. I threw a few stones at the three rats that were seemingly impervious to what had just transpired. They scampered a few feet away, but they didn't go far. One rat looked up at me with its beady red eyes, and I just glared back. "Piece of shit!" I yelled. Later that night, Marsha came to me and told me I did the most charitable thing possible. She said she was just grossed out and felt sick about not being able to help the bird. I didn't say anything other than, "Thanks." I wasn't sure whether or not I had truly done the best thing. I just did what I felt I needed to do, and maybe I got it wrong.

At the end of the summer, my little gang of friends threw me a small going-away celebration after work. We drank beer and laughed our asses off. It was a good way to end my childhood, I thought. I told them I'd be back to work with them again the following summer. Marsha kissed my cheek, and I felt different somehow. Maybe I had done some growing up that summer. Annie was long gone. I had earned my first real paychecks and had formed friendships with adults. They may have seemed like my age, but almost everyone at work was at least six or seven years older than me. I saved some money for college and was still painting on the weekends, usually around the clock. As I look back, it was odd that I had no incidents with the strange auras that entire summer. It seemed to coincide with Annie moving away. Maybe there was some connection with her or with going through puberty. All I know is I felt very different, grown up in some ways and looking forward to going away to school.

By mid-August I had packed my belongings and was eager to get to college. All out-of-town first-year students were required to live on campus, so I was headed for the dorms. Because of my early graduation from high school, I was once again leaving behind all the friends I had made, all the familiar faces and all the security I had. But that was exactly what I wanted. I was anxious to forget the heartaches of the past and glad to be rid of my little problem.

It was time for me to fly, and I was ready.

10

Life 101: A Ten-Week Crash Course

It took a little time to make new friends in college. Once again one of the misfits, I was a fine arts major in a technical school. Rochester Institute of Technology was a fast-paced vocational college that followed a ten-week trimester schedule. That meant the pressure was high for all students, and it was particularly challenging for first-year students to deal with. There was precious little time to goof off and relax. As someone who always pushed himself to be productive, it actually seemed pretty natural to me. But, over the course of the first year, I had my share of ups and downs. With overcrowded dorm rooms, some astonishingly terrible teachers and the dreadful male-to-female student ratio (9:1 when I entered), it was a culture shock. But, all in all, I enjoyed the experience. The freedom to make my own decisions was the best part of my first year. I still talked with my aunt and uncle over the phone a couple times a week, but other than that, I had few ties to my past. My future was a blank canvas, and I wanted to paint it my way.

I admit that I focused a lot of my attention and energy on losing my virginity as much as anything early in the year. As if it were a game, I circled the photos of every attractive girl in the handy printed guide the school provided. My roommate and friends all had a good laugh when they saw all the circled photos in my copy of the guide, which had been designed to help new students become acclimated. I thought of it as something of a shopping list, more than anything. There were a couple of girls I had my eye on, and I made it my business to find out what classes they were taking. Being in the fine arts program, a high percentage of the girls were in my classes anyway. That was the easy part. But being the competitive type, it was a fun challenge to become acquainted face-to-face with as many of them as possible.

Before long, I had established friendships with a handful of interesting young women. In the early months of my freshman year, I had become close friends with two girls in my program. One was a cute printmaking major named Rhea Ellerman. The other was a sultry, reserved girl I met in an auditorium during a presentation. Her name was Catherine Hutchings, and she actually had a girlfriend pass me a note during a typically boring lecture. I didn't even know her prior to that day, but when she revealed her attraction to me in the little note, I was more than excited to get to know her. The term *dating* seemed so inaccurate in my college days, especially during the era of the 1970s. How do you ask someone out on a date when you don't have a car or any spending money? That was my unfortunate predicament during my first year at RIT.

Beyond that reality, the early '70s were a time of sweeping and dramatic social revolution. Most of the freshmen women were either on birth control pills before they set foot on campus, or they quickly worked through the local Planned Parenthood office to acquire a prescription. Most of the female freshmen were obviously much more experienced with dating than I was; that was safe enough to presume.

Rhea was a lot like me in many ways. An artistic girl from a small town in Central New York, she didn't dress particularly well and was "without wheels," too. She originally caught my eye at lunch one day, with her big brown eyes and her shoulder-length blonde hair pulled back in a pony tail. She worked in the dining facility called Grace Watson Hall. A line server, she toiled behind the counter in a little white apron. I saw her a few times in the dining hall, and then I later saw her in my figure drawing class. Her shyness was quite alluring to me, and her magnetic smile was irresistible. I was convinced that she would never approach me, so I decided to roll the dice one day. It was during a lunch hour in October when I took the chance. The idea was hatched the previous night, and I came to lunch prepared. I had made sure to bring a felt-tip marker with me to the dining hall, and I grabbed a napkin from the line. I wrote a simple note in my neatest printing and slid it to her as I passed her station. It simply said, "I wish you would talk to me." She looked at me with a puzzled expression after she'd quickly glanced at the note.

Sitting in a booth with two friends, I had begun to eat my "gristle burger" when Rhea suddenly approached. At first, I was sure she was going to embarrass me in front of my buddies. Instead, she sat right down with us, directly across from me. She sweetly asked, "Is it okay if I join you?" and started to chat as if we were old friends. I asked how she was able to leave her position, and she said she was done with her shift and was planning on eating a bite before class anyway. This was ultra-aggressive behavior in my view, only because I had almost no experience with the opposite sex and had a preconceived notion that most girls my age would be far more aloof or intimidated than this. It was as much my *naïveté* as it was just a reflection of how well-adjusted and confident Rhea was. She was talking with my two friends as much as with me, and I instantly admired how open and honest she seemed to be. Almost as soon as I started to think she was only interested in forging new platonic friendships, she locked eyes with me.

In a second or two, I received an entirely different message from her expression. Her sparkling eyes were saying she understood what I wanted and that she wanted the same thing. It was a watershed moment for several reasons. I learned that I was capable of attracting the opposite sex, and also learned that it was a good idea to take risks because the outcome could be well worth the gamble. At the same time, I learned that women could be bold and aggressive, and that was definitely alright with me. I had previously thought it would be scary if a woman was as assertive as men traditionally were. That notion, however, was dissolved at that very moment. This brief interaction taught me so many things I didn't comprehend previously. I saw cleverness in Rhea's approach, as well, and I've always admired clever people. She made it seem like she was sincerely fascinated by all three of us. To an outside observer, it would have appeared that she was equally interested in and acquainted with all of us. But her eyes spoke to me differently, and only she and I knew that.

Rhea and I skipped almost all of the typical get-to-know-one-another posturing. We had known each other for less than a week and had only spent a few hours in each other's company when we had our first sexual encounter. Without going into too much detail, let's just say it was the first time for both of us, but you would never know it. She was the aggressor (naturally), but I was eager to comply. She whispered that she was "protected" and that she was a virgin. I said, "Me too," referring only to the virgin status. She was trembling, and I was awash in pent-up passion and anticipation. I was starting to get to know this girl, and I genuinely liked her. But it was the lure and excitement of finally crossing that forbidden threshold that motivated me more. I desperately wanted to know how it felt to be that close to someone. To be so intimate with another human being was more than amazing to me. Rhea's small breasts were in perfect proportion to her tiny athletic frame. She smelled like fresh flowers, and her flawless eighteen-year-old skin was as intoxicating as anything I had ever experienced.

In her cozy, darkened dormitory room, we both eagerly shed the trappings of childhood and hungrily devoured the promise of the future. The experience was tender, beautiful and rather artistically accomplished. I remember lying on my back next to her afterward, thinking it was far less traumatizing than I had expected. Throughout one's youth, the eventful moment is often built up to be frightening. Performance anxiety and worries about awkward fumbling fill one's mind. This experience had been anything but that. It was completely beautiful, and we seemed to mesh together as perfectly as any two individuals possibly could. No fumbling, no embarrassments, it was sweet and honest and good. What a relief, to get through it unscathed! It was not lost on me that we were probably fortunate in that regard. A bad first experience might have left a huge emotional scar to overcome, but this turned out to be lovely in every way, and I was so glad we had been willing. Rhea was laying there naked, smiling and looking up at the ceiling of her simple little room. She reached over to hold my hand, and we both soon fell asleep. Satisfied and exhausted in my new grown-up skin, I enjoyed the most glorious night's sleep I had ever experienced.

The next morning, I awoke to find myself alone. I tried to find my wristwatch on the floor, but it wasn't where I thought I had tossed it. Rhea had gathered up everything of mine and folded my clothes and draped them over the back of the musty overstuffed chair in the corner of the room. My watch had been carefully placed on the dresser next to the door, a handwritten note tucked under it. She had explained in her note that she needed to work from 6:00 AM to noon, so she got up and showered and was out the door well before I ever came to life. The note went on to warn that Rhea's roommate was due to return around 10:00 AM, having been off visiting her boyfriend in Buffalo the previous night. "Oh, that's where she was," I thought. (It's funny how I had never considered whether or not her "roomie" might walk in on us the night before. I was preoccupied with other thoughts.) It was almost 10:00, so I scrambled to get dressed. Because it was Saturday morning, I had no classes, but wanted to be sure to get out of there before Rhea's roommate returned. As I ambled down the hall, heading back to my building, I felt truly alive for the first time.

Rhea and I talked things over that Sunday. While we agreed that what had happened that Friday night and Saturday morning was wonderful, we decided to slow things down and get to know each other better. I honestly recognized the wisdom of that approach and sincerely meant to try to do just that, but the hormonal impulses of this naïve country boy were more than I could control. Catherine Hughes had been making eyes at me for weeks, during classes and any time we saw each other. I had never said more than a couple words to her, but I couldn't get her out of my mind. While Rhea and I had become good friends, we had resisted having sex for a while.

Cathy knew nothing about my relationship with Rhea. I admit I never bothered to offer up any information in that regard. That isn't necessarily something I was proud of, but it was what it was. I was hell-bent on exploring the wonderlands that other women surely possessed. Rhea's idea to work on our friendship and to slow down the physical relationship was a noble concept, but was fatally flawed. Cathy invited me to her dorm room one evening, saying she wanted to ask my advice on a drawing she was working on for class. I hesitated at first but eventually agreed to stop over mid-evening. She was very different from Rhea in so many ways. The only thing they seemingly had in common was that both came from relatively small home towns.

Cathy was an enticing mystery to me. She generally spoke more with her eyes than with words. Her warm, chestnut-brown eyes were large, expressive and very alluring. Her flowing mane of light brown hair was beautiful and kempt, and she was fond of wearing soft, fuzzy sweaters and tailored blue jeans. She had manicured nails and usually wore diamond earrings and delicate necklaces. Everything about her personal style was quite sophisticated compared to Rhea's simple girl-next-door ways.

Cathy was adept at saying little, yet projecting warmth at the same time. Everything about her was different from most of the girls I had known. I can't say she was the right type for me, but she was so different from the familiar that it was a powerful lure. We had some things in common (like our humble roots), but other than that and our inclination toward artistic expression, we had little to talk about. But the mutual chemical attraction was undeniable. She made me hot tea on a little electric hot plate and embellished it with honey and lemon. She told me her roommate was gone for the weekend and that I should relax. Even though I was new to all of this, I was aware she was seducing me. A powerfully intoxicating blend of aromas added to the romantic mood. Her perfume complemented the delectable scent of the hot chamomile tea, and the resulting blend was nothing short of hypnotic. I actually wondered if this country girl had somehow slipped something into my drink. While my thoughts bounced between the moment at hand and flashbacks of making love with Rhea, I admit I was fighting to stay in the moment.

I felt torn but reminded myself that Rhea and I were not seriously committed to one another and, since we had agreed to cool the physical relations for a while, I was aching to do it again. I guess I didn't care all that much with whom I did it. I just felt the need to do it again soon. Cathy was apparently similarly inclined, and she communicated that very clearly with her eyes and her body language. Soft, puffy comforters covered her bed, and I couldn't help but note the stark contrast to her roommate's disheveled-looking mess across the room. Everything about Cathy was feminine, well cared for and pretty. I sat in a folding chair next to her desk, just admiring her beautiful face and sipping my delicious tea.

As we struggled to find a subject to talk about, she motioned for me to sit on the side of the bed next to her. I obliged and immediately felt flushed and excited. I could feel the passion surging within me and was eager to kiss her. It was almost as if I had won a contest of some kind. Just months prior to this night, I never would have imagined such a lovely creature being interested in me. I had virtually no experience with women, and my self-esteem was not at all developed. I don't mean I had low self-esteem; I had no awareness what the term even meant.

When Cathy spoke with her honey-drenched voice, it sometimes felt like she was reading a script in her mind and then performing it in her signature style. On this cold night in the fall of 1973, we were just two young, inexperienced kids who were both getting accustomed to being away from home for the first time. I had finished wrestling with my conscience and feelings of guilt. I threw that aside when Cathy gently reached out, held my face and kissed me. I was unprepared for how different it felt to kiss her compared to Rhea. I enjoyed both; don't misunderstand me. But Cathy's lips felt very different: soft, full and indescribably delicious. Of course, she gave a lot of attention to her skin, her hair and her lips, frequently applying fruit-flavored lipstick or lip balm, whatever it's called. All I knew was I was lost in her floral fragrance and her soft, open mouth, and I didn't want to think. I wanted that feeling to last forever. Instead, it lasted only about five minutes.

Lying atop her gloriously warm frame in her nest of quilts and comforters, she suddenly pushed me away with both arms. I didn't understand what was going on. She blurted out, "What is *wrong* with you?" I was taken by surprise, to say the least. Completely innocently, I asked what she was talking about. "You know what I'm talking about: your girlfriend!" I was suddenly immobilized by her words. Playing coy and trying my best to appear unfazed by this accusation, all I could offer up was, "What girlfriend?"

As suddenly as possible, her mood had turned. After we sat up, she explained that she had seen me holding hands with Rhea. She had seen me kiss her one morning as we parted company along the walkway to the academic side of campus. I tried to describe my relationship with Rhea as more of a "friendship," without going into details about our pact of temporary celibacy. She didn't buy it. I asked why, if she was aware of my involvement with another girl, she invited me to her room and initiated the intimate moment we just shared. She said she was attracted to me and had been dreaming about kissing me for weeks. I asked why we couldn't have a physical relationship if we were equally attracted to each other. All she replied was, "Because you want it both ways. You want a girlfriend and you want someone else to mess around with. You *can't* have it both ways!" I didn't get it. "Why not?!" was my honest reply. I was actually pissed at her. Wow, things sure changed in one moment. Why couldn't we just enjoy our mutual attraction and leave it at that? I had no intention of getting overly serious about anyone at that point in my life. And I didn't understand why she wanted to ruin the moment. She made it obvious that she had emotionally shut down and was no longer open to any of my advances. I slipped my well-worn sneakers back on and thanked her for the tea. She looked sad, yet strangely satisfied with herself. I was getting an early lesson in the complexities of adult relationships, but I didn't quite appreciate the value of education at the moment. Instead, I was angry and frustrated while I walked back to my dormitory in the dark, crisp night.

I spent the next day sorting out my emotions and trying to understand Cathy's motivation. I concluded that she really was trying to get me to say I was a creep, but she also wanted me to promise to break things off with Rhea. I wasn't ready to do that. I enjoyed talking to Rhea because she was so "real" all the time. She was more mature than me in so many ways. We could talk very openly and easily. I didn't want to throw that away, even though I was very tempted if it meant I could sleep with Cathy. Oh, the torturous dilemmas of the post pubescent! I honestly had no clue what I really wanted or what I was doing.

Adding insult to injury, Rhea confronted me the next evening. She called to invite me to her room, even though she warned that she had a "steaming pile of stinky homework" to finish. Always eager to please, I shuffled over to her dorm in my sweats. I knocked my signature three knocks on her door and opened it myself. She was seated at her desk, surrounded by papers, drawing pencils and reference photographs. I noticed that her eyes were reddened, and it was obvious she'd been crying. I knew this wasn't good since I hadn't seen her cry before. "You need to tell me the truth," she said with a trembling voice. Dumbfounded, I didn't say anything. Instead, I looked at her with the puppy-doggiest eyes I could muster.

She went on to announce that her friend told her she had seen me coming out of Cathy's dorm room the previous night. Just my damn luck, her friend lived directly across the hall from Cathy's room. *Busted.* What could I say? I tried my best to say that I was just talking to her about a class assignment, but Rhea was very good at reading people, and she could tell I was lying. She told me she was disappointed but not surprised, and added that she didn't think we should see each other anymore. "Why are you doing this?" I asked in my sternest voice. She said, "I just can't trust you now, and I think you need to figure out what you want. We made a mistake, sleeping together so soon. Now you want sex, and you'll get it from someone else if you can't get it from me." I honestly couldn't argue. She was right. What surprised me was that she was so damn hip for someone so young and inexperienced.

Obviously, her instincts were right on the money. I felt like a disgusting jerk. I also recognized that at this point in my life, I just wanted to experiment and enjoy the things I could only dream of, previously. What I couldn't bring myself to do was lie to her or make false promises. That wasn't my style at all, so I admitted that I wasn't ready for a real relationship yet. We made no promises or plans to see each other beyond that night. I wanted to plead with her to reconsider, though, because the reality of the sudden breakup made my stomach upset. One look at her fixed expression of resignation was all it took for me to stop short of any begging. I said, "Okay, but I'll miss you," and walked out her door.

What a couple of nights that was. Cathy continued to cast flirtatious glances my way for a few more weeks, and she tried to strike up conversations with me now and then. But I was cool toward her, still resentful that she was indirectly responsible for my broken relationship with Rhea. Not long after this time, Cathy began regularly dating one of my classmates. She stopped the flirting, and I stopped noticing her completely soon thereafter. I saw her almost daily in classes and at the cafeteria or out in the quads near the dorms. She was always hanging out with her roommate or other girlfriends. She loved to play guitar and sing, and I went with a gang of friends one winter night to catch her performance at a campus talent show. There were no hard feelings after I realized we were never really right for each other.

During the spring of my freshman year, a strange thing occurred. On my way back to my dorm after an unusually warm morning, I went up the elevator to my room on the top floor. Upon exiting, I ran into one of my floor mates, Andy Levine. Andy was a computer science major from Philadelphia. He and I weren't great friends, but we played tennis together a few times and enjoyed challenging each other on the court. I asked if he wanted to play some tennis since it was so warm for the time of year. I was itching to do anything fun outdoors. He said he would possibly be able to play, but he was stuck here waiting for his friend to show up. The person he was impatiently waiting for was another guy I knew, David Croft.

He said he just needed to get his book back from Dave, who'd borrowed it. With no hesitation whatsoever, the words flew out of my mouth. "Why are you waiting up here? He's down on the first floor, in the lounge." He said, "Oh, cool!" and entered the elevator, in which I was still standing. I said I would go along for the ride since I wanted to find out for sure if he would be free to play tennis with me. I didn't tell him that I had no idea why I said what I said. I had run from the outdoor quad into the building and had just bolted into the waiting elevator, pressed the eighth floor button and gone up. I didn't see or hear anyone on the first floor. In fact, I wasn't even sure there was a lounge on that floor, still a bit unfamiliar with the areas beyond our immediate territory on the eighth floor. The way I blurted out those words with such confidence, Andy had no cause to question me. Certainly, he must have assumed I had seen Dave down in the lounge. The fact is, I hadn't. So as we made our way toward the lounge, I was baffled by what I had said. I imagined we would get there, no one would be around, and we'd just head back upstairs and wait for Dave in Andy's room. Don't ask me to explain this, but I was as curious as could be. The feeling I had was unlike anything I had ever experienced. I had just involuntarily offered up specific information on something I had no conscious knowledge about. I wanted to understand it but didn't even know how to begin. We got down to the lobby and headed toward the end of the long hallway lined with dorm rooms. The first floor turned out to be the same as all the rest, with a lounge area at the very end of either hall. I heard the unmistakable sounds of people playing table tennis in the lounge. Until we got to the end of the hall, we couldn't see the table or who was playing.

When we arrived, we saw that one of the two ping-pong players was none other than David Croft. There was no mistaking his long curly blonde hair and his mouth brimming with silver braces. "Hey, Dave!" yelled Andy. "What the hell are you doing? You had me waiting up there for over an hour. What gives?" Dave explained that he thought Andy meant they were to meet on the first floor in the lounge. He had just gotten his signals crossed, and he apologized. I was standing there, my mouth agape. For several reasons, this seemingly insignificant incident actually frightened me a bit. I had no advance knowledge of their planned meeting, and I swear I didn't see or hear Dave, nor do I think I would have even recognized his voice if I had heard it. Andy asked me if I was alright as I just stood there, staring. I brushed his question aside and asked Dave how long he had been there. He said he and his pal had been playing ping-pong for almost an hour. That told me he didn't happen to run past me when I had entered the lobby minutes earlier. Weird, but the weirdest thing was the very firm and sure manner in which I told Andy that Dave was here in this lounge I had never set foot in before. It kept me awake that night as I relived the experience, trying to figure out a plausible answer. Over thirty years later, I still have no logical explanation.

At the end of my first year at RIT, I was feeling depressed. I had been worn down by late nights, large quantities of cheap beer and the ups and downs of all the new relationships and the relentless onslaught of first-time experiences. A friend encouraged me to speak with one of the campus advisors, who in turn pointed me toward the health center on campus. Their services included psychiatric consultation, but I had occasionally heard negative comments concerning the qualifications of the staff. Since I'd been steadily losing weight and was feeling more than a little lost, I decided I would find out for myself. The consultation was brief, and the verdict was that I was suffering from the "common first-year depression," and no medication was prescribed. The staff psychologist instead encouraged me to make an appointment with my regular family doctor. I told him I didn't have one, and he just shrugged and said something about not being able to do anything more. I felt abandoned and betrayed. Was this the best care they could provide to students who were alone and going through these types of issues? Like drinking warm water on a hot day, this interaction provided no relief at all.

The end of the academic year was fast approaching, and I was torn between not wanting to go home and needing the comfort of family. On my way to my dorm, I was fatigued in every way and wanted to take a long nap. I never nap, so I knew I was depressed. As fate would have it, Rhea emerged from the dining hall just as I passed by. I was going to merely wave and walk by, but she came running over, clutching a letter in her right hand. She asked if we could walk somewhere together, and I said "sure" but warned her that I wasn't very good company at the moment. She asked what was going on, and I lied and said it was nothing. I didn't feel like getting into a lengthy discussion. She suggested we take a walk around the back of the campus. There was a nature trail cut through the thick grove of trees that lined the undeveloped part of the campus. This suburban campus had been constructed only five years before I arrived. The swamp it was built upon was previously untouched by man, and there were still many unaffected areas where deer and other wildlife flourished.

We slowly walked around the dormitories and made our way along a narrow, paved path toward the woods. Rhea couldn't contain her excitement. "My dad got the job!" she chirped. I recalled her talking about some new job her father had been seeking, but for the life of me I couldn't remember any details. This adorable little creature was nearly jumping out of her skin with enthusiasm. "What's the big deal?" I oafishly asked. She explained that her father had applied for his dream job and was finally offered the position. It was some great opportunity with a company he had always wanted to join. She was particularly excited because the job was based in Los Angeles.

A surfer girl at heart, Rhea had always talked about moving to the West Coast after graduation. Now she had a place to go and would be able to see firsthand what California life was all about. I asked if this meant she would leave RIT, and she said her father's job wouldn't have any bearing on where she attended school for now. In my heart, I wondered if she would really return the following fall when she could easily transfer to a California school. The news was exciting to her, but this was just one more heartache for me to cope with. I tried my best to support her and share in her excitement, but my heart wasn't in it. All I could do was focus on the thought of losing the one close friend I had made. It was bad news in my eyes, and those eyes reflected my sorrow over the thought of her departure. Rhea reacted by grabbing my hand and then hugging me tightly. She said, "Let's go somewhere and talk about it," and we walked along the nature trail deeper into the wooded area. It was peaceful there, and no one else was around. We came to a secluded clearing and sat together on the bed of leaves and pine needles.

Everything I had been suppressing just spilled out in a stream-of-consciousness manner. I told Rhea that I was "a freak and a

105

misfit." At first she smiled and said I was just tired. Then, I went on to confide in her about all the things I was worried about and afraid of. I told her the story about the kid in the lounge, and shared with her all of my memories about the weird blue lights and the aura I had seen. I even told her about the "little man" I saw turn off the TV set when I had my broken arm. I told her everything. I told her about the fight in high school and the "halo" over my head. I told her I was afraid because I didn't know what it all meant and that I was tired of being different. This all spilled into me rambling about missing my father and being cheated out of having a chance to really know my mother.

I told her I loved her in my own way, but I knew we would never be right for each other. She hugged me tightly again and tried to comfort me. She said she would try to help me. I didn't even know what that would mean. I wanted so badly to have a life "do over" if I could. I had not been honest with myself, and these outpourings of feelings opened my eyes to the realization that the incidents of the past that had made me feel like a freak were weighing heavily on me. For the first time, I was comfortable enough with someone to express my fears and concerns. I trusted Rhea because she'd always been honest with me. She tightly held my hand as I unloaded all of this on her. I could tell she was genuinely concerned. She told me she would try to help me, and she suggested I should talk to "a professional."

Resistant at first, I had serious doubts that anyone could help me. I also had no confidence in psychiatry or any form of therapy, but I considered her advice out of respect for her and out of my own quiet desperation. We held each other as friends do, and then we slowly walked back toward the dorms. She asked me if I wanted to have dinner with her, but I declined. I just wanted to sleep, so I headed directly to my room. Falling asleep the instant my head hit the pillow, I didn't wake up until the following afternoon, missing my morning classes.

Rhea called me that afternoon with a phone number and name of a local agency that offered family counseling to low-income clients. She urged me to at least contact them and see if they would talk to me. When I followed her advice and called to set up an appointment for the following week, the receptionist assured me that their services were generally billed on a sliding scale and that I would be granted a free initial visit. I asked a friend to drive me across town that day. Afraid but curious to learn something, I followed through and showed up despite the temptation to completely blow it off.

The Office of Family Counseling was housed in a small, modern brick structure, located in a busy suburban office park. A friend dropped me off in front of the building and, upon entering, I was promptly greeted by a polite receptionist who surprised me by saying I could go right in. I entered a brightly lit hallway and was summoned into the first office off the hall. A tall, thin, bespectacled bald man who appeared to be about 40 years old introduced himself and smiled as he gestured toward the couch across from his desk. He took a seat in the chair across from the couch, and we made our introductions. His title was that of Family Therapist, and I felt at ease with him right away. He had a scholarly appearance but was very humble and friendly, with a kind smile. He said we had as much as two hours for the initial visit, and I started talking. Mainly, he listened and nodded for a solid hour as I went through the highlights and lowlights of my childhood. He interrupted only occasionally, offering a lot of "I see" and "Can you please elaborate on that for me?" and "That may be an important piece"; you know, the stuff they teach in I Actually Am Listening to Your Bullshit 101.

He politely stopped me shortly after I had finished talking about the series of bizarre incidents involving the strange blue-tinged lights and such. He looked very concerned and puzzled. He had no problem sympathizing with the losses of my parents or the struggles I had at school, but he was rubbing his chin and scrunching up his forehead as I went through the various recollections of the mysterious ghostlike manifestations. He asked me if I had undergone any psychological counseling in the past. I was insulted, primarily out of ignorance. I incorrectly presumed he was implying I was insane or something. I said "No!" rather emphatically, and he tried to calm me by explaining it was just a standard question. While I felt comfortable with this man, I was also quite aware of his skepticism. At least I was fairly certain he didn't believe I could actually see any of these strange shapes and lights I tried to describe. I figured he probably concluded that I had imagined it all and was having psychological problems that led me to hallucinate. At the end of the first hour, he started to make some suggestions.

First, he suggested I make another appointment and asked if I would be willing to meet with him on a regular basis. I said I wasn't sure since school was soon ending and I was preparing to head home. He suggested that I return to see him in September, but, in the meantime, he urged me to see a medical doctor. I told him I would but expressed my strong doubts that it would help. I remarked that I didn't know of any doctors who specialized in dealing with blue auras and pulsating halos. He remained straight-faced throughout and seemed to take a genuine interest in me.

At one point, he asked if I was involved with marijuana or any other recreational drugs. I told him I had sampled pot once or twice but was not a chronic user of anything. He smiled and looked relieved. He asked me if I had ever had suicidal thoughts. I lied and said, "No, why would I?" Again, he smiled and nodded as he made some notes on his paper. I asked if he had any idea what the hell was happening to me, and he avoided saying much of anything. He said, as if reading from a script, "I wouldn't want to speculate on something I know so little about, Robert." Unsatisfied, I asked again, saying I just wanted to know if he had ever had a patient with similar problems and wondered if they were helped. He pondered my question carefully and then commented that some people have been known to have such unusually vivid imaginations that they were convinced others could see what they were "seeing." When I protested, saying that there were occasions where other people claimed they actually *did* see what I was seeing, he muttered something unintelligible and suggested once again that I ask my family doctor to consult with me on some tests he could administer.

I felt relieved to unload this stuff on someone who was unemotional and professional. There was some value in the process, but I still had no answers. I described the incident with the table tennis player, and he had a different answer for that. Once again, he cautioned me that this type of thing was not his specialty, but he made some interesting comments concerning my experiences. We briefly talked about the phenomena of extrasensory perception and precognition, and he said he couldn't personally conduct the type of tests that were used in certain circles or comment specifically on my situation, but he did say there was "some scientific support for it," regarding the abilities some people possess. Finally, he asked me if I had ever experienced trauma to my head, or, more specifically, to my brain. I thought for a moment and then told him of my skateboarding accident. He suggested that I review that and any other possibly related facts with my primary care physician. I thanked him for the free session, and he walked me out to the reception area. He handed me his business card and encouraged me to call again when I returned to school in the fall.

The session left me feeling a bit relieved, yet uneasy at the same time. Memories came flooding back, and I realized there had been quite a few unexplainable incidents over the years. Convinced that it was probably unwise to minimize their importance any longer, I was still unsure how to pursue the answers. I was concerned that I might have a physical problem that should be investigated. I had planned on taking a city bus back to campus, so I walked toward the closest bus stop as the sky opened up and a thunderstorm suddenly cropped up. It began pouring rain and, of course, I had no umbrella or hat, as usual. I ducked under a small overhang that I initially thought was part of a public library.

Desperate to get out of the worst part of the rainstorm for a few minutes, I stood beneath a vine-covered brick structure and wiped my eyeglasses with my sleeve. Turning around to get my bearings, I realized that the building was actually a church. Its two large doors were painted red, and a wooden sign on one of them announced, "Our home is open to all, every day of the year." I followed a sudden urge, opened the door and entered the tiny church. I didn't know what denomination it served, nor did I care. I mainly wanted a dry place to take refuge, but I was also curious to see what it looked like inside. To my surprise, I felt very much relaxed and calm the moment I sat down in the back row of pews.

The church was extremely small compared to the one I attended as a child, but it was very beautiful in its simple elegance. I picked a pamphlet out of the little slotted area in the back of the pew in front of me. The pamphlet told me this was actually a Catholic church, but I figured I was not technically trespassing since my mother had been raised Catholic. When she and my father married, they decided that each of them would change religions. His family was Baptist, and they were not pleased that he was marrying a Catholic. There was no way to please everyone, so they decided to pick a religion that was in the middle somewhere. I don't have a clue how they made their determination on that, but they settled on Presbyterianism.

I sat there and took in the atmosphere while I reflected upon many things. It had been a year of major milestones and transitions. I was no longer a boy, but I didn't feel I was truly a man yet. The year at college had given me the chance to begin to sort out who I was and who I wanted to become. I always kept the many memories of my father tucked away in a special place in my heart, and I had tried very hard to be brave and not miss

110

him too badly since his death. It was difficult, but I wanted to be strong for him. He used to sometimes tell me that he wanted me to be strong and independent so that when he was no longer around I would be happy and healthy. I used to put on my bravest face and assure him that I would do that. As I remembered so many of the good and bad times of my childhood, the emotional pain brought me to tears. It was the first time I had been able to catch my breath since the first day of school the previous September. Sitting there alone in the dark, deserted church, I broke down.

For a few minutes I buried my face in my hands and just let my tears flow. In this peaceful place of worship, I felt safe and vulnerable at the same time. Safe, because I felt no one could hurt me as long as I stayed there, but vulnerable because I was convinced that no one could save me from myself. The pain of growing up was wearing on me more than I cared to admit to myself, but in the darkened interior of this simple little haven, I was very aware of my inner sorrow. I missed my mother and lamented the fact we were cheated out of so many years and memories together.

The loss of my father had been emotionally devastating to me, and I had just not admitted it to myself until this day. The frustration of not understanding the weird things that had been happening to me for so many years was making me more and more worried. My fears and my loneliness seemed to catch up with me on this morning. I had never been much of a churchgoer or very religious, but on this day I asked God to please help me. I prayed for the first time in a long while. I asked God to let me not have any more deaths to deal with, and I asked Him why He always took the people I most loved from me. Whenever I truly loved someone, they always left me in one way or another. Mom, Dad, Nana, Annie and now Rhea was probably leaving me behind. I asked God if He was punishing me for something I might have done long ago.

Deep down, I was concerned that I was actually ill. Did I have a brain tumor or some other affliction that was causing these visions? Maybe something serious was wrong with me and I was not destined to live a long life. He took my mother when she was young, and my father was only middle-aged when he died. Maybe our entire family was cursed. And if so, wasn't God responsible for slapping that specter of doom on us? I was angry at God, to be honest. I was angry He plucked my father from me when I needed him most, and I was angry that He never seemed to provide any answers to the questions that ran through my mind all the time. Finally, I was consciously aware of my anger, and I thought some truly horrible thoughts. In my mind I was saying, "Just fuck you, God! Why do you do the things you do? Fuck you for taking my father from me. And fuck you for never answering my prayers!"

No sooner had these vile thoughts been thought that I felt a gentle touch on my shoulder. It was a clergyman who had obviously been observing me. I quickly attempted to wipe the tears from my eyes as he sat down in the pew in front of me. I instantly got up and turned to walk out the front door, head down. "Please wait," the voice offered gently. "Would you like someone to talk to?" "No," I replied in a very tired manner. "I'm not supposed to be here, anyway." I stopped in my tracks for a moment, with my back toward the man who I never actually saw. "But you are truly welcome here, my friend," he said. I had expected him to say something of that nature, but he sounded so sincere I had to acknowledge him. "I appreciate that," I said, but I didn't want to get into a long discussion with him. He softly and calmly said, "If you ever want to talk about anything, you will always be welcome here."

I paused for a second and then decided I wanted to just get back to my dormitory and go to my afternoon class. I was drained from crying and still reeling a bit from the morning chat with the therapist. With a whispered, "Thank you," I opened the door and emerged into the waning thunderstorm. I decided to ignore the rain, and slowly walked toward the bus stop at the end of the block. The rain actually felt good as it pelted my forehead and shoulders. I glanced back at the church and, for a moment, I regretted not telling the man in black my troubles. He was just doing his job, I figured, and maybe I should have trusted him. As I started to board the freshly rinsed bus, I had the urge to turn right around and go talk to him. But I was soaked and tired, and felt I had to get back to campus. During the bus ride back to campus, I realized how I'd allowed my anger to take me over, and regretted not being more willing to open up. The bus dumped me out directly behind the dorms and I sprinted for the sanctuary of the dry building.

As the bus pulled away and I ran to my dormitory, I felt certain I would see the man in the church again.

11

Why Object to Being an Object?

The first year at college came to a close, and my thoughts turned to home and returning to my summer job. I had been in touch with my previous supervisor and one of the company's owners. They told me they would have a night-shift job waiting for me if I reported during or before the first week in June. This worked out beautifully for me since I wanted to be able to draw and paint during the days, among other things: like swimming, fishing and playing tennis and golf.

Two of my professors had suggested I consider changing my major to Communication Design, which was more along the lines of commercial graphic design. They convinced me that it would be nearly impossible to make a living as a fine artist, no matter how talented I was. I guess I always realized that, but their words made me more seriously consider other options for the future. I wanted to give it a lot more thought and discuss it with my uncle and aunt. Rhea promised to write to me as soon as she and her family got settled in their California home. I made a vow to write back any time she contacted me. We said our goodbyes and then went off in opposite directions when my uncle showed up to take me home.

When Uncle Pete and I pulled into our driveway, I felt glad to be home. Sure, I had made several visits during the year, but it felt good to know I had a few months to relax and enjoy being a kid for one more summer. It was in my mind to rent an apartment in Rochester the following summer because I planned on getting a campus job and doing more freelance work. So this was to be my last summer living here with my aunt and uncle, and I

114

wanted to savor it. Over dinner one night, I expressed my desire to get going on earning more money so I could start to build a savings account. Aunt Elena mentioned that she had met a fascinating young man at the bank, where she worked as a teller. She described a tall young man who had just opened a business a few miles down the road in what we called "farm country." I was barely paying attention until she said, "He really wants to meet you, Robby." When I asked why some stranger was interested in meeting a teenage kid, she said they had a conversation in which he expressed the need to find an artist to help him with his business. I figured he might be willing to pay me to design business cards or something, so I said I was willing. Aunt Elena promised to call him in the next few days to set up the introduction. She said this man seemed to be exceptionally bright, and she thought if I did some work for him over the summer it might help me decide what direction to take with my education.

That evening, I tried to reach Annie on the phone. I'm not sure what possessed me, though, because we hadn't spoken in nearly a year. It didn't much matter since I discovered that the number was no longer in service. I gathered that her family must have changed their number and she had forgotten to give it to me. After I put my dirty clothes in the hamper and put the few clean clothes away, I went into the living room to talk with Uncle Pete. Reading the newspaper in his favorite chair, peering over his reading glasses at me, he eerily resembled my father. He asked me if I needed anything for my room, and I said everything was fine. He asked how it felt to be home, and I assured him it felt good, which was no lie. There was a peaceful quiet to the old house, and the mood was usually pleasant and relaxed. It was a reflection of the two good souls who made it a home.

Aunt Elena had gone to bed early, so Uncle Pete and I had a chance to talk. He surprised me by telling me he wanted to help me buy my first car over the summer. Of course I was completely in favor of that, no matter the cost. It was not so bad, being without a vehicle during my first year. I had always been able to get rides from friends whenever I really needed them, but it was an impediment in many ways, especially when it came to working off campus and dating. So I was thrilled at his generous proposition. He told me he'd take me to the city the following weekend to look at a few cars he had already briefly checked out. I told him I was set to start work at my old job the following Monday, and he was pleased about that. We agreed that he would pay for a "sensible" used car for me if it was within his budget, as long as I worked all summer and contributed to the insurance.

The following Saturday, we drove to a couple of dealerships and must have inspected a dozen cars, all under $1,000. Some were in dubious mechanical condition, while others had obviously been treated harshly by their previous owners. Finally, we saw a teal-colored 1966 Chevy Bel Air station wagon that looked almost brand new. It was not my idea of a "chick magnet" by any means, but it was in pristine condition. The salesman told us it was a "Florida car," picked up at one of the auctions they routinely took part in. It had low mileage, and the car didn't show one speck of rust. The only problem was that it looked like an old lady's car more than a college guy's. But after weighing all the factors, buying it was far and away the smartest thing to do. So we made the purchase, and I started to get excited to get it on the road. I told Uncle Pete I would pay him back some of the $900, but he told me to consider the car a belated high school graduation gift. All he asked of me was that I pay for my own gas and any repairs he couldn't do, in addition to paying half of the insurance costs. I enthusiastically agreed, of course.

What a thrill it was to be able to finally drive myself to work, my first day back in my old job! They told me to come in early so I could fill out some paperwork and meet the new evening supervisor. When I got there, I was greeted just inside the door by two women. One, Cindy, was the morning supervisor, and

I knew her from the previous summer. She was a bubbly little blonde of about 30 or so, with big blue eyes and a tight little athletic build. She reminded me of a high school cheerleader, the way she was so effusive about the littlest things. She was very cute in an all-American way, and I had suspected her of being romantically linked to one of the two partners who owned the little microfilm company.

I'll never forget my introduction to the new evening manager. Cindy made the introduction, saying, "Robby, this is Andrea. You'll be working under her this summer." At that moment, the two women burst out laughing and I was clueless until later, when I realized they were giggling over the phrase "working under her." I was naïve and had rarely had adults make lewd insinuations in my presence, at least not quite like that. I was still very innocent in many ways, but Andrea secretly had plans to do something about that. It didn't take long for her to start having fun with me. She would make suggestive comments with some frequency, especially if we were alone in one of the back rooms where we did all the photo work. I was eighteen, and I discovered Andrea was married with two children and was twenty-nine years old. Sure that she was just screwing around and having fun flirting, I went along with it and just snickered at her remarks. The flirting was fun, and I lapped up the attention.

Andrea was slender, about 5'5" and very attractive. She looked younger than twenty-nine but was certainly more mature, in many ways, than I. She never made many comments about her husband, other than talking about his frequent fishing and hunting trips. From what she and others said, my impression of him was that he was an avid outdoorsman who was often gone on the weekends with his friends. Andrea never made any loving remarks about him. I didn't really care all that much, since my attention was more focused on the excitement of my new car and looking forward to the long, hot summer ahead. I was also happy to be working the 4:00 PM to midnight shift again.

One day, I rode my bicycle to work, just for fun and to save some gas money. It was a dry, hot day in early June. Unseasonably hot, it was the type of day that makes it really difficult to focus on much of anything. The place was nearly empty that afternoon because the two owners were away on vacation at the same time. And, Doug, the evening supervisor, announced he was leaving to go home around 7:00 PM. He said he was not dealing with the heat very well. Overweight and a bit of a whiner, he seemed to complain a lot about any major shift in temperature or humidity. By mid-evening, the only people in the building, beside me, were Andrea and Sean.

Andrea was obviously vying for my attention all night, stopping in and interrupting my work numerous times. One time she asked if I wanted her to make popcorn, and then a half hour later, she leaned into the doorway and asked if she could bring me a cold drink. I was aware she was lonely and making excuses to talk. When she struck an alluring pose in the doorway and just looked me up and down, it made me feel strangely uneasy. She was an attractive, confident woman and had a way of flirting in an effortless, subtle manner. She sometimes wore a lonely expression on her face, and on this night, I saw her in a different light. I felt sympathy for her because she seemed so sad. She had two young children at home, yet she had to work these nightshift hours while her husband watched over them. Her husband worked days, so they barely saw one another. Andrea almost never even mentioned him, so I figured theirs was just another marriage that had lost its spark.

On this particular night, Andrea seemed younger and more playful than I had ever known her to be. She laughed over little comments I made and pushed me away in that flirtatious way a woman touches a man's chest and playfully shoves him away. I felt a surge of excitement and was surprised I felt this way about her. She locked eyes with me, and I had a very strong feeling she wanted more than just a manager-employee rapport. In retrospect, maybe I should have reconsidered it when she offered me a ride in her truck that night. But I didn't think, I just eagerly accepted. The ride to my house wasn't very far, but it was still muggy and hot at a few minutes past midnight. I threw my bike in the bed of her truck and hopped in next to her. In that desolate parking lot we were the only sign of life. She told me she was really not going out of her way since the same road led to her house, only five miles further. We made small talk, and the mood was relaxed and congenial. But I couldn't help but notice there was a different tone beneath her words. She suddenly seemed much more like a kid my age than a twenty-nine-year-old mother of two. Her tight shorts revealed beautifully toned legs, tanned from her "glorious afternoon sunbathing sessions in the side yard," so she said.

Along the way home I allowed myself to fleetingly wonder what it would be like to kiss her, but I tried to put those thoughts out of my mind because of our age difference and the fact she was married. When we arrived at my house, she pulled in and parked at the mouth of the driveway and I popped out to unload my bike. As I wheeled it alongside her black Ford truck, I leaned toward her window to thank her for the lift. Before I could react, she suddenly planted a very passionate kiss on me as I stood by her on the warm, steamy asphalt driveway. It was unexpected yet inevitable. It had been building up all day, and I probably subconsciously realized that she had been planning this all along. I pulled away, very confused about what was right and what was wrong. It felt right in that animalistic way, but my thoughts were very confused and I was afraid that we had just committed a mortal sin that would be impossible to live with.

She said nothing at first, but then we both burst out laughing at the same time for some reason. Just then, the light above the driveway was turned on, and our attention was diverted to that. We said goodnight, and she drove off down the road as I wheeled my red bicycle toward the garage. When I quietly entered the kitchen, my aunt was looking up at me from the kitchen table. She had made some iced tea and had poured me a cup and motioned for me to join her at the table. She asked me about the engine noise and was curious if I had gotten a ride home. "Everything alright?" she quizzed. I said I had been offered a ride by a coworker and let it go at that.

She had a weird look of concern in her eyes, and I immediately wondered how much she had observed. But the driveway was long, and I was sure there was no way she could have seen us sharing that forbidden kiss at its far end. I figured I was just feeling paranoid about it. That night I had a hard time falling asleep. These new moral dilemmas were all new to me. I felt like a child but knew I was about to cross over a new threshold.

And I was relatively sure I wasn't ready to deal with all the complex issues of adulthood.

12

The Genius and the Telepathic Mind Meld

Over the early part of the summer, I had begun work on multiple art projects. One of our neighbors called and asked me to paint a family group portrait. I agreed to take photos of the four family members and committed to completing the painting within a month. They offered to pay me $500, which was incredibly good in those days. This family had a lot of money, so I wasn't really surprised they could afford such a luxury. I bought all new supplies for the project and figured it would make a great piece for my portfolio. I took a bunch of photos of the family members all dressed up in their finest clothes. It went well, and I started working on the painting in our tiny spare room.

Meanwhile, my aunt had suggested that I contact the man she had told me about. One afternoon, before heading to work, I called and spoke with him. He sounded enthused to see some of my work, and we set up a meeting for the following Saturday afternoon. He told me he wanted me to bring examples of my illustration and design work, so I started assembling a representative sampling in a black, zippered portfolio I had bought at college. In it were a few photos of paintings I had sold, some logo sketches I had worked on for an assignment, and a lot of illustrations from high school and college.

Some of my initial work from Mrs. Gunther's 2D design class seemed to be most applicable for business, so I put those toward the front of the book. She had strongly urged me to shift my focus to corporate design work, such as logos, magazine advertisements and publication design. I could see that my style and approach were well suited to design work, but my first loves were illustration, cartooning and painting. I didn't know much about graphic design until I went to college, but I was considering all options and leaning toward shifting my major. I realized how much more realistic it would be to pursue a career in graphic design rather than illustration, and the encouraging words of teachers like Mrs. Gunther made me pause to reflect.

The following Saturday I followed the directions I had scribbled onto a scrap of paper and drove my shiny new "old lady car" several miles to the home of Mr. Stowe. My aunt had described him as an "Ichabod Crane type of fellow," and when he opened the screen door of his old farmhouse, I knew exactly what she meant. A younger man than I had imagined, he was very thin and tall, and he had little, round plastic-rim eyeglasses. He wore a short-sleeved white shirt and had it buttoned all the way up, looking uncomfortable through his crooked, closed-mouth grin.

I was not totally comfortable meeting strangers at this point in my life, so I was a little uneasy at first. Much of that trepidation was eased when he very eagerly said he wanted to show me some of his latest projects. As we walked toward the one-story "workshop" behind the house, I asked him why he had been so interested in meeting me. He said he had enjoyed talking with my aunt and that she had raved about my talents and intelligence. I was embarrassed and said that my aunt was a little biased. He said I shouldn't be concerned, and he started telling me about his business. As we entered his workshop, which in fact was a converted multi-car garage, he was bubbling over with enthusiasm. He showed me a huge stack of blueprints, unrolling them one after another in his frantic excitement.

When I asked him to explain what we were looking at, he apologized for his "childish lack of manners." The blueprints turned out to be actual schematics for amusement park rides.

One was a single-rail roller coaster that looked far more futuristic and amazing than any of the few such rides I had seen before. When I asked if they were real or just plans for things that were not yet built, he assured me that these rides had already been constructed. Most of them were already operating in theme parks in Europe and Japan, he explained. He had lived and worked in Germany and England for years before moving to America.

When I asked him what his business was focused on, he replied "engineering and innovative concepts." I admitted I really didn't fully understand what that meant, and he explained that he had a couple of engineering degrees and was a bit of a "nutty professor type of inventor." I was skeptical and kept looking through the complex blueprints and asking more questions. He described his work for a company in London, where he was responsible for initiating original concepts that were then fully developed by teams of engineers and other specialists. He told me that many of his inventions were in use around the world.

When he told me he was first hired in Germany at age fifteen, I was impressed. The more he spoke, the more I was a bit in awe. He went off on rants about the "evil bureaucracy" and the professional jealousy he dealt with in Europe, which convinced him he needed to break away and start his own business. He explained that he started his own consulting business about three years prior. He was doing business with firms all over the world and was recently bringing in more work from American corporations. He decided it would be wise to distance himself from his past and move to a small town in the United States. I asked why he moved to this small town in Pennsylvania, and he said he had sought anonymity and then added, "It really isn't very important where I reside since I'm always on a plane to one corner of the world or another."

I was a bit overwhelmed as his impromptu presentation continued. He showed me more blueprints and renderings of amusement park attractions, and I asked many questions. He was so genuinely excited about every project that it was infectious. I distinctly felt the power of his brilliance. He was a truly amazing person, and I felt lucky to have made his acquaintance. How odd that this type of rare individual happened to move to my hometown and that he had wanted to meet me. My head was spinning from the overwhelming array of incredible concepts unveiled before me. The open workshop had been carefully transformed, and electrical outlets completely lined the white interior walls above the waist-level work surfaces that had recently been constructed. He showed me plans for an automobile that used a new type of fuel that he described as "experimental, but inevitable." It operated on water mixed with something else I can't recall. Was this in some way a prototype for the modern hybrid technology? It was 1974 when I had the meeting with this bizarre, brilliant stranger.

I had been referring to him as Mr. Stowe, and he somewhat sternly urged me to call him Eric, so I complied. He seemed to possess a volatile temper, which had me a little on edge, but I was still poring over the papers he had laid out across the surface of the well-lit drafting table. When I asked him in what capacity he thought I could help him, he just asked me to show him what was in my portfolio. We quickly went through my humble little collection of work, and he barely commented. He asked what I felt were somewhat odd questions as we leafed through it. He inquired about my vision for my future and what I planned to do. I spoke of my desire to make my impact in some creative field, but I cautioned that I didn't want to be restricted to only one thing. As I showed him some of my work from my creative writing classes as well as all of my artwork, his eyes lit up. He said he had become curious about me from talking with my aunt and that he was impressed by my range of talents. It felt odd to me, albeit flattering, that this stranger was so impressed with me despite the fact that my abilities were barely developed and I had not yet accomplished much of anything.

He suggested we go into the house and have some lemonade or tea, and I obediently followed, my head still spinning from seeing all of his blueprints and sketches. As we ambled across the sun-soaked lawn, he told me he was in need of someone with the versatility I possessed to help him with all the aesthetic concerns he would be facing in the near future. He explained that he was more than capable of designing new technology or innovative products but admitted he was clumsy with words and didn't know what looked good or would help sell his new projects. I quickly said that I wasn't ready for that kind of responsibility, and he stopped to reassure me his intentions were more thought out than that.

"I realize it's still early in your development, but you possess a lot of talent and display versatility that's hard to find. I'm trying to find a complement to myself, and I need someone who can communicate in both visual and verbal form. I also need someone who will be able to work with me, and since I'm a bit unusual, it will be difficult for me to find that person. I think you can handle it, though. You can start by working on specific projects and can limit your involvement until you either finish college or come to understand that you probably don't need college." I was taken aback by that statement. "Why would I leave college?" I asked, stunned that he had even suggested it. He shot back, "You'll soon figure out that it's just a waste of your time."

He started to irritate me with what I felt was arrogance and impudence. I felt a little apprehensive, yet remained intrigued. This was the most unusual person I had ever met: one part boy genius and one part potential mentor. We entered into a bright, expansive kitchen, and he fetched lemonade out of the pristine refrigerator. As I surveyed my surroundings, I could see that he was a very organized person away from his mad scientist workshop, which was a cluttered mess.

His living room was oddly stark, with its shiny hardwood floor and sparse décor and furnishings. A small sofa seemed very alone in the center of the room and a couple of small stuffed chairs faced that. He informed me that he'd built the beautiful fieldstone fireplace with his own two hands and I expressed admiration for his craftsmanship. When he gestured for me to sit down, I took a seat in one of the chairs while he sat on the sofa. Abruptly, he held up a finger and said, "Hold on a second. I have something you'll really like!" and he briefly disappeared into the hallway, before emerging with what looked to be a stereo turntable. He was all smiles as he danced around, holding it high in the air. Plugged into a long extension cord, it was playing Aerosmith's "Dream On" on a vinyl LP.

Before I could ask any questions, he volunteered, "See this turntable? Ugly, right?" I thought it wise to say nothing, in case it might sound insulting, and he continued his fast-paced monologue. "It *is* ugly, but that's beside the point. See, I need a person like you to help me determine what this should look like so that its uniqueness is properly dressed up." I replied, "What's unique about it? It looks like a regular turntable." An impish grin quickly appeared on his face as he replied, "Oh, yeah? Ever see a turntable do this?" and he quickly sandwiched it with one hand below and one atop the dust cover.

Then, he suddenly flipped the entire thing upside down, and it kept right on playing the record, without so much as a scratch or a skip. He went on, through a big shit-eating grin, telling me how he developed the concept and design and even built it in his own workshop. I asked if it was in production, and he ignored my question. It certainly was amazing, and I was convinced he was telling me the truth. He said, "We have dozens of similar prototypes in the works, but I want to maintain control over how we produce them and where we market these things. I'm sitting on many more inventions and enhancements, but I have a lot of work to do, and I can't do all of it without help."

126

I had just noticed that there was no television in the room, which struck me as a bit unusual. But then I figured he was probably too smart to be entertained by the typical TV shows. Between sips of his lemonade he went into a whirlwind description of his vision for his fledgling corporation. He wanted to retain only the silent partners that currently helped support his research and development. He said they were located in different cities scattered throughout Europe and North America. He expressed that he wanted total creative control over what projects his company would work on and that he wanted to have a creative partner on board who would design all of the branding, advertising and packaging.

He kept stressing that he felt he was able to make the devices function but that he couldn't make them attractive to consumers. I asked why his clients couldn't provide that to him, and he snapped back at me, "I told you, I want control. I want everything to be a reflection of me and who I am, not some corporate distortion of that. If you agree to be that resource for the business, then I can be sure the image is consistent and recognizable around the world. That's what I'm after, and you can be part of it. It's not very difficult to understand!"

I felt a bit nervous and almost insulted with his tone. His behavior seemed way over the top for someone I barely knew. I kept reminding him that I was "just a student," and he kept countering by saying I had immense talents and didn't need anything but experience to realize my potential. He assured me that I could finish college and then come to work with him full time. His offer was open-ended. I didn't feel comfortable because I didn't completely trust him. I felt he was foolish to offer something so important to a snot-nosed kid who had completed only one year of college. That's when he shut down. His mood shifted rather dramatically as his face conveyed a sullenness and a darker tone. He stopped talking, and I froze up, not knowing how to defuse his obvious frustration. Then, the strangest thing happened.

Without actually speaking, I felt we were continuing a conversation, in great detail. He stood up and slowly began pacing behind the sofa. Rubbing his forehead, he seemed to be in pain at first. He eventually folded his arms in front of his chest and leaned against the wood-paneled wall on the far side of the room, then slid down until he was sitting on the floor. I considered that behavior odd for a grown man and thought to myself, "What a child!" In my mind I actually heard him react. His voice resonated in my mind. I did a double take at him as he just sat there staring at me.

"I'm a child?! You're the one who's throwing away the chance of a lifetime." I was in a state of shock as the voice in my head shook me up. I remember angrily glaring at him, feeling violated by the intrusion into my conscious mind. "You have a lot of nerve," was the sentiment I directed toward him with my mind. His expression changed, and that indicated he had received my thought. Looking embarrassed, he cast his gaze toward the floor. "I'm sorry," he thought. "You're a very special young man and you aren't even slightly aware of your true potential. It's too soon for you, I guess. I apologize for pushing you." Then, he paused, and all was silent as the sun began to set and the room was saturated in soft shadows of amber.

We sat there, across the room from each other, neither of us speaking or moving a muscle for many long, uncomfortable minutes. Still intrigued by this strange man, I was more impressed by the unique and bizarre experience of talking with our minds. I know it sounds ridiculous, but I'm not making it up. For an entire conversation, somehow, we were able to communicate in full dialogue, just as if we were speaking the words. How was this possible? Had he slipped drugs into my lemonade, something that made me imagine this was happening?

I had read about things like this in science fiction stories or heard people on talk shows refer to telepathy, but I never thought I would experience it. Eric started to appear more relaxed and comfortable as he continued to communicate with me. "You are an 'empath' and have unusual talents you don't yet understand. You will need someone to mentor you and help you to grow. I would be willing to help you, but you're too closed off at this point in your life. If we had met five years from now, it would've been better for us both. I'm not pleased, but I have to accept it." I felt nervous and was concerned that his intentions weren't completely honorable or selfless. I shot back, "I'm not a homosexual!" He immediately thought, "It doesn't matter. We have nothing to talk about now." I'm still convinced that he was looking at me as a potential solution to his loneliness as much as an answer to his advertising concerns.

I was concerned that my aunt and uncle would be worried about me if I prolonged the visit much longer, and I was emotionally and physically drained from all this non-verbal communication. Feeling increasingly exhausted and uneasy in his house, I began to make my way toward the side door. I heard him say, "Good luck," as I exited through the screen door toward my car. And a second or two later, I swear he sent the thought, "And I don't watch television. You got *one* thing right." I'm not absolutely sure whether he spoke those final words or *thought* them to me, but those were the last we ever shared.

I was intimidated by this guy, and although he and I had shared an extremely intimate encounter, I didn't want to see him again. Maybe it was my tender age or my preconceived fears, but it was far too much for me to deal with in any way. As I drove my old station wagon along the deserted dirt road toward the highway, I knew that I'd never be able to shake the memory of that afternoon.

To this day, I wonder what ultimately became of the genius and his amazing inventions.

13

Frequently Unanswered Questions (FUQs)

It was a very interesting summer of '74. As the days unfolded, there always seemed to be too many things happening all at once. The Watergate scandal was all over the news, with new revelations broadcast every day. Impeachment was a word I had not heard before that summer, but it had become all too familiar. One stormy summer night, at work, Andrea took my hand and led me out the back door behind the building. The door had barely slammed behind us when she forcefully grabbed me by the belt and pulled me to her. She kissed me so damn hard; I felt she would literally devour me. It was very different from the kiss in the driveway a few nights prior. This expressed a somewhat different intention, and it scared the hell out of me.

Before I knew it, I felt a sensation of heat surging through my chest, to my arms, and then down my forearms to my fingertips. It was an icy-warm electric sensation and, at first, I feared I was having a seizure. She tensed up and pulled back, looking down at our hands, which were clenched around each other's wrists. "Robby!" she exclaimed. "What's happening to us?" The bizarre blue glow was back, and it enveloped our intertwined hands and wrists. We both tensed up and stood there, arms extended, still holding onto each other. We both just stared at the strange blue-white aura, now dissipating into the air. "What *is* that?!" she insisted. I said nothing at first, just trying to come up with some response. I asked her if she was okay, and she assured me she was fine. But I saw fear in her eyes and felt responsible for putting it there. I had to ask her if she had felt any pain, and she claimed she only experienced a soft, tingly feeling. The same type of sensation had run through my veins from my neck down to my fingertips. At least that's how it felt to me this time. I told her I couldn't explain it but asked her to forgive me just the same. She clutched me and pulled me very tightly against her small frame. "Oh, baby," she said, "It's okay. Don't worry about me. I'm fine." Then she released me and walked toward the door, pulling me by my hand. She led me to the small break room, and we sat at the little round table there. Once we had both calmed down and caught our breath, I told her about the experiences I had previously had with the strange phenomenon. She listened intently as I tried my best to recount some of the past incidents when the odd light had made appearances.

While the stories sounded purely ridiculous to my own ears, Andrea seemed to accept them at face value. Feeling somewhat ashamed, I timidly asked her, "Do you think I'm a freak? Or crazy?" She reached out and put her hands atop mine on the table and said, "I was there and saw it and felt it for myself. You definitely aren't imagining it. If you are, then we're both having the same dream at the same time, and I don't think that's what's going on." "Then what *is* going on?" I asked. She just shook her head and said we should put it behind us for the time being and just get to work.

I felt a new admiration and affection for her because of how she made me feel accepted and didn't panic over this new development. She kept her distance from me the rest of that night, and I figured she needed to sort out her emotions. She must have been taken aback by the strange event, but I still felt she was my friend and was going to be there for me. A weekend came and went, and we both had time to reflect upon this unusual situation. On the following Monday evening, Andrea took me aside during a break, and she told me she thought I should definitely see a doctor. I told her I would probably do that, and we agreed that there was nothing to be afraid of since we had experienced no pain and there was no reason to expect it to happen again. We speculated on what might have caused the little "electrical surge" we both witnessed. I said I thought it might have had something to do with the wet ground we were standing on because it had indeed been raining just minutes prior to us going out the door. We agreed that it made some sense that we may have just picked up some excess static electricity from the carpeting in the hallway and it discharged when we had embraced, standing on the damp surface. That sounded somewhat plausible, but I didn't for one minute really believe it was the case. We were grasping for answers because that's what people do to make themselves feel better so they can sleep at night.

In the wake of that shared experience Andrea and I became even closer to one another. Ultimately, our mutual attraction overpowered us both. Maybe we were simply two lonely people who just needed someone, anyone to help us feel connected, but we couldn't deny our need to be together. Not more than a week after our strange interlude, we became lovers. While we both admitted feeling afraid and guilty, we pushed beyond that and embarked on an incredible odyssey of carnal discovery. She was the instigator, but I was an eager participant. We made passionate love in every setting imaginable. There were awkward yet exciting rendezvous in the storage room, in the parking lot after work, and even in the conference room. She was insatiable, ravenous and persistent. We had our friendship as a foundation, but this was really mainly about physical attraction, the thrill of the danger and filling each other's empty hearts.

We had forgotten the weird incident in the back lot, lost in a blur of kisses and sensual satisfaction. She had a tendency to call me her "Pookie" for some reason I never knew. But I liked it. I liked the way she made me feel and the way she said she needed me and loved me. While I was aware that I was nothing more than a stupid schoolboy exploring the joys of all things erotic, she was admittedly falling in love with me. I would dismiss those

132

declarations and would tell her to just "shut up and kiss me" whenever she started to get sentimental. We admitted to each other that we were doing something very wrong, in that she was a married woman with two small children at home, but we also admitted we weren't willing to end our relationship.

At work, we faked it as best we could, avoiding eye contact and trying so damn hard to not smile at each other too much. But, in time, we started noticing the raised eyebrows and had to endure some snide remarks from coworkers. Finally, one day, I heard Andrea talking very loudly, obviously engaged in some type of confrontation in the conference room. I was nervous, imagining that the jig was up. Sean, in the same room with me as usual, said, "That don't sound good!" I just kept quiet, trying to prepare myself for a scolding or for what I was sure would be an embarrassing conversation. I mean, it seemed ridiculous to me that no one accused us of anything over the course of this entire summer. It had to be obvious that something between us had changed. Andrea had been acting more upbeat and bouncy at work. I was probably also smiling way more than usual, although I had been a pretty happy worker all along.

I couldn't see the conference room door, but I could look out into the hallway, into which the door opened. Andrea finally emerged a few minutes after the shouting had subsided, exited briskly and immediately headed out the front door. She appeared to be crying. I then saw Gary, one of the owners, leave the same room and head to his office. He slammed his door shut, which sent shock waves through the building and down my spine. I knew in my heart that something bad was brewing. I wanted very badly to chase after Andrea but knew I couldn't be that obvious. Instead, I just continued working while Sean made his speculations about what might have just transpired. The whole thing was so bizarre because it had generally been a friendly and harmonious workplace. A little while later, Marsha walked in and dropped a file folder and a memo on my table. The memo said I was to meet Gary in his office during my next break.

I knew that the shit had hit the fan over something and all I could think was it must have had something to do with me and Andrea. I finished my work and turned off the camera.

I walked past Sean and then bumped into Marsha out in the hallway. She had a sad expression on her face. It was an unusual expression; it seemed like she was embarrassed, angry and sympathetic all at the same time. She looked down at her feet as I slowly eased past her toward Gary's office. He sharply said, "Come in!" when I rapped on the sturdy wooden door. I immediately knew this wasn't going to be a friendly chat, not only by the look on his square-jawed face but by the fact that he was holding a check in his hands. He proceeded to tell me in very plain English that I was fired, and said he had one week's back pay for me as he handed me the check.

At first I refused to reach out to grab the check, instead asking incredulously, "Why the hell are you doing this to me!?" He didn't change expression whatsoever as he matter-of-factly stated that my "production had suffered" and that he had to let me go because my "numbers were down." I instinctively smirked and may have even laughed in his face. My numbers, meaning the amount of images I was able to record on the microfilm, were always higher than any other camera operator. Sean would always bust my chops about how he was sick of never being able to keep pace with me. Andrea had kept me posted on my production every week that summer and had commented on my excellent numbers more than once. I knew this was a bullshit reason. I guess I was too young and stupid to realize what was really going on, so I said "It's a lie! There's no way..." Then, he put his oversized baseball mitt of a hand up to stop me and said, "Please stop. Just pack up your property and leave out the front door. This check gets us all caught up, including tonight. Good luck back at school, Rob."

I angrily snatched the check from his hand and never said another word. Instead, I stormed out and just made a beeline for the front door. I didn't have any belongings to speak of so there was nothing to gather up. I was so pissed; I didn't even care about saying goodbye to Sean or Marsha. Now I knew why Marsha had that look on her face. We were friends and I knew she liked me. She may have suspected the little affair I was involved in, but she had never said anything. I guess she knew in her heart that something might have been going on, but now the proverbial cat was out of the bag. I figured it would be far too embarrassing to face her, so I turned and strode down the hallway and out the front door into the evening air. Andrea was waiting out by my car. I could see she had been crying as I stomped my way across the pavement.

Through her tears, she just kept saying, "I'm so sorry. I'm sorry this happened." Obviously, she knew I was getting fired. "What the fuck just happened?" I angrily asked. She just kept shaking her head, saying, "I'm sorry." It took me a few more seconds to figure out she had just been canned, too. "Damn it!" I said. "Why would they do this? How could they do this?" She was taking all the blame, and she described how the owners had been informed about our torrid love affair. She said they had a hard time with it, mainly because they thought it was scandalous and disgraceful. "Holier-than-thou assholes!" I yelled. She put her hand over my mouth, and a tear trickled down her cheek. I expressed concern for her and the loss of income, and she assured me she would get another job quickly. She said I needn't worry since her sister had always told her she had a standing offer at the store she managed in a local mall that was soon opening.

I suddenly realized that all of this meant the end to us working together. We would never again be able to enjoy those stolen moments we had enjoyed all summer. It felt like a piece of me had suddenly been ripped out. She was having trouble stifling her tears, so I just held her close to me as we leaned against the side of my car. I had tried to be good to her but, but I never had anything to give but my willing body. She had always made it clear that was all she really expected I could give. But on this night, I think we felt like two little kids who just knew we weren't ready for the story to end.

It was only about 8:00 PM, and neither of us had to be home just yet. She said she needed time to come up with a story to tell her husband, and I was petrified to admit to my aunt and uncle that I had just gotten fired for the first time in my life. Andrea said, "Come on, Pook," and led me by the hand to her truck. I just followed her lead, and off we went. She and I didn't say much as we drove toward the river. She held my left hand in her right along the way, and I felt like I never wanted to let go of her. My favorite song of that summer, Rufus' "Tell Me Something Good" was playing through the truck's radio as we pulled closer to our destination.

We finally arrived at the river's edge and parked in a secluded spot atop a small hill. From that secluded and quiet location we could see for miles. She and I just fell into each other as we had done time and time again, and I quickly forgot the anxiety and anger of the past hour and was once again lost in her hungry arms and willing mouth. She squeezed me so tight I felt she would crack my ribs. We took a blanket from the backseat and laid it down near the row of lilac bushes. The flowers had long since closed up for the summer, but the plants provided a secluded sanctuary for our lovemaking. In the afterglow of our latest senses-shattering interlude, Andrea confessed her love for me again. I finally really understood the depth of her devotion to me.

I imagined that I was so very different from her husband in that I was open and trusting and willing to be vulnerable to her. From the fragmented details I knew of him, he wasn't a very sensitive or compassionate man. I truly cared about Andrea, and although we went through with our forbidden dalliance, I had expressed my genuine concerns about not wanting to contribute to destroying anyone's marriage. I knew we were treading on dangerous ground for so many reasons, and I worried that our reckless behavior could somehow hurt her kids and destroy her marriage. That was something that admittedly ate at me all along. It didn't stop me from following my urges, but it did frequently enter my thoughts. She understood my concerns and once in a while we talked it out, but she would invariably tell me that I didn't need to worry, and we would make love for hours. At the end of those marathon sessions, I was too damn exhausted to think about anything. On this memorable night, we made love until past midnight and then she returned me to my car and I sleepily drove myself home. When we parted, we promised to call each other the next day. With her scent still in my hair and on my hands, I staggered my way to my bed and just collapsed.

I didn't break the news to Aunt Elena and Uncle Pete until just before the following evening, as soon as both of them were home from work. They didn't really sweat it as I explained that I felt I was let go because the company was struggling to keep its doors open. They bought it, and I felt it was a harmless white lie. I couldn't tell them the real reason, obviously. That evening, I called Andrea and we talked about the future. She said her sister had already paved the way for her to work days at her women's clothing store in the new mall in Mount Lebanon. She told me to be happy because soon I would be returning to school. I felt better about it after I had processed the disappointment of being fired. A few things went through my mind. I had always thought that Gary, one of the owners of the company, had a crush on Andrea. He seemed to really light up any time they talked. I guess he saw in her the same charming qualities that I enjoyed, but he was married, too. They had worked together for several years before I had ever come into the picture. I had always felt a little negativity coming from Gary toward me, and it had escalated a bit in the recent weeks.

Andrea never even hinted at any such thing, and I never asked her for fear she would take it the wrong way. Anyway, it was "only a job," I rationalized, and soon I would be returning to

137

school for another year. I had made previous arrangements to share a small off-campus apartment with my friend, Jon, who was a fairly cool guy, although a bit nerdy and awkward. Andrea asked me if I had made an appointment to see a doctor, and I lied and told her I had an appointment for the following week. She said, "Good. I think it's a good idea to try to get some answers." I agreed and had every intention of making an appointment the next morning.

After we ended our call, I went and talked to my uncle in the basement workshop where he spent much of his time. He started the conversation. "Only a couple more weeks of freedom, huh Rob?" I smiled and shook my head affirmatively. He said, "I remember how it felt to be your age, y'know. It's a tough time. Things change so fast. People sometimes expect you to act a certain way, and you're still not really sure who you are. It's not easy, I know, but the main thing you've gotta do is just try to learn a little every day and to especially learn from your mistakes." I tried to reassure him that I was learning a lot, and I expressed my anger about being "unfairly" fired from my job. He just said in a matter-of-fact way, "Never crap where you eat." That told me he either knew or suspected the truth about the reason behind my termination.

I realized it was time to drop the subject, so I asked if we could talk about something else. He stopped his puttering and, in the warm glow of his cozy domain, he took a seat on a stool. It probably worried him a bit as I began to recount stories of the strange experiences with the unusual glowing aura. I told him pretty much everything, starting with the incident immediately following my skateboard accident, with the "little man" and the television set. I didn't tell him all the details about the most recent incident with Andrea, but I changed the story and still got it across to him that this was still happening to me. He was genuinely concerned but tried his best to absorb this incredible story. He said, "Well, I can't say I saw *this* coming. It sounds like you've bottled this stuff up for a long time. Why'd you wait so long to say something? If this has been going on that long, you should have told someone about it long ago. Or *have* you told others about it?" I told him I had only shared a little of it with different people over the years but had never opened up like this. He slowly stood up and thanked me for confiding in him. When he suggested I talk to Aunt Elena about it, too, I protested, saying I wanted to wait on that since it was difficult enough to open up and share all this with him.

I was trembling as I slumped down onto a stack of cardboard boxes that were filled with auto parts. He looked pretty concerned when he realized this confession had shaken me as much as it had. He said he thought it would be wise to have our family doctor check me out. "Maybe it's time to have your first complete physical," he calmly suggested. I agreed, saying I was tired of not knowing what was happening to me. He offered to set up the appointment and drive me to the doctor, but I insisted I would do it alone. He kept telling me there was probably nothing to worry about. I was concerned that he thought I was crazy, and I was even more concerned he would tell Aunt Elena I was losing my mind or something. He reassured me he wouldn't say anything to anybody, even her. At that moment I realized how much he had filled the void my father had left. While I still missed my dad, I saw such genuine compassion in his brother; it often felt as though my father were still here with me. I made an appointment for a few days before school was to reconvene, and on that morning I drove myself to the doctor's office.

Our family physician, Dr. Henson, was a middle-aged man with almost no bedside manner. He wasn't surly or anything, he just came across as very dry and robotic. He never showed much of an emotional reaction to anything. While I hadn't exactly been a frequent visitor to his office, I had been to see him a few times over the years. I had to wonder if he was always the same way, even in his personal life. He kept me waiting for what seemed to be an hour before his assistant summoned me from the tiny waiting room.

Dr. Henson had treated my concussion and broken arm back when I was eleven. He was a thorough, gentle and attentive doctor, despite his cool demeanor. He efficiently went through all the obligatory tests, including taking my blood pressure and pulse and listening to my heart. He had his nurse draw some blood and said it would be a couple of days before they checked it out, but he anticipated no problems. In fact, he said I was in excellent condition. When he asked me if I had any recent illnesses to tell of, I took the opportunity to tell him about the unexplainable episodes I had been having the past several years. He listened intently while I went on about all the occurrences I could remember. Still sitting atop the examination table, I felt a great relief just letting it all out. It was at this time that I realized how much it had been weighing on my mind. With all that had been going on in my life, I had not given myself the luxury of taking the time to seek some answers. He listened intently to every word I said and barely seemed to react.

When I had finished listing all the times I had witnessed the weird phenomena, he was still stroking his white-whiskered chin and carefully considering my story. At first he asked if I had been having headaches, dizzy spells or any issues with my eyesight. I replied that I had not, while he looked into my eyes with his small penlight. He asked if I had experienced any additional head injuries in the years since my severe concussion. I informed him that I had never really struck my head again, other than a few bumps incurred while playing touch football. He asked me to look up and down and side to side, and then had me follow his penlight with my eyes as he moved it all around. He asked if I had been nauseous or feverish recently, and I said I had not. I informed him that I hadn't really been sick with a cold in years. He seemed pleased with all the answers, and paused to look through my file as he relaxed into his leather padded chair. He swiveled back and forth a little, and then he asked if I would be willing to undergo another set of tests. I said, "That depends," so he went on to describe them. He said he didn't know if it was completely warranted, but he wanted to examine me with something called an electroencephalogram. He explained it was a rather routine test and that there would be no risks or discomfort. According to him, doctors often recommended such tests for people who had previously experienced brain trauma.

The doctor went on to describe how the test recorded the brain's electrical activity using special electrodes attached to the patient's head. When asked if he thought this test was necessary, he said he felt it might provide me with some peace of mind if we could rule out such possibilities as epilepsy and other types of seizures as the root cause for my "hallucinations." I informed him that I wasn't the only person who had seen these hallucinations, and he furrowed his brow and looked up at me over his half-frame glasses. "Mr. Chandler, are you saying that other people have had simultaneous hallucinations?" I said, "No, what I mean is these are *not* hallucinations. They are something real, something tangible and visible to anyone, not just me!" He seemed unimpressed and very skeptical. He strongly suggested that I undergo the EEG exam and said he could get it scheduled for the following day, as long as my uncle or aunt would drive me. I agreed somewhat hesitantly because I was afraid of what the test might uncover.

The next morning I got showered and dressed, and Aunt Elena drove me to the hospital. I was nervous yet hopeful that the test would finally provide some answers. The wait wasn't very long, and the test itself was as simple and painless as promised. The attendant attached little plastic sensors to my head and kept assuring me that I would feel nothing during the exam. A small machine was off to the side of the exam table, and he told me it would register irregular lines that would indicate my brain's electrical activity. It sounded interesting, and I was fascinated to see the patterns my brain would create.

During the hour or so the test took to complete, the doctor administering the test asked me several questions. At certain times he had me look at a flashing white light he held in his hand. At other times he told me to inhale or exhale to change my breathing pattern. Before long, the test was over and the attendant removed the small electrodes from my scalp. I was glad it was over and anxious to find out what the test indicated. Before they let me leave, I was asked to take a seat, and the doctor came over to speak to me. He asked if I wanted water or had any questions, and I said I just wanted to know if he saw anything weird. He said the full results would have to be interpreted and then sent to my family doctor. He told me he had not seen anything to concern him during the exam and that Dr. Henson would be contacting me. I was happy he hadn't seen anything "weird," and I was looking forward to returning to school in a few days. I figured I would save any questions for my own doctor since he was the only one I had really told about all that had been happening.

The next day we got a call from Dr. Henson's receptionist, who asked if I could come in that afternoon. I had only two more days before I needed to be back at school, so I eagerly agreed to come in the same day. I was anxious to find out what the test showed. I drove over to the doctor's office and was pleased that Dr. Henson greeted me promptly in the waiting room. When we sat down in his office, he opened up my file and had the results of the EEG test on top of the pile of papers. Before I could ask anything, he said, "I'm happy to report that your test results appear quite normal." I breathed a sigh of relief, and he continued, adding, "But I have some concerns, nonetheless."

That caught me off guard. He went on to explain that there was nothing obvious in the test results to indicate epilepsy or any type of seizures. He said that my physical exam had also revealed nothing to alarm him, but he was hung up on the stories I had told him, and he expressed serious concerns about what that might indicate. "Mr. Chandler," he dryly said, "There is definitely something unusual going on, and we can't ignore that. You may still be suffering some ill effects from the concussion of seven years ago, and there may be some other ways we can get to the bottom of it. While it is encouraging that you do not exhibit signs of seizures, you do have a family history, evidenced by what I have in my records, of mental illness." "Are you saying I might be mentally ill?!" I exclaimed. In typical fashion, he calmly responded, "No, I'm not jumping to any conclusions here. I've just been reviewing the records we have from your family, and the only thread worth pursuing at this time might be the fact that your grandfather was diagnosed as schizophrenic. That's just something we should not overlook or ignore."

When I calmed down and asked what that meant, he explained that schizophrenia is a mental disorder that sometimes causes symptoms such as paranoia and hallucinations. He said it was not generally believed to be hereditary, but he felt it was something we should investigate. I said it didn't make sense, though, because other people had also seen what he kept referring to as my "hallucinations." But I could tell he didn't believe that was true. He said it was conceivable that I might have imagined others saw the same things I saw, but he seriously doubted the possibility of a shared vision. I was a bit ticked off but had also started to tire of all this testing and talking. I wanted to get myself back to school and away from the fruitless guesswork. I was satisfied we had ruled out epileptic seizures and chose to assume the episodes were all in my past.

Dr. Henson suggested I might want to look into talking with a psychiatrist or therapist, too. I was offended because I felt he was jumping to conclusions, but I admit I thought it made some sense, considering I had felt depressed at times during the past few years. I thanked him for all he did and told him I would consider his recommendations. He stopped me before I left, to offer to make arrangements for additional tests, but I said I wanted to hold off for now. He said it was not urgent to have these tests, but he told me to keep him informed if I were to have "any additional episodes." I left there with mixed feelings and still no real answers.

I saw Andrea the night before I was to go back to school. We drove across town in her truck and got takeout from a fast-food place. We walked through a quiet park and sat on a bench to eat. Then, we talked about us and our plans to see each other in the fall. We talked a bit about the strange thing that happened between us that day, earlier in the summer. I said I had no faith that the doctor could help me, and I expressed my feeling that he didn't really believe what I told him. She asked me what I thought could be the root cause of all the strange episodes I'd experienced.

The best I could come up with was that I wondered if it might have something to do with the concussion I had when I was a kid. I explained that as I looked back upon the various times I saw these strange things, I realized they had never happened prior to the accident. Although I had no idea how it was possible, in my mind I was convinced something within me had changed or gone awry. I told her I felt a surge of what I could only describe as heat or electricity in my body whenever I experienced an episode. She asked me if it only happened when I was really angry or excited, and I stopped to reflect. I said, "Maybe that has something to do with it," and felt as though it could be a clue worth considering. I was growing tired of all the fruitless speculation and just wanted to put my head on her shoulder and inhale her perfume for a while. We just sat there, holding each other and not talking for the longest time. The gentle breeze felt soothing, and I felt fortunate to share this last peaceful night with Andrea.

She surprised me with a box full of gifts when we went back to her truck. She had bought me several new shirts, a small chain necklace of braided gold and a desktop statue of Groucho Marx. I had told her how much I enjoyed watching old Marx Brothers movies, so she had gone out of her way to find this caricature-style statue for my desk. All this told me how devoted she was to me. I felt guilty because, in my heart, I knew I would soon have to separate from her. She was a summer fling, and because of our age difference and her being married, it was obvious to me this couldn't result in anything but heartache. Still, she was able to convince me that it was conceivable that another human being could truly love me and could feel genuinely concerned for my happiness.

All Andrea ever brought me was pleasure and joy. On this particular night, we expended all our energy talking for a change, and she asked me about the incident when we saw the aura dancing around our arms and hands. I still had no real answers for her, but I described the test I had just undergone. There was no way she could fully appreciate what I was going through inside, but it was clear to me that Andrea truly cared about my well-being. She was convinced something unusual was affecting me, and expressed her desire to help me through it as best she could. She was protective of me and was worried that something was trying to take me from her.

Andrea hugged me very tightly saying, "I just don't want anything to ever hurt you." Neither did I.

14

Friends and Wannabe Lovers

My second year at college was vastly different from my first. By the fall of 1974, the campus atmosphere was all very familiar, and I really hit the ground running as I plunged headlong into my school work. Long hours in the studio were far more productive and satisfying. I took courses in printmaking, 3D design and communication design, the latter of which became my new passion. I enjoyed learning about page layout and publication design for the first time.

I was very disappointed with most of my teachers in day school, but I was taking some elective evening classes taught by working professionals. These adjunct professors were far more engaged and talented than any of the teachers I had to suffer during the regular daytime sessions. Unfortunately, the evening classes were in illustration, so I was not getting much worthwhile instruction in graphic design and layout. I gained some insight by talking with upperclassmen and by reading a few books they recommended. I wasn't worried that I couldn't learn what I needed to know, but I realized I wasn't going to learn it in the classroom. I started to toy with the idea of leaving school after the year was over. I had borrowed a lot of money, and it made me nervous, wondering how I would ever pay it all back. There was no money coming from home, so I was eager to start earning money on my own.

As I suspected, Rhea decided to enroll at a California school, and we didn't communicate often. But, I enjoyed meeting new people and made some good friends that fall. Andrea called me fairly frequently, but I was thinking I should distance myself

146

from her. I was concerned that if we kept pushing our luck her husband would eventually figure things out and come looking for me. She insisted on coming to stay with me one weekend in October, and I guess I went along with it because I knew how awesome the sex would be. It made quite an impression when guys who lived on my floor got wind of the fact that she was thirty years old and married and that she was coming to spend the weekend. Her husband had gone away for a week, and she convinced her sister, who knew nothing about us, to watch her kids while she "got away for a girls' weekend with some friends." She had to lie to pull this off, and I didn't argue.

The guys teased me pretty badly for a few days, and when she arrived, they all made sure to check her out. A lot of winks and snarky expressions were cast our way when we went to the cafeteria for dinner. I didn't want to take her there, but she said it would be fun, so we went. My better friends were very cool about it, so we had some friendly company during the meal. Horny as hell (as usual), Andrea was ready to go back to my room very early. We only stopped at the Cellar for a beer because I was thirsty for one and thought we should stall until at least 9:00 PM before turning in for the night. I had arranged for my roommate to stay with a friend on the other end of the floor, and he was fine with it. What I didn't know was that some wiseass short-sheeted my bed while we were eating. When we tried to get under the covers, our feet couldn't get past the folded pleat the culprit had cleverly prepared. Funny stuff.

The weekend came and went, and Andrea had to leave. She kept declaring her love for me, but I wasn't really interested in that kind of talk. I enjoyed her, but I felt we had a relationship based primarily on sex; at least that was what it meant to me. We both admitted that there was no way we had a future together, but we were certainly compatible in the physical sense. I walked her to the parking lot, kissed her goodbye and started thinking it was probably the last time I would see her.

147

For a while, I avoided getting involved with anyone new. Instead, I became infatuated with producing better work in my classes. One of my favorite teachers was an illustrator named Richard Blair, who was a working freelance artist with a growing reputation. At one point in the middle of Winter Quarter, I asked him if he'd be willing to review my portfolio, which I had worked hard to fill with more varied pieces. In my communication design class I had created some very polished corporate logos and symbols. The portfolio contained a collection of realistic pencil renderings, a couple of pages of figure drawing sketches, quite a few printed posters and some of the cartoons that had been published in *Reporter* magazine. He invited me to come to his house in the city, which doubled as his studio for his freelance illustration business. I was flattered that he would give me the time, and I stuffed even more work into my portfolio. He was the first working professional who gave me his focused attention and seemed to truly care about me as an individual.

He didn't just quickly leaf through the portfolio, as some of my daytime teachers had done. Instead, he carefully reviewed most every piece and asked the type of questions that indicated he was really thinking about what he was looking at. He said he was impressed that I was exploring graphic design as a possible career direction, although he was quick to compliment my innate illustration skills. He applauded the fact that I had the confidence to go out and solicit freelance work around town. He took note of the corporate symbols and logos in my book, and when I told him I was "new to it," he just smiled and said, "It doesn't matter, you have good potential in that area." It was the first time anyone had implied that I was possibly good enough to make a living in the field of design.

None of my full-time professors seemed to care enough to really consider anyone's potential or suggest what one might do for the future. In school, over the years, I only seemed to receive warnings, admonishments and negativity from the faculty. As a freshman in college, a couple of my professors said things like, "You can't make a living as a painter in this country, so you're crazy if you stick with that dream," and, "No one cares if you can draw. You need to have a backup plan." Gee, thanks for the pep talks, guys. Some of my professors were bitter because they were never able to make a name for themselves, or they were forced to teach because they couldn't find any work in their preferred area of expertise. And some of them were flat-out talentless asses who should never have been granted the privilege of teaching.

This man had been a successful commercial illustrator for years. He told me how he enjoyed working with young artists and giving private lessons to supplement his income, although he was always very busy with commissioned work. In many ways, we mirrored each other with our versatility and drawing talent. He was focused on portrait work and had developed some national notoriety in that area. A masterful painter in the tradition of Norman Rockwell, he was able to get work from regional and national clients with the help of his agent, who was based in Chicago.

There was real tangible warmth to his paintings, and I was in awe of the portraits he showed me. He could draw or paint anything and make it look appealing. The difference between us was that I really wanted to maintain a diverse repertoire of styles and genres. "It's pretty rare," he told me, "to have both the graphic design ability and the illustration talent that you seem to have. If anything, I would encourage you to keep working to develop skills in both areas. You can make a living in commercial art and design and still do illustration projects on the side, since it's harder to find that type of work." Those words helped me lay out my plan of action.

It might have been that conversation in Richard's quaint little city house that eventually gave me the impetus to leave school to pursue my dreams. I figured that my varied abilities were my ticket to earning a living. If I could get a job as a graphic artist in a business or in an advertising agency, I could possibly continue to get some work as an illustrator, too. What I didn't even mention to anyone was that I had always been a good writer, and I felt there were going to be a lot of opportunities to utilize that talent too. Suddenly, it seemed possible that I could actually prove a lot of people wrong by earning a living in the field I chose.

I would often work on projects in the art building late into the evening, sometimes forgetting the time and missing dinner. Other times I would be playing tennis or Frisbee or some other outdoor game and would lose track of time because I was having so much fun, and every now and then I'd meet some new girl and become infatuated yet again. I had developed a major crush on my friend's girlfriend, Kristen. They had been dating as long as I knew Tony, who had been our resident advisor, a student position of authority in the dorm. He was a great guy, and we became friends in my first year, although we didn't see each other for long stretches of time. He had a lot of obligations, with a part-time job off campus, RA responsibilities and his studies.

Tony was a senior in the winter of '75, and I was already aware that I'd miss him when the year ended. Kristen was always hanging around our dorms. She attended college in Brockport, which was about 45 minutes away, but Tony would either go pick her up or she'd bum rides and seemed to be around every weekend and sometimes during the week, too. They had been high school sweethearts and had been talking about getting married in the future. She was about three years younger than him and was an adorable young woman with sparkling, expressive eyes and light brown, shoulder-length hair. I had a huge crush on her from the minute we met, and had always envied my pal Tony. I told him how lucky he was all the time, and though I imagined he suspected my ongoing lust for Kristen, it never seemed to bother him. He was mature for his age and stood out among the rest of the guys in the way he calmly dealt with everything.

I never seriously considered declaring my feelings or making a move on Kristen, out of respect and loyalty to Tony. It was just something I would never do. She would often talk to me, and we'd laugh and have great times together. She grew from being a wide-eyed, shy freshman to a more confident and mature person. I saw the two of them on the first day back after Christmas break, and she was irresistibly magnetic, as always. Kristen ran over to me as soon as she spotted me exiting the elevator, boxes in hand. She snatched up the smaller box that had been balanced atop the heavier one, and carried it to my room, a few paces ahead of me. It was impossible to not be infatuated with her. She had a happy attitude, a ready smile, and gorgeous hazel eyes. A bit of a tomboy, she was also purely feminine in the best way. She was naturally a little timid deep down but seemed to be learning to be more assertive. I always felt so alive around her, probably because she was so spritely and energetic.

A couple of weeks after the holiday break I saw a surprisingly different side of her. One bitterly cold evening in January there was a gentle knock at our door. I was working on an assignment for class, and my roomie sprang to his feet to answer it. I instantly recognized Kristen's voice, but she sounded weird to me. She walked in and asked if I could go somewhere with her, and when I asked where Tony was, she didn't answer. She said she wanted me to take a walk outside with her. Of course I was happy to oblige. She was a friend, after all, and I was curious about the strange tone in her voice. We had just exited the back of the building when she started talking. Despite the crisp winter air, being in her company made me feel impervious to the elements.

She told me that Tony had been saying he needed some space recently, and that she suspected he had been seeing someone else over the break. I asked if they had discussed breaking up, and she vehemently said, "No!", so I suggested she might be imagining that he was cheating since that really didn't seem like his style. I probably said that because Tony often expressed to me how lucky he was to have Kristen and that they had been a solid couple for the three years I knew them. Tony also never outwardly eyeballed other women, at least not that I observed. He seemed completely devoted to her, and I thought it was preposterous to suggest he might be straying. She reluctantly agreed with me but said she was worried because he did seem a little distant and that they were not together as much during the holidays as she would have liked, despite living in the same town. They lived in a small town in the Southern Tier of New York, called Vestal, and had known each other since Kristen was a high school freshman.

She seemed pretty bummed out, but by the time we finished talking and walking, she was becoming her old self again. Finally, I asked her where Tony was, and she said he was working at his new off-campus job and he would be back to have supper with her. She invited me to eat with them, but I declined because I'd previously made plans to have pizza with my roommate and a group of other friends. I actually felt bad for her because I knew how committed she was to Tony, and I never wanted to see anything ruin that. She thanked me for listening and said she'd bring Tony to meet up with me and my friends in the Cellar after dinner. I agreed to join them there.

That evening I was looking forward to seeing old friends and was very ready for a cold beer or two. I had unpacked most of my crap and quickly got showered and dressed. I dragged a few pals down to the bowels of the dorms and into the Cellar where they proudly advertised "25-cent beer Night." The place was pretty packed, and the same damn songs were still blaring from the battered, old jukebox in the corner. "Brown Sugar," "Free Bird," and "Layla" seemed to be playing any time I was down there. The place thoroughly reeked of spilled beer and pizza, but there was an undeniable charm to it anyway. When I spotted Tony over near the bar, I hurried over to welcome him back. He was all smiles and said he was going to miss these nights after he graduated at the end of the academic year. We got caught up a little, and he told me he felt he had lined up a potential full-time job during the holiday break. After telling me a bit about his recent co-op experience at IBM in Endicott, he gestured over toward Kristen, who was alone at a long picnic-style table across the room. He said she was "a little grumpy," but she waved enthusiastically at me when I caught her eye. He didn't know that she and I had talked earlier. Everything seemed normal between them, but I started to sense that maybe there was something going on with him. He seemed a little distant, and I figured he was just so used to being part of their two-headed tandem; maybe he was merely guilty of taking her for granted.

We were quickly joined by a few friends I hadn't seen in a few weeks, and we all drank a little more than we should have. Kristen rarely drank alcohol, but she downed a couple of cheap beers herself that night. Someone said there was a party going on up on our floor, so we all headed up to the eighth floor of the building. Getting off the elevator was reminiscent of a circus car regurgitating a gang of drunken clowns. Loud music was flowing from the far end of the floor, and we all staggered toward it. People were yelling out names, greeting friends they had missed during break. The atmosphere in the hallway was cloaked in a strange smoky haze, as the "Reefer Madness Twins" were up to their old tricks in their dorm room. Queen's "Bohemian Rhapsody" blared out of two enormous speakers that someone had stacked atop each other in one corner.

I was semi-inebriated, and the scene was a kaleidoscopic blur of colors, sounds and smoke. I was the last person out of the elevator, and I quickly ducked into my room to see if my roommate was in there. But he was already down in the lounge, unbeknownst to me. As I re-entered the hallway, Kristen suddenly appeared in my face. Giggling and staggering, she slurred, "There you are! I was looking for you!" She took my hand and dragged me down the hall. Just before we reached the packed lounge, she pulled me into the restroom off to one side. I thought it was a ballsy thing to do and was laughing because it seemed out of character for her to be so impetuous. Before I could react, she pulled me into one of the shower stalls and kissed me. It wasn't a brother-sister-type peck, either. I mean, she really put her all into it. I was absolutely unprepared for it and was frozen in my tracks. It was a weird deal because it was something I had wanted for a long time, but I never suspected that she wanted it too. Then I remembered that Tony was only a few yards away, and I immediately felt like a horrible traitor. I kissed her back – don't get me wrong – and I really enjoyed it and savored the fact that this was a forbidden thing we were doing. But, then, I suddenly felt so guilty about it I dragged her out of there as fast as she had dragged me in.

Out in the hallway, we were swallowed up by the chaos before we eventually spotted Tony and the rest of the gang. People were talking over the music, wading through the blue smoke and having a great time. I was feeling incredibly conspicuous, imagining that Tony knew what had happened, but that was just paranoia on my behalf. Kristen and I stayed cool and avoided each other the rest of the night. I relived that kiss for the longest time afterward and wondered about her intentions. Part of me had always been jealous of Tony and had fantasized about having someone like Kristen for my own. Hell, I admit I used to wish they would break up because I always suspected there was at least some mutual attraction between us. Now this came out of left field and I wasn't prepared for the mixed emotions it created.

After that evening, I didn't see Kristen for several weeks, until one night when she called. She said she wanted to talk to me on Saturday and asked if I had time. I immediately agreed, but started to wonder what she wanted to talk about the minute we hung up. I was worried that she had told Tony what we had

154

done, and wondered if he would be furious and come to confront me. I imagined that Kristen was feeling regret about kissing me and wanted to tell me it was a mistake. She didn't own a car, but she borrowed her roommate's junker to come see me. I offered to go to her, but she said she didn't want to have her friends tell Tony we were on her campus together.

I met her out in one of the parking lots, and we walked to the Student Alumni Union and bought some hot chocolate. Once we found an out-of-the-way place to sit in the cafeteria, she showed me a photograph that one of our friends had taken on move-in day the previous August. It was a picture of the two of us hugging each other out in front of my dorm. We were a little sweaty but otherwise we looked happy to be reunited. I thanked her and then asked what she had on her mind. She started crying and said that Tony had informed her that he had been seeing another girl since the previous July. At his summer job in their hometown, he had met someone who kind of threw herself at him, according to Kristen. I figured that might have been the way Tony portrayed the situation to her, but I kept my mouth shut. She went on to say that he asked her to understand that he didn't want to break up with her but needed time to sort things out regarding their future.

Obviously, she was hurt and angry. I asked if she felt she could forgive him, and I credited him for being up front with her about it. She said, "I don't care. I can't go back to him and don't want to now. He ruined everything, and he has to live with the consequences." Though teary-eyed, she quickly composed herself. When I suggested she give him some time, and predicted he'd come back to her after he realized they had it pretty good, she clearly didn't want to hear it. Instead, she said he could "go to hell" for all she cared. She surprised me with what came out of her mouth next when she asked, "Do you have feelings for me?" I replied, "Of course I do!" because I truly did like her and had always been very attracted to her. She said, "I want us to be together. Do you feel those types of feelings for me, too?" I was stunned more than anything. This was honestly a dream come true for me, because I had fantasized about Kristen ever since meeting her. On every level, I was probably more attracted to Kristen than I had ever been attracted to anyone else. I flat-out lusted after her for years. She was pretty, funny, charismatic and fun to be with, but Tony was such a good friend that I never allowed myself to really think about her as much as I would have liked. I always felt guilty when she looked at me and my heart would begin to race. I had trained myself to think of her more as a sister or a cousin rather than a potential girlfriend. It never seemed right, and it never seemed possible before. Now, suddenly, things had changed, and here she was, offering herself to me on a silver platter. I must be the biggest loser of all time because I told her, "No."

What a fool I am. I told her I was flattered and incredibly tempted, but reminded her of the one thing I firmly believed over anything else, concerning her. I said, "You and Tony belong together. You've always been destined to be together, and it would never work with us because, ultimately, you would go back to him. I know him well and I know you, and the two of you belong together. Every couple goes through their ups and downs, and sometimes they just need a break. It's not the first time it's happened, but you guys have something I have not seen much of. You really are meant for each other, and I still believe you'll be married within a few years."

She didn't want to hear it that day. She was arguing the point; actually, she was arguing and declaring that she wanted me. When I look back and hear her words echoing around in my brain, it still kills me that I refused her. She was angry and hurt, which I realized, and I did the altruistic thing and felt sympathy for them both. But I always wonder: if I had taken advantage of the moment and talked about how great things could have been between us, everything might have turned out very differently. A few weeks later, Kristen and Tony had a major blowup and decided to separate. That lasted about a month. They ultimately got back together, and a few months after Kristen graduated, I attended their wedding. They've been married ever since and have three beautiful kids together.

Sick and depressed in late February, I was feeling the strain of looming decisions that needed to be made. I had borrowed so much money for tuition and room and board I feared I would never be able to dig myself out of debt. My roommate had grown tired of my increasingly surly demeanor, and he received approval to transfer to another room. I subsequently had a room all to myself, but it wasn't good for me to be even more isolated. The school's doctor gave me a prescription for penicillin, and I went underground for a week to try to get over a case of walking pneumonia. I slowly began to feel better physically, but my outlook was clouded, and I was becoming increasingly depressed. Friends suggested I go get some help, and I thought I had better do something because I was unable to pull out of my funk for the longest time.

My car was out of commission with a dead battery, but I was able to hop on a bus and go down to that family counseling center in downtown Rochester. I felt like I needed to get away from campus, so I planned on walking in to see if I could set up an appointment. Because I had no money, I planned on asking them if their sliding scale could slide all the way down to my level. I dragged myself off the bus and shuffled my way down the snow-covered sidewalk on this brilliantly sunny Saturday afternoon.

The sun glare was tremendously intense, and it glinted off of millions of tiny ice crystals blanketing the area. It was so distracting to me I didn't notice the makeshift sign until I tugged at the front door. The door rudely refused to respond. Then, I read the sign taped to the inside of the glass door. "Family Counseling Center now located on High Street in Fairport." The phone number was written in red ink, but I didn't bother to write it down. I didn't have a pen on me, and I was just plain ticked off. "It figures!" I thought, as I shoved my hands into my coat pockets. It felt as though nothing was working out for me and no one cared. It was just a bad time in my life, and I was tired and frustrated.

I didn't even react when I bumped into the man in the long, black coat. With my head down, I was turning up the collar on my worn winter coat when I walked right into him on the sidewalk in front of the building. I was not in the mood to apologize, so instead I just sidestepped the man and continued toward the bus stop. A vaguely familiar voice called out from behind me. "Son, can I help you?" I craned my neck to see if the voice was addressing me and suddenly realized I had just run into the same priest who I had spoken with in the church the last time I had been on this street. I had barely gotten a glimpse of him back then since it had been so dark and I was trying my best to avoid eye contact. I recognized his voice and, for some reason, I stopped in my tracks. He gingerly approached me and asked if I would wait while he fed a letter to the nearby mailbox. I didn't reply, but I didn't move either.

He dropped the letter into the blue box and slowly returned to me. He said he remembered me and asked how things were going. It was so refreshing to have someone sincerely inquire about me and my needs; it encouraged me to want to talk. He appeared younger than I had originally thought, maybe about thirty-five years old. He had thick, wavy black hair and grey eyes. He was a ruggedly handsome man with sharp chiseled features and a strong clean-shaven chin. He smiled and suggested I join him for a bite to eat at the diner across the street. At first I said I couldn't, but when he insisted, saying he could use my advice, I was intrigued.

As we made our way across the hard-packed, slippery road, he said he would treat me to lunch if I would be willing to help him with a few simple questions. He said he wanted to talk with a local college student who was not a member of his congregation.

When I asked him how he knew I was a college student, he just smiled. I remarked that I wasn't Catholic, but he said that was fine with him. I didn't want to admit that I was starving, but that wasn't the sole motivation for me anyway. The fact that someone was interested in my opinions and my story was very appealing to me. At school it seemed everyone wanted me for something that fulfilled their immediate need. Professors were often aloof and uncaring. My family was there for me, but I wasn't always comfortable being totally open with them. I missed my father and longed for a mature, caring person with whom I could confide. This priest, who politely introduced himself as soon as we sat in our booth, struck me as very reminiscent of my father in some ways.

He firmly shook my hand and said, "I'm Father Gilberto Reyes, but please call me 'Father Gil'. That's what most everyone calls me." He had a gentle smile and projected a warmth and sincerity I really appreciated. When he asked me how school was going, I briefly told him of the long hours, lack of sleep and money and the challenges I'd been dealing with. He listened intently and nodded understandingly. We ordered some food, and he remained silent as I expressed my stress level and told him I was leaning toward leaving school at the end of the academic year in May. He said he would never tell anyone what they should do and that I had obviously been giving a lot of thought to my decision. I admitted that some of my motivation was fear of taking on so much debt, and he just raised his eyebrows appropriately.

He then asked me to tell him some positive things about my college experience, and I couldn't come up with much. I guess I was too depressed and feeling negative about everything. He encouraged me to think of the best things about the past several years. I was in such a bad emotional state that I couldn't come up with anything substantive to say. He was doing all he could to stay objective and understanding, and I appreciated that, but I wasn't in the mood to be scolded. If he had started to lecture me

159

about appreciating all the good things I had, I probably would have left him sitting there alone in the diner. Instead, he kept telling me it was understandable to feel depressed and scared and that things would work out in time. He refrained from any religious talk, which I was relieved about, too. While we ate our club sandwiches, he talked about his work in the parish, and told me of his devotion to working with the young children he served.

He did a lot of work in the inner city and especially wanted to help educate underprivileged children – not just about God and the Bible, but to educate them about life. He was obviously very passionate about his work and was dedicated to helping people. He seemed younger than his age, and it felt like I had known him for years, even though we had just met. He was such a great listener, and he cleverly drew me into explaining why I had come downtown to the counseling center. I described my feelings of depression and opened up to him in a way I had not done with anyone else in a very long time.

I quickly felt comfortable talking with Father Gil, so I told him a condensed version of my life story. Over the course of the next couple of hours, I told him about the puzzling incidents I had experienced with the bizarre auras and blue electrical charges. He barely reacted as I recounted all of the incidents I could recall. He smiled when I told him about the first time it happened, when I saw the "little blue man" who was turning off my tiny television set. His eyes kind of sparkled as I described the strange glowing shape that seemed to form into the shape of a human being from a nebulous mass. He refrained from asking any questions and just nodded and stroked his chin and sipped his hot herbal tea. I asked him if he thought I was crazy, but he didn't answer right away. Instead, he stared at his tea cup and spun the spoon around and around with his index finger for a while. He then looked up at me and said, "Robert, this is nothing I would ever make light of. To me it sounds as though you have an awful lot going on. Your thoughts are a bit confused, but you

160

don't seem like a crazy person to me. I work with a lot of young people who have dealt with major life crises at very tender ages. They sometimes ask me if they are losing their minds, too. Life can be harsh and even cruel sometimes, and when young people are dealt more than they are ready to process, things can easily get overwhelming."

"What are you saying?" I asked. He looked me in the eyes and calmly stated, "You miss your father. I know" It stopped my heart for a second. I felt a slight pain in my chest as the words crossed from his lips to my ears. "Yeah, I do," was all I could eke out. I knew I missed him terribly, but I had been trying to avoid thinking about my father for a long time. "You're also smack dab in the middle of becoming a man," he added. "The transition is no small challenge, and the world just keeps dealing you curve balls, regardless of what you're going through." It was refreshing to hear this from someone who really seemed to understand the pressures I'd been wrestling with. My mother's absence, my father's sudden death, and all the changes I had been coping with were obviously taking a toll on me. But I didn't understand what the strange phenomena had to do with anything. I described some of the other mysterious incidents I had experienced and went into greater detail about some of the unexplainable mind-reading and ESP-like memories I had.

Father Gil didn't skip a beat as he tried to reassure me that I was not losing my mind. He said, "There are many, many documented cases of super-sensitive people; at least, that's the term I use for them." "What do you mean?" I asked. He went on to describe some of his experiences and several case studies he had researched as part of his education. "There are people who can be categorized as 'empaths', for lack of a better term. They seem to have highly developed sensitivities far beyond what the average human being possesses. These individuals can literally sense or feel another being's emotional or physical state, and there are documented cases of people whose abilities are so acute they can discern another individual's illness or disease. It is not regarded as scientifically substantiated, yet there are many reports that are too remarkable to be summarily dismissed. From the stories you've told me, I have to wonder if you might have similarly overdeveloped sensitivities. It could help explain some of these incidents." He then paused for a moment to drink a few sips of his tea.

He went on to ask, "Robert, do you believe in God?" I said I kind of did but that I had become doubtful since my father died. He said that was a typical and understandable reaction to a traumatic loss such as the death of a parent or child. "What about the human soul? Do you believe in that notion?" he inquired. I replied that I didn't really know. "I guess I do believe each person is unique inside, and if that's what people consider the 'soul,' I guess I do believe it exists. What are you getting at?" I asked.

"Well, I'm not sure myself," he answered. "It's just that I can't help but wonder if what you've been experiencing for years could be a reflection of your own soul. And what I mean is not that it is a literal reflection, but maybe you are imagining or feeling so vividly you see this little person or 'aura' as you call it, in your mind's eye. From what you've told me, it seems that you experience the phenomena at times of heightened emotional reaction. I think we can both agree that you have a tendency toward heightened sensitivity. You feel things very deeply and are in touch with your emotions and your environment in ways many are not. If a person's soul is real and thereby made up of energy or some form of matter, as all things are, then maybe it is possible to actually see a physical manifestation of it. Many millions of people adamantly claim to be able to see auras surrounding living things. I've often wondered what those auras truly are composed of. And what are they indicative of? Is it the tangible representation of the human soul? Is it electrical energy being discharged from within the brain? There are a lot of unanswered questions. I happen to study these things and…"

I held up my hand and cut him off mid-sentence. "Whoa, whoa, whoa," I injected, "But *other* people have seen these things at times, too! How can *that* be?" I shouted. He took another sip, rubbed his forehead and took a deep breath. "My friend, I wish I knew the answer to that. I really do. As preposterous as it sounds, it could be that you're able to project thoughts into the minds of others. Or it could be a "shared experience phenomenon" in that the power of suggestion causes a group of people to think they see something that isn't there. It's impossible for me to know what happened since I wasn't present. Even then, it's likely beyond my realm of expertise to analyze it."

It suddenly dawned on me that this could be a clue to something I had never considered before this moment. "Father Gil, what if there is some connection between the concussion I had when I was a kid and these repeated episodes. Or maybe I am schizophrenic, after all, and that's playing a part in this. There must be an explanation somewhere..." Now it was his turn to interrupt me. He raised an eyebrow, and a look of revelation came over him. "It might actually make some sense, after all," he sort of muttered. "What?" I asked. "Your concussion. If it was severe enough in nature, it may have caused some long-lasting damage. Have you had headaches during the ensuing years?" I quickly replied, "Not especially."

I could tell he was becoming more intrigued by our discussion by the minute. We had lost track of time, and it was already getting dark outside, but I needed to press the issue and find out what else he was thinking about. We requested more tea and coffee, and he continued his hypothesis. "The brain is a complex mass of relays and electrical impulses, right? In my opinion, it's not ridiculous to consider that a concussion could temporarily or even permanently affect the brain's 'wiring,' for lack of a better term. What if a concussion diverted the electrical signals in such a way that they formed a field of energy external to the host body? I don't think that's completely unfeasible. What if your concussion did something to focus some of the electrical energy in such a way that it manifests in a tangible visible field outside the confines of your brain?"

"And you're saying this image projection could be a physical representation of my soul?" I asked. Father Gil replied, "Well, I'm not quite ready to make that assumption completely, but is it impossible? That's what I'm considering at the moment. We can physically see electrical surges from various sources all the time. What if your brain was affected in such a way that the energy within it is sometimes focused and projected externally? Under duress or in a heightened emotional state, our physiologies do change. Blood pressure increases; the brain starts firing messages at an increased rate of speed. It all sort of makes sense to me. I just wonder if it's possible, and can't honestly dismiss the possibility. Certainly makes for some interesting conjecture, huh?" he uttered through a half-smile.

A bit overwhelmed at all his musings, I put my hand to my forehead and said, "This is just too far-fetched for me to believe. I mean, it's an awfully huge leap to make, to connect the concussion to these different incidents. It's so complicated it makes my head hurt just thinking about it." The kind man in the booth across from me said dryly, "Well, it's quite possibly very simple after all." "Oh yeah," I shot back, ultra-sarcastically, "Real simple, minus the 'imple'!" We both laughed heartily as tears trickled from the corners of our eyes. At that moment I had an odd feeling that I'd heard those words before: minus the imple. I said, "Hey Father, maybe I should assign that as a nickname for the little blue man I saw when I was eleven years old." "What's that?" he asked through his diminishing giggles. I said, "'Minus the Imple.' It sounds like a name for some strange little being from another dimension or world. You know, Minus is his name, and he's an 'Imple' from some strange world." "Well, I guess we *have* been here too long after all!" he quickly offered, and we both laughed almost obnoxiously as we simultaneously got up and started to put our coats on. It was now quite dark, and we had been at the diner a very long time.

The snow had begun to fall in the form of enormous flakes slowly floating earthward. My new friend, Father Gil, walked me to the bus stop on the corner, and we said our goodbyes. He turned and walked toward the little brick church, a solitary shadow against the lonely concrete stage that was the cracked sidewalk. My mind was reeling from all the new possibilities that had been planted during our conversation. Was it possible there was a purely logical scientific explanation for some of the things that had puzzled me for years? Or was it a blending of the physical and the spiritual that really intrigued me most?

In my heart, I knew what I knew but could never say to any other living soul. My feeling was that I had always been able to discern things that many others could not. I had always had a knack for reading people, for feeling what they were feeling, even without speaking to them. I took a lot of it for granted since I had always had these abilities and figured that everyone had them. As I got older, I started to realize that not everyone feels the way I feel. My hands were shaking as the smelly bus careened around a bend in the road. It was an evening that would profoundly alter my future and, even at the time, I suspected just that. I slept the last few minutes of the trip back to campus and had a dream about angels flying around in heaven and my grandmother sitting in a white rocking chair. She was knitting and humming an old traditional Italian song. She never looked up while she just continued rocking and knitting, humming and rocking and knitting. I felt a smile come to my face as I was jostled awake when the bus came to a stop in the loop behind the campus dorms.

That night, I felt reborn. Finally, someone truly understood me and accepted me despite all my quirks.

165

15

And Furthermore, Father

I moved my meager belongings into the dorms for the last time in late August of 1975. The room I shared with Tommy Curtis wasn't far from the elevators on the top floor of Nathaniel Rochester Hall. During my last months at home, I had finished several new paintings and a slew of sketches, and the two portfolios I dragged down the hall were bursting at the seams with new work, so it was a relief to dump them in my closet. I had arranged to switch majors and was now enrolled in the Communication Design program, which focused on graphic design and corporate communications. I still retained my Illustration minor and planned to take some additional courses on illustration in the evenings. I knew it would be a pivotal year as I tried to come to terms with what I wanted to do with my future.

I had been working on various illustration techniques and was convinced that I needed to develop a signature style of my own. One of my good friends, Rick Wehl, was the best cartoonist I had ever known. For such a young artist, he had developed a very refined and identifiable style. He drew in a style very similar to Disney artists of the '40s and '50s, and I admired the way he rendered with such definitive line strength. He was a good kid with a heart of gold. We were very different, in that he was very religious and interested in the ministry, but we connected over our mutual fascination with cartooning and illustration, so we learned from each other, in the classroom and on our own. He inspired me to work harder to improve my rendering abilities, and everything started to come together early in my third year at school.

166

I had become graphics editor of the school magazine, called *Reporter*, and that gave me a great opportunity to gain some vital experience. Once in a while I was able to do some page layout work, but I made a bit of a name for myself by creating illustrations and cartoons for the student-managed magazine. I sometimes designed concert posters for the College Activities Board, and that led to some freelance work for a local ad agency. They liked my poster designs and especially liked my "cartoony" illustration samples, so they called me in to do some projects for various clients. There wasn't a lot of work, nor was there much money involved, but the experience taught me that people in the industry would willingly pay to have me involved in projects. I began to aggressively seek the advice of my professors about my future. A couple of them told me they felt I was at the top of their class, and they wanted me to do some freelance work with them or for them. I still wanted to do illustration and cartooning, but I did find graphic design and publication layout fascinating. And there were many more employment opportunities for designers than illustrators, most of whom had no alternative but to freelance. That meant no salary, no benefits and no security whatsoever. I didn't think that made any sense for someone who wanted to eventually be married and have children, as I did.

Most of my third year was spent working my ass off on class projects. In the middle of winter quarter, I got very run down and depressed from the workload and the stress coming at me from every angle. I never had much money for even the simplest needs, and I never asked my uncle and aunt for any support, although they would have gladly helped. I was stubborn about getting by on little sleep, little emotional support, and even less money. I got sick again with a mysterious virus, and the bottom kind of dropped out of everything once again. I became more secluded and introspective. For hours on end, I would work in the studio in the art building or spend time creating illustrations for the magazine. I had less and less time to hang out with friends, and the weather was so brutal, there was no opportunity to go outside and have fun. I didn't go home to see my family for long periods of time, especially once we got beyond Christmas break.

My final months as a college student were mostly filled with classroom and freelance work. There just wasn't much time for anything else. I built a decent portfolio filled with a wide array of project types. I had a couple of strong logo designs I had done in class. My illustration techniques had been refined a lot during the year, and now I had several printed samples to include in the book. I had examples of a few published articles I had written, and some of my freelance publication design work rounded out the portfolio. I was tired of wasted days with weak classroom instruction, and I was very afraid to borrow any more money. By the end of my third full year, I had incurred a sizable debt that eclipsed the limits of my anticipated financial burden. Even a couple of my professors suggested I drop out and pursue my career, rather than return for a fourth year. I was torn, but in the end I made the decision that the spring quarter would be my last one at RIT.

During April of 1976, only a few weeks prior to the end of the quarter, I met a pretty girl at a party. Her name was Erin Zimmerman, and the minute I saw her walking toward me, I felt as though there was something very special about her. When she first spoke to me, I just felt like I knew we would become much more than mere acquaintances. We spoke only briefly that evening, but I knew in my heart that I'd see her again.

At one point during the spring, I realized it had been a long time since I'd spoken with Father Gil. I had called him once or twice the previous fall, but it had been several months between conversations, so I made plans to go see him. We agreed to meet at a downtown restaurant for dinner. He told me he'd meet me at 7:00, on a breezy Friday night in April. It had been unseasonably warm for days, and the wind was really whipping as I guided my trusty station wagon through the pothole-pitted streets. The radio played Peter Frampton's "Show Me the Way" as I neared my destination. I looked forward to telling Father Gil about my scholastic successes and was also anxious to report that I'd been free of any strange episodes for a long stretch of time.

I parked in a lot adjacent to Blades, which was a popular new restaurant on University Avenue in the city. The wind pushed me back a full step as I eagerly approached the restaurant. Father Gil was already seated at a small table in the far corner, and I spotted him immediately. Shooing the hostess away, I quickly brushed by to embrace my friend. We had established a very strong rapport since meeting by happenstance that one fateful day. We corresponded by mail during the summer and had pledged to try to see each other at least a few times during the year. Previous plans for dinner had been cancelled when he was called out of town to attend to his ailing father, so this reunion was a bit overdue in our eyes.

While we waited for our entrees to arrive, he asked about my family, and we made all the requisite chitchat before he sprung it on me. "They're moving me to Boston," he announced. I nearly choked on my breadstick. He went on to explain that the church in Rochester was closing its doors, and he was being transferred to a much larger church in Boston before the end of summer. It didn't please me in the least to hear this. He was a symbol of stability for me, and his impending departure really upset me. My appetite left me when he made his declaration, and I couldn't finish my meal. He could tell I was upset, and he tried to make light of the situation. "Look, I don't like it any more than you do, Rob, but I have no choice but to make the best of it. We'll still stay in touch, assuming you're willing."

I nodded and whispered, "Of course," but I was really taken by surprise by this bombshell. He had replaced my father as a beacon of honesty and strength. Father Gil was never one to soft-pedal his opinions, and he always treated me with respect. Our relationship had been built on mutual respect and open communication. Over time, I had confessed to him all my fears and dreams and had even gone to him for advice on women. Because he listened and genuinely cared, he always had some valuable wisdom to impart. Now that he would no longer be a short drive away, I suddenly felt vulnerable.

"Rob, you and I will always be friends. There's no reason to feel bad. I promise to call you once a week, and we'll probably get together as much as ever because I'll be flying back and forth to Rochester on occasion. My parish is being split up between two other churches, and I can't just turn my back on so many people I care about. We'll work things out so I can come every other month or so to take part in services at the two churches. I'll never be far away, and if you ever need me, I can always make a special trip."

I had no choice but to accept it, but it hurt to think yet another important person in my life was being taken away from me. Here I was again, being left behind by someone who meant so much to me. We talked a bit about my father and how his steadying presence had helped build my inner strength. Father Gil said, "You had a very strong bond with your father and his spirit remains with you, all these years after his passing. You also have your grandmother's spirit with you all the time, don't you?" I had to agree. He added, "Rob, you take pieces of all those you love with you when you part ways. Your mother is here with you and will always be, as I see it. She's in your heart and mind, and you sense her watching over you to this day, don't you?" Once more, I had no doubt that this was true. He went on to say, "When two people connect and their lives become intertwined, they leave behind little strands of their souls. One person touches the heart of another, and that imprint remains. I look at it as though we leave indelible impressions on each other's souls. The deeper the relationship, the stronger and more lasting the imprint."

"So, you believe our souls are like 'fingerprints'? Is that how you would describe it?" I asked. He thought for a second or two before replying. He leaned toward me, over his cup of hot coffee, and said, "Yes, I believe we each have a unique 'fingerprint' that's a product of all the people who have touched our lives, from the day we're born until the day we die. Your closest influences and loved ones make a very powerful impression and are a big part of your makeup. They are, in many ways, the architects of your soul as much as God and your parents are. You retain the innate qualities you're born with, but through life experiences your soul is continually shaped and developed."

My heartbeat seemed to slow down as I was fixated on his words. The way he described it made perfect sense to me. I said "You know, it does make sense the way you say it. We all seem to change and take shape through our experiences. I feel a lot different compared to last year's version of me. The experiences I've had with other people have changed the way I think, the way I feel and the way I behave. I do feel as though I've absorbed energy, both positive and negative, from the people I've encountered. My father's strength is still within me. So is my grandmother's peaceful nature, at times. It's as though I carry them with me wherever I go."

"Rob," he said, "you have a good understanding of what I'm talking about. You seem to have grown a lot this past year. I see you as a man, now, ready to make a difference in the world. Your parents would be very proud of you, if they could be here to see you today." I didn't skip a beat as I declared, "They *are* here. They're with me all the time."

That was the last time I had dinner with Father G for a long time. He and I spoke on the phone many times the rest of the year, and when he moved to Boston that summer I helped him load up his car with his belongings. Saying goodbye hurt a little, but I knew there was no doubt we'd remain friends and would see each other again before long. As time went by, we did just that and remained great friends for many more years.

Most of my friends had plans to return for their fourth year, but I had decided upon a different direction for myself. I had made my mind up to get a summer job on campus since I still had student status. I needed a steady paycheck, so I applied at RIT Facilities Management for a carpenter's assistant position. They immediately hired me since I promised I would work throughout the entire summer and beyond. They assigned me to work with their team of carpenters, who were assigned to a wide range of projects, from painting to repair work.

I had arranged to go home for a week, and during that break, I informed my aunt and uncle of my intention to leave college after three years. They were not very keen on me dropping out, but they agreed to stay out of it after I informed them of the magnitude of my increasing commercial art business. I told them I had rented an apartment near campus that I would be sharing with my friend Jim. They reassured me that I could always live with them if I ever needed a place, but I packed up almost everything I owned and drove it back to Rochester at the end of that week.

Finally, I would have my independence.

16

Struggle for the Barely Legal Tender

Summer came and went. The time went by in a flash. I earned minimum wage as a carpenter's assistant in RIT's Facilities Management Services department, doing whatever they told me to do. Some of the full-timers were decent toward me, but one guy, in particular, was a major-league asshole. He always yelled at me and never once called me by my real name. He usually called me "college boy" in that smug, sarcastic growl he usually employed. He was a fat slob with no future and no dignity. I was shocked to learn that he was married. I couldn't imagine who could have been that desperate. Anyway, I made the best of it and got a great tan working outdoors half of the time.

Our tiny apartment was across campus, on the opposite end from where I punched in and out, and I usually ran to and from work. At the end of the typical day, I would run at full speed back to the apartment (about a mile or so) and jump into the shower. For much of the summer, I didn't do much other than work days and screw around in the evenings with friends. It felt great to have that level of freedom and independence. Money was tight, though, and I lost weight until I was as thin as I've ever been as an adult. I almost never had lunch but would eat leftovers or extra food the other guys would offer. For dinner we ate a lot of franks and beans and bread and soup. Once in a while, someone would stop by, and we'd all chip in for pizza, but we generally had very little to go around.

That July, fate swooped down and changed my world again. At a friendly impromptu volleyball game out behind our apartment complex, I saw Erin again. There were about twenty people playing volleyball in the intense sunshine, and I was beckoned to by another girl I knew. I didn't immediately recognize Erin, but she caught my eye as the only person there who really gave any attention to a small boy who had been clamoring to join in on the fun. She held the little guy up high so he could feel like he was playing along with all the "grown-ups." Some of the others were annoyed by the little six-year-old, but she felt sympathy for him and made the effort to include him. It touched me for some reason, and I saw it as a reflection of who she was. Beyond the beautiful hair and the pretty, freckled face, she seemed to possess a good heart. I was content to just watch from the other side of the net, and I didn't ever speak to her that afternoon, but for some reason I felt we were destined to know each other better.

To make a long story short, we were reintroduced that fall and soon became inseparable. There was a profound connection between us that couldn't be denied. She was entering her second year of college, but she eventually admitted her heart wasn't in the Medical Technology program she had entered. We were both in a hellacious hurry to become adults and to establish our independence from our families. Over that winter, we decided to marry, and in May of 1977, we fought every obstacle from family to finances and were married in a simple outdoor ceremony. She was only 19 years old, and I was 21 at the time of our wedding. Even though neither of us were Catholic, Father Gil performed our wedding ceremony in the middle of Highland Park in Rochester, at the height of the annual Lilac Festival. The day was gloriously sunny and hot, and was one of the happiest of my life. We had such high hopes and great intentions.

I recall feeling extremely nervous as we spoke our vows. The tiny hairs on the back of my neck rose up like so much wheat in a windstorm. That tingling hot feeling that sometimes rushed from my heart to my head was starting to surge in that now familiar way, but I had learned how to suppress it over the years, and was now better able to contain it through force of will. I didn't want anything to spoil the day, especially some freakish episode that might further alienate me from my future in-laws. They were already opposed to the marriage and made it clear that winning them over would be nearly impossible. We had no money, so there was no honeymoon, but we didn't care a whole lot about that at the time.

We rented a two-bedroom apartment unit in an old but quaint building on Park Avenue in the city, scraping coins together to put together the required security deposit. An older brick structure with on-street parking and antiquated plumbing, it looked as grand as the Ritz Carlton to our young eyes. Over the next few years, I was able to build a freelance client list that brought in enough income to allow us to maintain our small downtown apartment. I made hundreds of cold calls, and tried my hand at just about everything, from courtroom illustration for a local television station to working as a substitute illustrator for Gannett Newspapers. In those days, they had a team of full-time artists creating custom illustrations for articles published in the two local papers.

Over time, I gradually acquired numerous design and illustration projects for clients such as Xerox, Eastman Kodak, Bausch and Lomb, as well as ongoing assignments from nearly every advertising agency in the region. Before long, my reputation grew and I got a lot of repeat business from a small collection of local clients. Erin worked at a hospital for a brief time, but then realized she didn't want to be sticking people and drawing blood all day long, so she found another entry-level position, this one with a small company that made dentures. Neither of us earned much, but we both kept plugging away, always looking for an opportunity to increase our income.

We barely made ends meet the first year of our marriage, until I landed a full-time job in a small design studio. All three of us who worked there were former RIT students. We all learned a lot from each other and from the fairly steady workflow from our blue chip clients, while it lasted. About a year and a half later, that design studio abruptly moved out to California, and I was hired as art director for a full-service ad agency in downtown Rochester. At the time, I was the youngest art director in the Rochester region. Working on everything from corporate logos to billboards, it was another great opportunity to learn and expand my versatility. We did photo shoots in studio and on location. I designed publications, created original illustrations and even wrote some advertising copy for various projects. They allowed me the freedom to use my cartooning skills as often as possible, which I greatly appreciated.

Erin went to work as a bank teller and, for some time, our offices were actually across the street from each other. No situation was ever very secure for long, though, in that the advertising business was inherently so volatile. The agency lost three major clients in successive months, and they were forced to lay off seven of its employees. What was once a promising future dissolved suddenly one afternoon, and I was left with no means of steady income once again. The loss of that position created tension at home, and I had no choice but to scour the newspaper classified ads and make phone calls trying to ferret out work.

It was a very lucky day, in the winter of 1981, when I spotted an ad in the newspaper seeking a graphic designer for a department at RIT. The timing was perfect since I was in my third month of being laid off from a full-time position and feeling desperate for another opportunity. Erin was a few months into her first pregnancy, and our priority was to achieve some financial stability. It turned out to be the best possible timing, when I was hired to join the staff of the Communications department at my alma mater. It was both strangely familiar and completely new since I was now seeing the campus and the college experience from a completely different perspective. I had previously met the department's manager, as he had hired me to work on a couple of freelance illustration projects before this opportunity had opened up. We enjoyed a great rapport, and I spent four years working with a great bunch of people within this very busy on-campus department. We eventually won our share of awards and drew accolades from our internal clients throughout the campus.

The services we provided to the campus were similar to those traditionally offered by a full-service advertising agency. Once again, the education and experience I gained were priceless. Our first child was born during my second year on the job, the same year our department was moved to the downtown campus, which was hard for any of us to accept. Being removed from the entire suburban campus was not what any of us wanted, but overcrowding forced the Institute to exile us to a somewhat dreary location in the city. We had our new daughter, Violet, to enjoy, so I took the move in stride and decided to make the best of the situation. Erin had quit working, a decision we had agreed upon before Violet was born.

My freelance work was picking up in volume, and I was aggressive about trying to pull in more work to help cover expenses at home. I was promoted to senior graphic designer during that same period, but my pay was still just barely adequate. The workload at RIT kept increasing, but my pay never kept pace. With the pressure on to earn enough to support three people and a mortgage, I had to keep bringing in more freelance projects. That created a lot of exhaustingly long workdays and it began to take its toll on me. After four years of this, I decided it made sense to leave RIT and start my own business. Against the objections and warnings of many, I established my own corporate design studio. Erin was uneasily supportive, as she was obviously concerned that I was leaving a stable, steady paycheck for the unknown. But I had been working many fourteen-hour days, between my eight-to-five job and the freelance work that was pouring in. I felt I could make a better income and build something for the future by leaving my day job and concentrating on building my client base. With my versatility, I figured I was better equipped than many to be able to survive dry spells. When there was no illustration work, I could get graphic design and layout work. I could even take in writing and editing work, which helped keep me busy.

In retrospect, maybe it was a gamble for which I paid a heavy price, but my intentions were pure. I was convinced that I could make a success of it, and my confidence was never shaken. It worked for ten years, but it was a challenging and stressful journey at times. Our second child arrived in 1985: a beautiful son, Michael. We had just bought our second house, and I thought we were going to continue building for the future. But life throws us many curveballs, and everything began to unravel before long.

Computers were becoming more prevalent, and the effect on the advertising world was being felt rather swiftly. I maintained a client base of a half dozen steady customers, from Eastman Kodak to Xerox, and a handful of small businesses in the area. RIT was still a fairly steady source of freelance work, too. But, over time, the financial rollercoaster ride was a huge problem for our family. Erin was frustrated that we always had to struggle to pay our bills. The stress was wearing me out, too, but I stubbornly wanted to make it work because I had wanted my own business for a long time. A perfectionist, it had always been frustrating for me to be held back by coworkers who settled for mediocrity. I wanted full control of the projects, and now that I had that, I didn't want to give it up. I knew that once I relinquished it, I would never get that control back. That decision ultimately cost me dearly, as Erin didn't have the luxury of ignoring her feelings of insecurity and fear. She insisted upon a divorce in 1988. I saw it coming but never wanted to recognize it. While I realized I wasn't the husband and provider she needed me to be, I didn't know how to change.

As I look back upon our 11 years of marriage, I find it puzzling that there were almost no incidents involving Minus. In fact, I can only recall one fleeting episode closely leading up to

Violet's birth. There's no way to know just why the unsettling appearances had ceased for such a long period of time. If it had something to do with the fact that I was more settled and had the benefit of a life partner to share my burdens, I can accept that. But, perhaps the reason had little to do with any of that. Maybe there had been some important physiological changes within my body that relegated Minus to the past. With our busy lives and excitement over our growing family, perhaps so much of my energy was diverted in such a way that there was no energy left for Minus to draw from. It's all just wild speculation on my part. The fact is, I had been free of the strange episodes for over a decade, so I had assumed I would probably never see evidence of him again.

Over time, the pressures of running a business, juggling the responsibilities of parenthood and dealing with the myriad of challenges that came our way caused stress that our relationship couldn't overcome. Erin and I had grown further and further apart through all of the stress and disappointments, and it was inevitable that one of us would finally crack. Not that I blame her, because she was justified in feeling helpless and threatened by our financial situation. Coupled with my inadequate management of the business, which survived but rarely thrived, she had reached her limit that spring. One day, she finally told me it was over, and that she wanted me to move out of the house. At first, I couldn't believe the words even came out of her mouth, but I quickly realized she had been holding back the anger and disappointment for a very long time.

The harsh reality her statement represented felt like something from a nightmare. As ridiculous as it must sound, I never really imagined that the day would come. In the weeks immediately following her declaration, I would sometimes go into our bedroom and stare at the framed document that stated, in part, "Those whom God has joined together, let no man put asunder." It was a statement that had previously made me feel good and warm and safe inside. I knew that our relationship had become

179

tattered over the years, but I never knew how to fix it. I wanted to, but was just too stupid to figure it out.

At one very low point one night, I was feeling particularly hopeless and desperate, so I called Father Gil from my office in the basement of our house. I told him I was lost and didn't know what to do next. In my frustration, I asked him why God did things like this to good people. He just thought for a moment and replied, "Life does this to good people, Rob. Life does things like this to everyone." I told him that I had begged Erin to reconsider and she had repeatedly insisted that she couldn't picture us having a future together any longer. Father Gil thought for the longest time before suggesting that I accept her decision and try to come to terms with accepting a new image of the future. I was too emotionally exhausted to listen to reason, and I just slammed the phone down on my dear friend.

Once again, I was being left behind by someone who meant everything to me. I had to face the very real possibility that my wife and children were turning their backs on me, and I couldn't believe it was really happening. Even Minus had apparently abandoned me, and I admit I mourned that loss, too.

I would have done anything if I could have turned back the hands of time and made things right with Erin. Now, with her at the end of her patience and out of love with me, it was far too late to repair anything.

17

No Kidding?

By April of 1988, I wanted to die; that much I was sure of. If you've never experienced that level of emotional pain, trust me, you do not want to. As it became obvious to me that we weren't going to be able to patch things back together, I was beside myself with sorrow. I still felt love for Erin and was convinced that I could never accept living apart from our children. It was unimaginable to me. Angry and frustrated, I suffered what can best be termed an emotional meltdown, and could barely function anymore. Our relationship had deteriorated to coldness, frustration and disdain. Amid the stress and confusion of the recent years, I had not been there for her as a husband. Emotionally distant, I was a horrible partner, so I completely understood that she had little choice but to be the one who would finally end the madness of going through the motions. That lucidity may have helped her in some important ways, but I was in a different place, emotionally, at the time. It felt like I was just being jettisoned, and I blamed myself fully for all bad things.

One blustery, rainy morning, I guess I reached my breaking point. I called our family doctor, and he expressed great concern over my state of mind. When he asked if I felt suicidal, I didn't answer. He promptly made an appointment for me to see a therapist at a nearby office. At first, my anger and depression kept me from agreeing, but, finally, I said I would take his advice.

During our discussion the therapist asked me if I had considered hurting myself. For some reason (maybe I was finally desperate enough to be honest), I said, "Yes." He then rather clinically and dispassionately informed me that he was admitting me to the hospital for evaluation. When I said I wasn't going to let that happen, he informed me that I had no choice. He explained that he had the legal authority and the obligation to "place" me in the hospital, regardless of my cooperation. He tried to reassure me that it was in my best interest because, as he said, "You don't want to leave those two children without a father, do you?" I broke down when he mentioned my children, and then, as a pair of orderlies helped me onto a gurney and wheeled me into an ambulance, I realized I was never going to return to the life I had known for so long. I wept and thrashed about in agony as my emotions finally poured out. I had held it all inside for such a long time, abusing myself by never facing the truth. As the ambulance worked its way through the rain-splashed streets, all I could think of was my wedding day and how different things had been in the beginning.

Upon arrival, they told me I was not going to be released for a minimum of thirty days. At first I was resistant and angry, and I told them they couldn't keep me against my will. The ambulance had delivered me to Rochester General Hospital, and I was rather quickly admitted to the psychiatric unit. It was all surreal to me. All I could think was that it was just like the movie "One Flew over the Cuckoo's Nest," only I was playing the Jack Nicholson role instead of watching it from a seat in the theater. I admit I was afraid and feeling decidedly suicidal. The first thing they did after getting me signed in against my will was give me an antidepressant medication. Later that first night, I met a young doctor they had assigned to my case. He introduced himself as Dr. Wynne and informed me that he was a child psychologist who handled adult cases in this particular ward. I thought it was appropriate, in that I've always acknowledged that I think like a child. I was assigned to a small single room at first, one they used for all new arrivals. Most of the rooms in the unit had two beds in them, but there were a few rooms like this that they used for evaluating new patients. The nurses had me remove my shoelaces and my belt. They told me I would get them back eventually. It felt like I had been incarcerated in a prison. At first I was so set against everyone in that hospital that I didn't open up to Dr. Wynne at all. I just kept telling him I wanted out or that I wanted to die. He took it easy on me at first and just wrote down a lot of notes that first session. He tried his best to reassure me that it was not uncommon for people who were going through a rough patch in their lives to come here for help. He explained that it was standard practice to admit someone who was threatening to harm themselves, for their own protection.

For whatever reason, I slept like a baby that first night in the looney bin. Maybe I was relieved to be free from the tension at home. Maybe I needed to let everything crash at my feet. I was in the middle of multiple work projects when this happened, but I didn't care. I had been so deadline-conscious for so long. The pressure was relentless, but I had no energy left for those clients now. This was about survival, and I knew that was the most important concern at the time.

Everything was a blur those first few days. They gave me antidepressants several times a day, but I never felt any effect. The doctor scheduled me for a consultation every couple of days, for thirty minutes at a time. The rest of the time was made up of mornings in the workshop; breakfast, lunch and dinner at the same time every day; and specified visiting hours. There must have been about twenty or more adult patients at any one time in this part of the hospital. Some were in and out, but the majority seemed to be in my predicament, interred against their will. Many were on antidepressants that were substantially more powerful than what I took. Some took lithium regularly, and others had to eat a veritable smorgasbord of pills several times a day. At specified times of the day, usually following each meal, it was "meds time."

We lined up and the nurses dispensed the pills *du jour* in little paper cups. Someone always observed each of us as we ingested our medications, to ensure we didn't spit them out. On one occasion I hid the pill under my tongue and was successful at faking the nurses out. But I rethought it after proving to myself that I was so smugly smart, and I ate it anyway. I felt I should play along while people were willing to give a damn about me.

The first few days went by, and I was still very depressed and angry. I was angry at myself most of all, but I felt a lot of anger for others, too. I was angry at Erin for being the one to pull the plug on our relationship. I was very angry at God, who I blamed for allowing this to happen to me. I sometimes made immature comments to other patients, some of whom were fairly lucid most of the time. A few seemed very "normal," and we forged loose friendships. No one openly trusts any relationships made in a nut house like that, though. You never know what people have going on in their minds, so you have to be cautious.

A couple of the patients were obviously plagued with severe mental illnesses. One black woman, who was about 45 years old, had a serious obsessive-compulsive disorder and dementia to boot. She constantly shuffled around in her worn blue slippers, always straightening items and picking up any stray trash she saw. She did everything in super-slow motion, which made her behavior slightly less disturbing. She was almost in perpetual motion, but would just go about her business, cycling around the lounge and only sitting when she finally became exhausted.

Rick was a fiery, crimson-haired young guy, probably my age, and he was someone I could actually talk with. He had a colostomy and would complain about it quite a bit. It was uncomfortable, and it made him cranky a lot of the time, but he was an interesting character who amused me. He was a tough nut, and he was full of colorful stories. I was also one of the few people who could hold a conversation, so we were drawn to one another by default. There were a few older women who seemed fairly sane, too, but there weren't many. Most of the people were extremely quiet, and they kept to themselves.

They moved me into a double room after a few days, and I had a roommate for the first time. The first guy they put in with me was very old. He was only in the room with me for about two days, and then, suddenly, he was gone. He and I never spoke once. Hell, I don't believe he ever spoke to anyone, now that I think about it. Another patient told me that he died immediately after being moved from our room, but I never received any confirmation on that.

My new roommate was brought into the room very late one night. His name was Carl, and he introduced himself to me the next morning. I was relieved that he seemed pretty sane, and we told each other a little about our situations. He had a bipolar disorder and had some issues with depression. According to him he had a bad temper that had gotten him into trouble. He attributed that temper to being on the wrong medication for a long time. To hear him talk, you would think he was absolutely sane and reasonably normal. He had three kids and a wife, for whom he expressed great love and concern.

I asked him how he ended up in here with me, and he mumbled something about "making threats" to his family. But he stressed that it was the messed-up medicine that put him in that state of mind. He said he was worried he wouldn't have a job when he got out, which concerned him as much as anything. I felt bad for him because he seemed to be a sincere and honest man. His wife and children came to visit him a couple of times at the end of his first week there, and I caught a glimpse of them leaving one afternoon. The kids hugged him, and his wife kissed him goodbye. Observing them made me very sad since no one had come to visit me during my entire first week there.

My doctor asked me if I'd had many visitors, and he became visibly angry when I informed him that my wife had not brought my kids in to see me yet. He actually called her and asked her to consider bringing them. I think he impressed upon her that my outlook would only worsen if I wasn't reminded that I still had something important to live for. At least he was willing to be honest. He kept telling me that I had to accept it if my wife was no longer willing to continue our marriage, but he quickly reminded me that my precious relationship with my children was what I should focus on. I acknowledged it as good advice, but I still couldn't stand the thought of living under a separate roof. I had never formed any image of a broken family, and I couldn't accept that as our future. I was so angry at myself for failing the marriage and, therefore, failing my children. I still wanted to die and had convinced myself that everyone would be far better off with me planted in the ground. I felt that my children would be infected by me if I lived and I didn't want to be the bad influence I was convinced I would be. Obviously, I couldn't imagine any other outcome but failure, and I didn't want to let anyone down in such a profound way again.

On this particular evening in April 1988, I decided to take matters into my own hands. Carl remained asleep throughout everything, until I had confessed my actions to the nurse in the office and she organized a systematic search of the room. It crossed my mind that they had obviously done this before. A pair of orderlies and two nurses entered the room around 2:00 AM. They woke Carl and walked him down the hall into the lounge while they inspected my bed and examined everything else in the room. Another nurse interviewed a somewhat disoriented and confused Carl, while I was examined by an on-call doctor. He shined a flashlight into my eyes and performed a physical exam on my throat and neck. He asked me a list of rehearsed questions and made me follow his finger with my eyes. He asked me if I planned on trying anything like this again. I assured him I wouldn't, that I had learned a lesson from it (which was only partly true). Then, he had the nurse record my vitals. The doctor instructed the nurses to move me to a private room and to give me a sleeping pill and some anti-inflammatory medicine.

The doctor then told me I didn't do any permanent damage, but when I looked in the mirror later, I was taken aback. My face was covered in hundreds of tiny red dots. I looked like someone had used my face as a pincushion. The attempted self-strangulation had caused blood vessels to rupture all over my neck and face. There was a visible rope burn where the sheet had squeezed against my throat. My eyes were bloodshot and teary. I was left with a bit of a raspy speaking voice, too. I thought it was amusing that I now sounded a lot like Carl when I spoke.

I had a very sobering conversation with the psychiatrist the next morning. He asked a bunch of questions about my children and wanted to know when they had last been in to visit me. I had been "locked up" for well over a week, and, as I informed the doctor, they had not once been brought in to visit. I remember being stunned by his reaction. He asked if my wife had been by recently, and I told him that she had not come to see me yet. "Not once?!" he exclaimed. I was so far in the dumper at that point, I was actually defending my wife and making excuses for her not coming to see me or bringing the children in. He would hear nothing of it and began railing against her for being "selfish." I told him that I did not want my children to come to this awful place, and he argued that I was unnecessarily worried. He said, "You need to see your family. You need to know that someone does care about you. Your children can handle this place. Kids are more resilient than you might think." Being a child psychologist by trade, I had to respect his contention, but I still had very mixed feelings about having my kids come for a visit. I missed them terribly but was worried that they might be scared by the sight of some of the other inmates.

One new female patient constantly moved from chair to chair, never sitting for more than a few seconds. Another woman was prone to yelling out random, nonsensical words at the top of her lungs. There was one old man, who must have been seventy-five, who would stare at you until you thought he might burn a hole in your brain. One of the younger patients was a somewhat attractive teenage girl who had just been admitted. Reluctant to speak to most of the patients, she and I made a friendly connection one morning in the arts and crafts room. She made a few complimentary remarks about the wooden toy car I was building for my son, and we talked for a while. On the surface she seemed completely healthy and balanced. Maybe she was a little introverted, but nothing unusual as far as I could see. We spoke on several occasions over the following several days, and I couldn't figure out why she was in this facility. I vividly remember that thought crossing my mind one afternoon when I stopped by her room to ask her a question.

As we talked, I finally noticed her arm. A mass of thick scar tissue encircled her left wrist. I was able to catch a good view when she had reached over to catch a plastic cup she had inadvertently knocked off the nightstand. There were literally layers upon layers of both old and what appeared to be fresh scars around her slender wrist. Some were deep, jagged and bold, while others were a mass of wispy strands of broken skin. Thinking quickly, I tried to make sure she didn't see me staring. But before I could completely gather myself and attempt to distract her, I caught my first glimpse of her other arm. The fresh bandage peeked out from beneath the discolored blue flannel sleeve of her ratty bathrobe. I could discern a dark red discoloration soaked into the front edge of the thick gauze mass that protected the wrist of her right arm. For what seemed like an eternity, but was probably a split second in reality, we locked eyes. She self-consciously turned away and said something about needing to change her clothes. "My father's coming to see me in an hour or so," she blurted. I excused myself and went to the lounge to read a magazine. It was obvious that these wounds had been self-inflicted.

What would bring such an innocent young girl to abuse herself like this? How could she endure that type of physical pain? What could I or anyone else do to help her?

Despite being exposed to some forms of mental illness throughout my younger years, this was a shocking revelation. Seeing this girl's tortured skin was a very sobering moment for me. All I could think was how normal and well-adjusted she appeared to be, yet she was clearly very experienced at cutting herself. How many other seemingly balanced and healthy people did this type of thing? How could she and I be engaged in trivial chitchat while, all along, she was aware of her history of self-abuse? It didn't add up for me, as I was naïve and unprepared to deal with this reality. This honey-haired, bubbly teenager was only with us for a week. Her father visited her about three times and then returned to take her home on a sunny, warm Saturday in May. She and I never spoke about her injuries. While I was curious, I never felt it was my place to bring it up. She waved goodbye to me as I watched her climb into her father's car from my second story window. I couldn't help but focus on the large bandage on her right arm.

During the scheduled session with my doctor the next morning, he informed me that he had called Erin and that she had agreed to bring the kids to visit me that afternoon. I said I didn't want them to see me with my "pincushion face." He said it was vitally important that we see each other right now. I knew he was right, so I decided to do my best to get ready for their visit, and I began to get excited at the thought of holding them close. I was concerned about protecting them from any of the crazier patients, but the doctor arranged for us to have some privacy in the smaller lounge in the unit. There was never a time in my life that brought such mixed emotions. It was so incredibly necessary to see my children again, and they ran into my arms as I knelt on the floor of the austerely appointed room. All I could focus on were their smiles and their shining eyes as they both ran and latched onto me. "Daddy!" they both exclaimed loudly.

189

They literally bowled me over with the sheer force of their small bodies. The three of us embraced and laughed, as they kept vying for a tighter squeeze from me.

When things calmed a bit, I acknowledged Erin, seated on the other side of the little room, and thanked her for bringing them to see me. She looked very uncomfortable and refused to smile while she nervously watched our reunion. The kids asked about the "polka dots" on my face, and I said I had just strained too hard, working out in the gymnasium. We talked for a while, and I tried to assure them that I would be coming home soon, even though I couldn't imagine how Erin and I could ever cohabitate again. She was decidedly detached and cool toward me, and I could tell she was also a bit fearful at the circumstances I had obviously found myself in. She wasn't comfortable in this place, and I could understand why. The kids were a bit creeped out, but once we started talking and making jokes, they quickly relaxed. We visited for about twenty minutes, and then Erin abruptly said they had to get going. I didn't want them to leave, yet I wanted to limit their exposure to this place. I walked them out to the exit, and I hugged each of the kids so hard they probably couldn't breathe.

After they left I took stock of all that had happened and started to blame myself for all of the failures in my marriage and in my business. I felt angry and depressed and wanted to sleep forever. In my hospital room, I turned off the lights and just lay in bed, staring blankly at the ceiling. The children became my focus, and I replayed all my fondest memories of better times with them. Violet was five years old and getting ready to enter kindergarten. Michael was about to turn three and was still struggling to speak in complete sentences. They were so young and vulnerable. I realized I had to snap out of this funk and be there to help them get through this world. They needed me for so many things. I finally stopped being selfish about the emotional pain that was ravaging my spirit and shifted my attention to the two people who truly relied on me. It became a lot clearer to me that I was necessary to someone. Even though my wife had come to realize that she didn't need or want me, that had nothing to do with my relationship with the two children we had brought into the world. They needed my financial and emotional support, and I realized that I had to somehow fight through my sorrow.

The level of emotional pain I had experienced during the previous year had caught me by surprise. Before the strain associated with the breakdown of my marriage, I had never known such intense pain. It hurt more than any physical pain I had ever endured. And it was almost all related to the children and my fear of being separated from them. I also felt an intense amount of guilt and shame over what I considered failing them, because I never wanted to be responsible for anything that would bring them pain or disappointment. My father had never done anything to cause me strife. Hell, it wasn't his fault that he died. His illness and ultimate passing were pretty much the only incidents associated with him that brought me sorrow. Otherwise, he was always there for me. I wanted to live up to his example, although I felt in no way equal to him when it came to character.

When I awoke early the next morning, things seemed different somehow. While still very confused and depressed, at least I felt convinced that I was no longer going to try to kill myself. That was one significant step toward my recovery. The warm memory of the previous day when I had wrapped my children in my arms still lingered. My psychiatrist had realized the importance of reconnecting with my children, because he had understood, from several conversations, that my affection for them was more powerful than anything else. He knew that I hadn't seen them in a long time, and he wisely determined that seeing them again would have a profound effect on my attitude. It did seem to wake me up, in a sense, but I still felt horribly lost. How in the world would I be able to leave this place and go on? I felt so uneasy around Erin, and she had made it clear to me that there was no way she would ever be able to love me again or tolerate living under the same roof. And I knew it would be horribly stressful for us all, especially the kids, if I came back home to them now. But all I wanted to do was just that. More than anything, I wanted to turn back the hands of time and do it all over again. If only I could change things and make it all turn out good in the end.

There was no desire within me to ever live apart from the children and Erin. The house we had bought together was my home, too. Where would I go, and how would I adjust to a whole new life without the three of them by my side? It was truly unimaginable to me at the time. I started to sink deeper into a state of depression and anxiousness. My appetite was nonexistent, so I skipped breakfast and walked down the colorless hallway toward the nurse's station. I knew that the greater hospital had its own chapel, and I asked permission to go pay a visit. The staff had always reminded me that we had some freedom to come and go as we pleased (some of us, anyway), and we could even leave the grounds if we wanted to. Most patients didn't stray too far because we felt dependent upon the medical staff and none of us had any money. There was little purpose in escaping because almost all of us had self-admitted or been brought to the hospital by loved ones or a medical professional.

On a few prior occasions, I had gone outdoors for long walks with Rick. We would walk down the block, and it felt so strange to be among the "normal" people, all going about their daily business. Seeing a woman coming out of a dry cleaner storefront or watching a father carrying his young son on his shoulders seemed so surreal. When you have the self-image of an inmate, you're acutely aware that you are no longer part of the social structure you had previously taken for granted. I felt like a stranger in a strange land.

One Saturday morning in early May, I put on my jeans, T-shirt and sneakers (sans laces) and took the elevator down to the main lobby of the hospital. It was very early, maybe 6:00 AM or so, and the place was eerily quiet. When I eased open the outer door of the chapel, I noticed it was quite dark inside. Small stained-glass windows adorned the far wall, on either side of the humble little pulpit. The centerpiece of the chapel was a large crucifix mounted on the wall facing the door. There was a small electric organ off to one corner, and the narrow, darkened room housed several rows of narrow pews. Once the heavy wooden door shut behind me, all noise from the outside hospital corridor was completely shut out.

I sat down in the second row of the pews and took in the atmosphere. The place reminded me of Father Gil and his little church in downtown Rochester, and for some reason, thinking of him made me sad. Words he had said to me came scrolling back through my mind, and I felt resentment that he had not contacted me while I had been incarcerated. His faith was powerful, and I was jealous that he had that to guide him through life's ups and downs. Alone in the silent chapel, all I had to accompany me were my fears, frustrations and loneliness.

My thoughts were a jumble of both painful memories and disturbing projections of the future. Where would I go next? How could I move forward without my children and my wife? What about my business? How would I make a living? Why had I messed up so bad in my relationship with my wife? If I lose everything I had worked so hard for, what will keep me going? I started to get agitated and angry, mainly at myself. I still hated myself for letting everyone down. That's how it felt at the time and I started to fantasize about doing myself in again. Convinced that I was the root of all evil, I thought it would be best to eliminate the problem. Envisioning my children attending my funeral, I thought, "You'll be better off without me."

I grabbed a pencil and a Bible out of the wooden rack attached to the pew in front of me and, in my frustration and anger, I violently stabbed at the cover with the pencil. I flipped open the Bible and slashed at some of the pages, ripping gashes in them. With my blood boiling, I tore a handful of pages out and threw them to the ground. The anger was swelling inside me. I didn't deserve this fate, I thought. What had I done to deserve to be exiled from my family, to be feeling so completely alone and isolated? I hurled the Bible across the room, where it smacked against the wall and dropped to the floor, pages fluttering like the broken wings of a bird. I formed a fist with my right hand and repeatedly slammed it against the wooden pew upon which I sat. Needless to say, I was just losing it. All the stress and tension and anger were erupting, and I was having a hard time controlling it.

The powerful surge of energy I had come to recognize began swelling and churning in my head. The first evidence appeared around my neck this time, and suddenly I was almost blinded by the blue-tinged electrical field that encircled my head and shoulders. Growing, moving and intensifying, this energy became larger and more impressive than ever before. Within seconds, it had stretched to encompass my entire upper torso, and bands of white-blue light shot out from my fingertips. Very frightened, I was propelled into a state of shock.

All of the hairs on my arms were sticking straight up, and I could actually taste the electrical energy. There was a crackling electrical noise as the blue aura blossomed to surround my entire body. Unaware, at first, that I had stood up in place, I stretched out my arms and gawked at the glowing aura that covered every inch of me. In desperation, I ran toward the front of the chapel to the crucifix hanging on the wall in front of me. Slamming my entire body into the wall, I smashed both arms against its surface, along either side of the crucified Jesus. The sheer force of the impact created two very noticeable indentations in the painted drywall. The light from whatever this energy was illuminated the area in which I stood. I slammed my arms against the wall again and again, pleading "Why? Why? Why are you doing this to me?!" directing my anger toward God.

My body slumped to the floor, facing the now ravaged wall. Legs askew, I leaned my head against the wall and smashed my forehead against it. I was so full of rage and self-hatred; I truly wanted to injure myself. I felt something strange as my forehead slammed into the hard surface the second time. My vision suddenly cleared and I no longer saw the blue-tinged light when I opened them again. Glancing over my shoulder to my right, I saw something that reminded me of a time long ago.

There, floating in the room's darkened corner was a small amorphous shape made up of crackling blue-white electrical energy. At least that's how I can best try to describe it. I had a flashback to the time I was recovering from my skateboarding accident. Back then I had been convinced that I saw a "little blue being" turning off my little television set. This pulsating shape was reminiscent of what was still tucked away in my memory. Lighting up the immediate area surrounding it, the little aura shifted shape and floated from me toward the wall across from where I sat crumpled on the floor. In utter fascination, I just stared as it gradually seemed to take the form of a child or small person. As I stared directly into it, I marveled at the shifting colors and sparkling pin pricks of intense light. It seemed to have no tangible substance, yet it did. It was morphing and shape-shifting and its edges intensified and then started to dissipate. Staring intently into its core, I wondered if Father Gil was right when he theorized that this phenomenon might have some connection to the human soul – in this case, maybe my soul. As I stared wide-eyed into the glowing aura, I got a sense of something very familiar, something uniquely 'me.'

Memories peppered my consciousness like so many raindrops in a windstorm. I saw Nana, sitting at the foot of my bed, telling me a story about a little wooden puppet named Pinocchio. All he ever wanted was to become a real boy, and he was willing to do anything to realize his dream. It made me think that I was all too willing to throw away the greatest gift of all. In my flood of memories, I saw a young Annie running up the driveway, her tiny porcelain-like arms outstretched. "Look at me!" she squealed. "I can fly faster than you, Amazing Boy! See?" And she soared right up to my face, smiling exaggeratedly and giggling through her teeth." I had to smile, too, despite the bizarre situation in which I found myself. It was clear to me that Annie would somehow always be with me.

I saw a vision of my father as a young man, before he ever dreamed of having a family of his own. He was lacing up his baseball cleats, and then he stood up straight and grabbed his mitt. He held the leather glove up to his face and breathed in its aroma. It was a slow, deep inhaling of a thousand hours of running bases, throwing and catching, laughing and savoring the tiniest moments of joy. How he loved baseball and the joy of competition. I could actually smell the wet grass and the worn leather as I closed my eyes and pictured myself at his side. Wouldn't it have been great fun to have spent even one day on the ball field as his teammate? I thought that for a moment but then quickly revised the wish to be able to have one more day at his side, as his son. Nothing would have been better than that.

In my imagination I saw my wife on the evening of one of our first dates. Strawberry-blonde hair glistening in the sun, she was unaffected and pure and required no makeup to be beautiful. In her blue jean shorts and simple white tank top, she was a natural wonder to me. Innocent and honest, she was my perfect partner. At least I thought so back in the beginning. Picturing her in my mind reminded me of what I had won and what I had now lost. Yet I smiled warmly as thoughts went to me reaching out and taking her hand for the first time. I thought of my mother and the last real memory I have of her. All I recall was her kneeling in front of me in our little kitchen hallway while I was fussing about, eager to get outside to play in the snow with my friends. She buckled up my boots and then wrapped the thick blue scarf around my neck. "Bobby," she said in that gentle voice of hers, "Will you please be extra careful out there today? It's so windy and icy, I'm worried you'll be swept across the yard and we'll have to send a search party to find you!" She then pulled my scarf down and stuck a chocolate chip cookie in my mouth, tapped the tip of my nose with her finger and turned me around to point me toward the front door. Off I went to play with my friends, never realizing it would be my last clear memory of her.

My thoughts turned again to Father Gil and our long conversation at the diner. He had planted the idea in my head that it's conceivable that we could actually see a physical manifestation of our own soul. I looked into the nebulous glow and thought, "Are you part of me? Are you me?" Nothing much changed, but I felt convinced that this incredible substance was somehow a collection of my memories, my thoughts, perhaps my very essence. It didn't seem foreign in any way to me, and that was finally clear to me. After all the strange little episodes of the past, I finally realized that I never felt fear and never felt as if I was dealing with something external. It now made more sense, and I finally realized that this phenomenon was of my own creation. Inadvertent though it was, it was a part of me after all. I felt a great sense of connection to the little shape, which slowly but surely had been dissipating and forming a wispy cloud-like form. Within a few minutes it was almost completely gone.

I laughed to myself through tears as I recalled the discussion with Father Gil. "Real simple, minus the 'imple,'" I had once said. "Minus the Imple, is that what you are? Or who you are?" I asked rhetorically. I stared deeply into the center of the remnants of the glowing form, trying to come to grips with what was happening. I was nearly hypnotized by the beauty of the crystalline blue light at its center. Then, it was gone. Nothing but the blackness of the empty little chapel surrounded me.

Exhausted, sitting on the floor, propped up against the wall I had nearly demolished, my back now rested against the damaged surface. I slowly picked up the Bible I had defiled and located the stubby, eraser-less pencil next to it on the tile floor. I tried to piece the torn pages of the book back together, fruitlessly attempting to right the wrong for which I felt guilty. I finally collected myself and slowly stood up, realizing my head was hurting. It felt like a dull headache, and I felt extremely fatigued, despite having slept soundly the previous night. Peering up at the clock on the wall above the organ, I saw that it was now close to 9:00 AM. Time had passed very quickly, and although it felt like I had only been in the darkened chapel for a few minutes, it had actually been close to three hours. Completely drained of energy, I slumped down in the front pew and put my head in my hands. I returned to reality and ran though the list of challenges I now faced. In my mind I reviewed the checklist and started to feel very sad again. I wanted out of this hospital, and I wanted to be able to see my children again. In my heart I knew I was destined for something better than this, but I couldn't imagine how I would ever get back on my feet.

My freelance business needed to be rebuilt since I had left some clients swinging in the breeze when everything came crashing down around me. Where would I live? With very little money in the bank, it would be nearly impossible to establish a new residence. I still believed I wanted to patch things up with Erin, too, but was also convinced there was no way she would ever consider that now. Only thirty-two years old, I felt like I was eighty-two, and the dense pattern of broken blood vessels on my face and neck made me *look* old, too. I was confused and afraid and simply stuck in neutral. The thought kept running through my mind, "I need your help, God! Please give me a sign. Show me what to do. I need you to help me. Please, show me the way!" What happened next honestly freaked me out. Despite all the strange occurrences with what I now refer to as "Minus," this was very different.

As I sat there with my head in my hands, tears flowing from both eyes, I literally heard a voice in my head say, "The Lord helps those who help themselves." It was a deep, masculine voice delivering a strong and clearly spoken message.

It certainly wasn't my own voice that I heard. It wasn't that familiar internal conscience that I've heard a billion times. This was foreign in origin, and yet I heard it as clearly as if someone had been standing in the room with me. The message was powerful and delivered with simple conviction. It resonated through my spine, and I felt a tingling sensation in my chest.

It seemed as if there had been someone in the chapel speaking to me, and I raised my head to look around and behind me. No one was in the room with me. In fact, it was completely silent. As I wiped tears from my eyes, I looked up toward the crucified figure on the wall and instantly found peace. I realized that this was a turning point. I had reached rock bottom, and now I was ready to stand up and do something. "Yeah, I get it," I thought. "The Lord helps those who help themselves." It makes sense. I had felt helpless for too long. How could I expect the answers to come to me? I now realized, finally, that I had to go and seek the answers for myself. And only then would I have any chance of recovering from this setback. I thought to myself, "God isn't going to waste His time on anyone who isn't willing to take the first step. I guess I would feel the same way if I were Him."

I actually smirked and shook my head at my own foolishness. Realizing that I had been so busy feeling self-pity I had lost faith in myself, it was now clear to me what I had to do. I had to form a plan and take action right away. The clarity was returning to my mind, and I made a vow to remember those words I heard. I swear I actually *heard* the words spoken by a voice other than my own. It made a profound impact, and that's all that really matters. Whether it was all in my imagination or not was unimportant. The renewed energy I felt was rejuvenating, and it seemingly transformed me immediately. It was as though Minus disappeared, but his energy found its way back into me. Weird, but I was not going to question it since I felt powerful again.

The evidence of my tantrum in the chapel was something no one "dreamed up," though, and I confessed responsibility for the damage to the nurse staffing the main reception desk in the lobby. It surprised me that she didn't seem upset with me. I apologized profusely and offered to pay the hospital for the damages. She told me not to worry about it, but she insisted on walking me back to the psychiatric wing. She kindly escorted me up to the psychiatric area and walked me directly to the nurse's station. The heel of my right hand was cut slightly, but otherwise I was intact, despite my tantrum in the chapel. As I walked toward my room, I could barely make out a conversation between her and the other nurses on duty. No one ever mentioned a thing about the damaged Bible or the destroyed drywall in the chapel. It amazed me that the hospital never sought remuneration for the damages.

Everything felt very different when I returned to my routine that afternoon. We did our crafts in the workshop, and I put the finishing touches on the wooden car I made for my son. Despite going through the motions of what the staff expected me to do, I felt like I no longer needed to be there. I decided it was time to start getting serious about making plans to leave the hospital. The next morning, I had my scheduled appointment with my doctor. He asked me about the visit with my children, and I thanked him for making it happen. He examined my face and said he was glad the red specks were beginning to fade. When asked how I was feeling, I said I felt ready to get out of the hospital. He was thrilled to hear that but cautioned me it was nothing to rush into, and he said he'd have to evaluate me in order to authorize my release.

Although he admitted being pleasantly surprised at the dramatic turnaround in my outlook, he recommended that I fulfill the thirty-day period for which I was admitted. I protested, but then he helped me understand that it would be in everyone's best interest if I stayed one more week and started to line things up from within the hospital sanctuary. It made sense. With no place to go and no idea what I wanted to do, I understood that I needed to think it through and make some plans before I could be released. The doctor was supportive and seemed genuinely very happy about the epiphany I had experienced. I told him the whole story, and he never once indicated that he thought I was imagining it all. Here was this trained psychiatrist listening to a story about a glowing blue mass that resembled a child and a disembodied voice speaking to me in the darkness, and he never flinched or disputed any of it. That made me feel good, and it only served to embolden me to begin my recovery and re-entry into the "real world."

As our session drew to a close, I asked him, "Do you believe in the human soul?" He said, "Yes, I do," with no hesitation. "Well, in your opinion, what is it?" I probed. "Hmmm," he muttered, "I never really gave it a lot of thought, but I guess it stands to reason that it would be composed of some type of matter like everything else, right?" I agreed, but then pressed him a little more. "But what *is* the soul?" I insisted. He repeatedly tapped his ball-point pen against his shoe as he sat cross-legged at his desk. The young doctor thoughtfully replied, "I think it's what makes you 'you' and what makes me 'me,' and it has something to do with our connection to something bigger than us."

I returned to my room, exhausted from the previous 12 hours, but at least slightly hopeful about the future.

18

The Girl from Zelienople Goes Walking

The fresh air in the courtyard was the sweetest fragrance I had experienced in my life. Finally free of that hospital interior and its stale atmosphere, I drew in a hugely satisfying deep breath. The flower garden out in front of the hospital was in full bloom that sunny day in late May, and I swear I could identify each variety by the individual scents swirling about my brain. My friend, Jim, had come to pick me up. From the hospital, I had arranged to rent a one-bedroom apartment in a suburb not too far from our home. It already felt wrong to think of the place where Erin and the children lived as my "home." I knew I would never be able to return there, as much as that pained me. We had so many dreams tied up in that house, and now they would never come true. I put those thoughts out of my head for a few days while Jim helped me move my small quantity of possessions into the new place. He helped with the physical transporting of boxes and hand-me-down furniture, but I was left to set the place up by myself. A couple of other friends offered to help me, but I wanted to do it alone.

After the intense mental and physical exhaustion of the previous month, I slept the most restful and peaceful night of my life that first night in the new apartment. In a few short days, I had set up the entire apartment and begun to contact my clients by phone. To my pleasant surprise, the majority of them were not even aware I had been out of commission for more than a month. Slowly but surely, I regained my client base and actually began to add some new clients.

202

Erin and I negotiated visitation schedules, and we agreed that I would see the children every weekend and on Wednesday evenings, too. It gradually became the norm, and it eventually felt like we had 50/50 custody much of the time. Violet was having a bit of a tough time with our long periods of separation, but she was mature for her age and, once she resigned herself to the inevitability of our arrangements, she adjusted. Michael was naturally easygoing and never had a problem getting accustomed to our new lifestyle. Our weekends together were almost always happy, through illnesses and scrapes and cuts and all the troubles of everyday life. The three of us got along so well; there was always laughter and a lot of affection between us. As the years went by, I realized how grateful I was that I had not killed myself. I would have missed so much, and the kids would have missed a lot, too. Money was always in short supply, but love was always abundant.

Much of my business involved graphic design and publication layout work, but I always seemed able to maintain a following for my illustration work, too. I had coined my own term, "corporate cartooning," for the crisp, Disney-esque drawing style I employed for my corporate clients. I promoted that style every chance I got, and many were willing to give it a try when the style was suited to the project. I continued to work at developing my skills and was supremely confident in my cartooning abilities as the next several years passed.

At one point during the fall of 1990, I sketched out a rough pencil rendering of an original character. I had created numerous characters for various clients over the years, but this one wasn't designed for any client but, rather, for me. It was a cartoon representation of Minus the Imple, a little blue character from another dimension. Initially, I had several simple pencil sketches stashed away in a special little notebook. I toyed with the little character's details, but I had always had a basic image in my mind. I guess because I knew "him" so well after all these years, it was nearly impossible to deviate from my preconceived notion of what a cartoon version might look like.

Although the real Minus seemed so much more complex than a simple cartoon figure, I felt there was an unmistakable charm about the little blue alien I was sketching. In the beginning, I didn't have specific plans for the character, but I just felt it was fun to mess with him. It had been a couple of years since I had last seen Minus in the hospital chapel, and I wondered if I was finally rid of him. That made me sad for some reason. Although it had been a source of serious concern at times, Minus had become a large part of my life. It was a very strange phenomenon, but no harm ever came from it.

For some time, I put the sketches aside and tried to push on with my life as a single father, because the children were always my primary concern. There were school plays, concerts, music lessons, vacations, and ten years of Little League. Nothing was ever more fun than watching little Michael pitching on a balmy summer afternoon. He was one of the smaller boys on his first team at age six, but by the time he completed his final season ten years later, he was a tall and sturdy young man. Catching his fastball seriously stung my hand since the time he was about nine years old. At the tail end of his Little League career, it hurt my palm way more than I ever let him know. He was a smart player who always seemed to crank up his focus when the chips were down. One day, as I watched from the dugout, where I assisted the coach, I marveled at him as he mowed down three batters after loading the bases. His eyes bore the quiet strength of my father. I saw him thinking out there. He knew how to stay calm and become more focused while others were unraveling. "Your grandfather would be proud," I thought to myself. Michael always loved anything to do with cars, trucks or motorcycles. Eventually, he decided he wanted to learn to be an auto technician, and he went to college in pursuit of that goal. It seemed so effortless for him. I'm proud that Michael has always possessed the best work ethic of anyone I know.

Violet had grown and blossomed after going through her years of awkwardness and toothless smiles. She had always been the inquisitive scholar and writer in the family, authoring numerous short stories, poems and her "little books" ever since she could pick up a pen. Her imagination has always seemed boundless, and she never ran out of creative ideas. In school she was known as the little quiet one in the back, who would rarely speak up in class. Every parent-teacher meeting would inevitably include a comment from a teacher about encouraging her to speak up in class. One day, when she was in fifth grade, we were stunned when she attained the lead role in the play. Words can't describe the shock I felt when I saw her enter the room from behind the audience and take the stage with fearless confidence.

She projected very well and displayed a never-before-imagined sense of style and flair. I was speechless. She drew such enthusiastic applause from all the parents and children; it must have made a profound impact on her. She went on to act in other productions in middle school and then began to pursue her passion for music. Whatever she wanted to do creatively, she seemed able to do well. Clarinet, guitar, keyboards and then singing; her impressive talents in art, music and writing have always been inspiring to me. I've grown to admire her writing ability above all her other talents, as she's demonstrated truly amazing ability to weave a compelling story. I couldn't be more proud of my children and their individual growth. They turned out to be very different from each other in their interests and communication styles, but their unique qualities have made life all the richer, because I've learned much from them both.

I had never been fond of dating, so I struggled with the notion of trying to become socially active. I tried Parents Without Partners but never enjoyed their group meetings. Many of the members seemed so desperate. The women all had children, of course, and I was resistant to adding to my already daunting obligations. Many of the women I met were clearly willing to say almost anything if it meant they could find a meal ticket to help support their children. I understood their motivations, but the disturbing lack of sincerity was a huge turn-off to me. Over the years, I attended various "singles" meetings, functions and parties, but rarely felt even remotely entertained or even comfortable. There were a few brief moments when I was mildly interested in someone, but it never lasted long. My heart was still with Erin for quite a few years after our divorce.

On February 10th of 1993, a strange twist of fate occurred. I was renting a tiny one-room office in an old warehouse that had been converted into an office building. One of the neighboring offices was home to a business-oriented publication which employed a handful of writers and a pair of account executives. One day, an AE named Will knocked on my door. He was a bright, good looking kid with wavy blonde hair, Windex-blue eyes and a charming personality. We had just become acquainted that year. Most of the employees in that office didn't stay long, so it was rare that I got to know any of them very well before they moved on. Will popped into my office, clearly excited about something. He went on to tell me that he wanted me to meet someone, and he described a young woman who was a freelance artist and designer who had recently relocated to Rochester from New York City. I said I was always happy to meet a fellow artist in the hope we could network or perhaps collaborate on a project. He kept saying he thought we would enjoy each other's company, which I thought was oddly overstated, and he said he would bring her over when she finished her 10:00 AM meeting with his editor the next day. I agreed, thinking nothing of it other than it might be fun to meet someone new.

The next day was a Thursday, the 11th of February. I had actually forgotten about the morning meeting. I had a design project to finish, and arrived to work at 7:30 AM. By 11:00, I was tired and hungry and just about ready to call my friend Craig to see if he wanted to get lunch with me. A gentle knock at my door startled me, and then I suddenly remembered I was supposed to meet some designer from New York. I braced myself for anything as I said, "Come in!"

You can imagine my reaction when the door opened. Leaning into the room from behind the partially opened wooden door was a petite young woman wearing a black wool coat. I couldn't make out her features at first, but when she lifted her head and said, "I can't believe it!" I knew those haunting, green eyes immediately. It was Annie, my long-lost childhood friend! It felt like a dream. She really looked nearly the same as she did when I had last seen her in 1970. She very gingerly entered the tiny office, blushing and smiling from ear to ear. It was a surreal moment, to be sure, and I was filled with joy as I helped remove her coat.

She awkwardly hugged me and then eased into the chair set aside for guests. She smelled like spring flowers and was simply breathtakingly beautiful. I was amazed at how pretty she was. Her little turned-up nose was adorable, and she had the most infectious smile I have ever seen. I saw she was blushing as she became aware of my clumsy gawking. All I could eke out was "I...I can't believe it's you! Annie?" She just laughed and rocked back in the chair in front of my desk. "How can this be?" I asked, still stunned at the surprise. Just then, the door suddenly popped open, and Will stuck his head halfway in to say, "I had a feeling you'd be glad I asked you to meet her!" He disappeared just as quickly as he entered, and returned to his office down the hall, while I still couldn't take my eyes off Annie.

We had stopped communicating years before, both of us involved in busy lives in different cities. I stopped grinning long enough to ask about her family, and she told me they were doing well. Her stepfather had been relocated by his company several times. They had lived in Atlanta for a few years, but then he was transferred to Orlando, Florida before finally ending up in New York City, where they resided for eight years or so. Annie had majored in graphic design at Pratt Institute, and had also taken a lot of writing courses there. She was not an illustrator like me, but, otherwise, the similarity of our interests was uncanny.

She asked me about my business, and I got her up to speed quickly. I didn't want to bore her with the details. She jumped up from her seat when she spotted the wall of photos of the kids. "Oh...my...God!" she whispered intensely. "They are beautiful!" She wouldn't stop gawking at the photos adorning the wall. She asked about my wife, and I had to break it to her that things didn't work out. It still pained me to talk about the disintegration of the marriage, so I glossed over most of the details. Annie generated such a positive presence; I had almost forgotten how comfortable I felt with her. As crazy as it sounds, within a few minutes of becoming reunited, it felt as if we had been together all along. She finally sat back down, and we talked about what brought her to Rochester.

Annie told me she had decided to move to Upstate New York for several reasons. She had grown tired of New York City and its hectic lifestyle. Her brother had moved away, and that broke the ice for her to finally test the waters herself. She chose Rochester for the size, location and business potential. Her plan was to establish her own marketing and advertising business with an emphasis on writing and public relations. When I asked her where she was setting up shop, she told me her plan was to work out of her apartment for a year and then evaluate whether or not she had enough clients to establish a separate office. I couldn't hold back the question any longer, so I finally asked, "You're not married?" She sort of laughed and said, "No," and wiggled her ring finger in front of her face. "Oh. I'm surprised," was my ultra-witty retort.

She insisted on looking through my portfolio, so I cleared off the top of the drawing table in the back corner of the room and opened it up for her to review. We stood side by side while she leafed through the oversize polypropylene sleeves. She was impressed with many pieces, especially the corporate design and publication work for my larger clients. In my portfolio, there were quite a few annual reports, and Annie was very interested in how I acquired that type of work. She thoroughly enjoyed the cartooning and was impressed that I was able to get paying work on such a regular basis. She kept saying, "We should do some projects together!" as she went through the rest of the samples. I gave her my promotional brochure and business card and said I would help her in any way I could. Since she was still new to the area, I offered to introduce her to my clients and to help her create a list of other potentials. She eagerly agreed. When I asked if she had a portfolio to share with me, she said "Not really. Not yet!"

She sat back down and we chatted about work for a few more minutes. Finally, she looked at her wristwatch and said, "Oh wow! It's noon already! I should go." I figured she had to rush to another appointment, and I felt seriously disappointed to have to end the conversation prematurely. As she rose to start assembling her belongings, she asked, "Do you have plans for lunch?" I was thrilled at her question and immediately suggested, "No. Let me take you for Chinese food!" She agreed wholeheartedly, asking how I knew she was craving Chinese. "Lucky guess," was all I replied.

We went downstairs on this snowy, beautiful February day, and she opened the trunk of her car to stow her belongings. She had parked her car, unknowingly, right next to mine. I gestured for her to ride in my car, and she scooted over and hopped in. It felt so unreal to have my Annie sitting next to me in my car. Here we were: two adults, still feeling like kids and still full of wonder. It was obvious that the two of us had somehow retained our youthful curiosity and sense of adventure. The conversation flowed effortlessly, from my office to the parking lot, throughout the short drive to the restaurant and during the lunch. We went to a nearby Chinese restaurant that I had frequented. It was dark, quiet and, although usually busy at lunchtime, service was reliably efficient and friendly.

209

We were talking while we put our winter coats on the backs of our chairs, and we never stopped talking. There was never an awkward silence, never a moment we weren't talking or laughing. The friendly Chinese waitress got a kick out of us for some reason. I guess we were entertaining to observe in that we were quite obviously having such a great time together. The waitress asked if we were married to each other, and we both laughed hysterically. After apologizing, we assured her we were just old friends who hadn't seen each other in years. I'll never forget that this gentle little woman made it a point to say, "You make a good couple. There is joyful energy here, I think."

Time slowed down for a moment, and I took a hard look at Annie in the semi-lit corner of my favorite Chinese restaurant. She looked so gloriously young, with skin as flawlessly smooth as porcelain. Her dark hair was as beautiful as ever, and it made her green eyes stand out. She had a face that made people smile. Pretty and feminine, she was definitely a head turner. In the few minutes we had spent in the restaurant, I noticed how people looked at her. Men did a double take, and women stared for a moment. Annie was magnetic. Not only was she strikingly pretty, but her quiet charisma was tangible. Maybe it was her smile; maybe it was the way she was so quick to laugh and react to what others said or did. She was someone who instinctively knew how important it was to be in the moment.

We had one of the all-time greatest lunch meetings. We never discussed work, as had been our initial intent. Instead, we talked about her life, my life, my children, her family and a lot of other stuff that we had experienced. She expressed her brand of spirituality, which is something I would struggle with explaining to anyone else. She was a kind and gentle soul who was aware of the universe around her, sympathetic and interested in helping others. I admired the ideals she expressed, and I knew she was completely sincere about everything she said. She seemed fascinated by my children and said she hoped to meet them before too long. I referred to them once as the "kiddie-winkles," and she liked the term so much she just started to refer to them that way, too. We laughed about some of the crazy stuff she saw in the Big Apple, and she said she had a lot of similarly funny stories about Atlanta. I wanted to hear them all.

As we opened our fortune cookies, I blurted out an awkward question: "Do you have a boyfriend?" I assumed she had someone special at this point in her life. How wouldn't she, right? A more serious expression came over her, and she said, "Not really. Not right now." I asked, "What does that mean?" And all she said in reply was, "It's complicated." Well, that was good enough for me. You can understand how I felt, I'm sure. Here was this blast from my past, just suddenly walking into my life after so many years. She relocates to my city and is in the same field of work I have been in for years. She seeks me out and sets up a meeting to surprise me. As we get reacquainted, she tells me she is not married and not really in a serious relationship. She adjusts her plans for the day to go to lunch with me on the spur of the moment, and we have the most fun I have ever had over a meal. She is drop-dead beautiful and expresses ideals and ambitions that seem incredibly similar to my own. Enough years have passed that I can stop thinking of her as only a little girl. No, this was a full-grown woman, and the new Annie was far more compelling than the old version. I was never so excited in my life. I hated to end our lunch, but we both had mid-afternoon appointments to get to. She said she had a meeting at the bank, and I had to deliver a finished project downtown.

Some of the restaurant staff seemed particularly enamored with us. As we walked past the hostess desk near the door, three of the staff members were awaiting us. They all smiled enormous smiles and said, "Thank you. We are so glad you come here. Come again, okay?" We smiled back and said, in unison, "Of course," and opened the door into the blinding sunlight. The memory of that simple moment still lingers in my mind. There was something about our combined energy they reacted to, and it was something very powerful. At least that's how it felt to me.

We reluctantly parted ways in the parking lot of the Old Pickle Factory, home to my tiny office. I sprung from my driver's seat and rushed to open Annie's door to help her out, not that she needed any help. I grabbed the brush from the back seat and started to wipe all the snow off her car while she started the engine. She was waving at me as if to say I needn't bother, but all I could think was I wanted to protect her at all costs. When someone places a diamond in your hand, you ought to take special care of it.

Off she went, and I stood there in the ankle-deep snow of the parking lot, just watching her little light blue Nova getting smaller and smaller. One of my friends from the building, Lenny, was just coming down the front steps toward his car. He asked, "What the heck are you doing?" when he noticed me just standing there, ankle-deep in snow. It must have been a peculiar sight, the way I was standing still and staring out toward the access road across the lot. "I'm in love," was my reply. He laughed and said something like "Oh, brother!" but he could tell I wasn't joking by the way I said it.

I finished my delivery and returned to the building. When I got back to my office, it was around 5:00 PM, and I couldn't think of anything but Annie and our lunch. It was the most wonderful time I had experienced in many years, and I wanted to do something to express my feelings. I knocked on Lenny's office door and went in to tell him a little about Annie and about the lunch we'd just had. He said I needed to slow down, but I didn't know how. My emotions were running wild, and I needed to do something about it. Good or bad, that's just the way I've always been. I need to express what I'm feeling; otherwise I feel I'll burst.

I asked him if he knew of a nearby florist, and he offered to take me to a place nearby, if I would drive. I eagerly agreed and we made the short trip to a quaint little shop called Eve's Garden, where the owner greeted us warmly. A friendly middle-aged woman partly hidden beneath a mound of platinum blonde hair, she said the shop would only be open for a few more minutes, but I assured her it wouldn't take us long. To speed things up, I told her I was going to rely on her advice and assistance to impress a young lady I'd just "fallen in love with." She was obviously touched by the brief story I shared and said, "I know just what to do. How about if I describe it all and then we'll put it together early tomorrow with all fresh flowers? And then we can deliver everything to her in the morning, if that's what you want." I enthusiastically agreed to the plan, and she proceeded to show me all the individual elements she planned on assembling.

I really liked her ideas and appreciated her enthusiasm in creating a uniquely customized array of flowers. She described how she would add some green elements and some baby's breath to round it out. I then spotted something on a small table off to the side of a display. It was a small ceramic cherub, a simple and delicate statuette. The little angel was posed as though he was flying. I suggested that it would be a perfect addition to the flowers, and the manager enthusiastically agreed. She promised to arrange it in the delivery box in a tasteful and artistic manner. I didn't care about the cost and gave her the go-ahead to do everything we had discussed. Thanking her profusely for her kindness and patience, I paid and we headed back to the office building. Lenny was smiling, almost laughing at me. He was more cynical than I, and he clearly felt I was overreacting and setting myself up for a big letdown. At least that's what he hinted at as we walked up the entry stairs to our offices. I knew he would make fun of me, but I also knew myself and realized this was a reflection of my outlook on life: if you feel it, be willing to say it.

Friday morning was very busy for me. I had a string of appointments with clients that kept me out of the office until about 11:00 AM. When I returned, there were a few messages on my phone answering machine. One was from my son, asking if I could take him to Little League tryouts on Saturday. The next message was from Annie. She had just opened the box of flowers that one of her neighbors had signed for that morning while she was out at the store. She was gushing in her message. It had obviously made the impact I was trying to make. She alluded to the angel and the message on the card, which I had written myself at the florist. It read, "How convenient: falling in love just a few days before Valentine's Day." Her voice message was brief and was a sincere expression of gratitude, but the tone of joy resonant in her voice was what stood out. So much so that I recorded the message into a tiny handheld tape recorder so I could play it back again and again.

Just then, my phone rang. It was Annie. She wanted to take me to lunch to thank me for the flowers, and of course I accepted. We laughed at our impulsiveness, and she said she would pick me up in front of my building in about a half hour. We went to a quiet little vegetarian restaurant in the village of Pittsford, not far from my office building, where the Erie Canal gracefully wound through the collection of unique shops. The humble little eatery was only a stone's throw away from Eve's Garden, which I pointed out to Annie. She was as electric and charming as ever, and while we enjoyed our artichoke appetizers, she told me a little more about her years in New York. She shared memories about becoming ill from some chemicals contained in the carpeting of her Manhattan apartment. Her condition had improved greatly, yet she still had to be careful with her diet, needing to avoid certain types of preservatives. It concerned me because I was very protective of her and wanted to shield her from life's harshness. That was the feeling I had, for whatever reasons.

We had another wonderful time together. I told her I didn't want the fact that I had been so bold with the flowers to make her uncomfortable in any way. She reassured me that there was nothing to be concerned about because she fully understood why I felt compelled to do it. She said she had thought about me all night long and remarked that it was amazing how we seemed to so seamlessly connect. Our conversation never lagged, yet we were strangers to each other in many ways. She said she liked my smile, and it made her smile every time she looked at me. She told me how impressed she was with my devotion to my children, and she reiterated her desire to meet them. I told her we'd arrange for that when the timing was right. Always protective of their feelings, I was cautious about introducing them to new people until I was certain it would be right for them.

Over our meal I had the urge to ask her about her personal life. She seemed hesitant to divulge much, and that concerned me. She did offer that she had never been married but came close to accepting a proposal once. She said her plan had always been to establish her own business before really settling down. One thing she did say was that there was a man in her life until very recently, but they had decided to call it quits a few weeks earlier. When I asked if he was "still in the picture" she said, "Not really, but there's some stuff we need to work out." I didn't know what to make of that, and it made me wonder what she was leaving out. But despite those little nagging concerns, I was still encouraged. The reason for my hopefulness was the fact that she could have said something to completely dissuade me from any amorous notions, but she didn't. She clearly seemed interested in continuing our relationship.

This may sound unbelievable, but I still maintain that nearly every moment we spent together was euphoric. That's a strong word, and I could never describe any other relationship I've had in such a way. We smiled and laughed all the time. Who knows why some people click and others don't? We certainly clicked in a profound way, and it was blissful. Every time I saw her I not only felt the urge to hug her and pull her close to me; I felt like I wanted to absorb her into my body. I wanted to melt with her and become one with her forever. My inner voice would warn, "Be careful. You're setting yourself up for a big fall if this doesn't work out." I recognized the risk but simply refused to try to control my emotions when it involved Annie. The pure joy I felt in her presence was unlike anything I had ever experienced. Why deny myself? In a life that had always been peppered with disappointments and "going without," I needed this refreshing dose of happiness and was in no way interested in over thinking it.

The weeks ahead were filled with phone calls at all times of the day. Annie would pick up her phone and call me as frequently as I would contact her. She would apologize for bothering me too frequently but, as she said, "I always just want to see you and can't seem to resist calling. Is that so wrong?" One afternoon in late February she called and invited me to her apartment, under the guise of showing me her business setup. I couldn't help but wonder if that was all she had in mind. Trying to keep my head screwed on tight, I told myself it was just that, even when she added that she would make us dinner after we talked business. I didn't do anything rash, but I did bring a bottle of wine to add to the meal.

I can never forget the image of her when she answered the door. Having been held up at an afternoon meeting, she had returned to her apartment a little later than she had planned. She had hurriedly jumped into the shower and had just emerged moments before I rang her doorbell. She buzzed me into the building, and, as I reached the top step, she opened the door to her apartment. With one hand, she held the white door open while she was frantically rubbing her hair with a bath towel held in her other hand. Just dressed, she had not had time to dry her hair before I showed up. Here she was: bent at the waist, vigorously trying to absorb the excess water from her long, beautiful hair. She rose up quickly and tossed her hair back in one smooth motion. Standing there, laughing at her own imagined rudeness for "being a bad time manager," she was the most beautiful woman I have ever seen. My heart nearly stopped beating. At that very moment, I realized how hopelessly in love with her I was. She stood there, barefoot, hair still mostly wet, no makeup, no perfume, just a graceful young woman with an undeniable charm. She couldn't have been lovelier. No one could. Apologizing for her tardiness, she turned and scampered into the bathroom to finish drying her hair. She told me to make myself at home, which I did. I felt such excitement and love for her at that moment.

I found a corkscrew in a kitchen drawer and opened the wine to let it breathe. In the moments I had been waiting, I walked the perimeter of her living room, which also doubled as her office. Along the windowed wall was a drafting table adjacent to a desk. There were two Macintosh computers in the room as well as a very expensive-looking printer on a stand next to one of them. I spotted a flatbed scanner and a new word processor, too. Everything looked to be extremely new, and I added up the costs in my head. There was a lot of money tied up in all this equipment. It was none of my business how she financed it all, but I admit I was curious. It had taken me several years to save up so I could buy my lone computer, and I even had to borrow additional funds to afford that.

On her drafting table I spotted one of the ribbons from the flowers I had sent her. The little card that bore my hand-written declaration of love was positioned atop a stereo speaker, in an obvious spot. I couldn't help but notice a greeting card she had laid upon her desk. It was open, and I was able to read the brief message written inside by one of her girlfriends. It stood out to me because it said something like, "I can't wait to see that beautiful face of yours again." I thought to myself, "Oh, I guess I'm not the only one who appreciates how beautiful she is." I admit that I wasn't just killing time but trying to get a more complete picture of Annie's world. I was acutely aware that I didn't spot anything that indicated she was involved in any romantic relationship. There were no photos that would say that, no letters from possible boyfriends among the others on her desk, only notes and cards from her parents, her friends, and me. I was relieved, to be honest. Maybe she was keeping those out of sight, but I wanted to believe there was no one else in the picture.

Annie's one-bedroom apartment was located in Brighton, not far from RIT's Henrietta campus. It was tidy and pleasant with a spacious, open living room between the kitchen and the bedroom. She rather rapidly finished brushing her hair, and when she came out into the living room, her hair was still a little wet. I was still awestruck by how beautiful she was. She gave me a quick tour, and of course I posed a suggestive question when she walked me up to the threshold of the bedroom. She turned a little red but was not offended. She already knew what was going through my mind.

We had a discussion about her plans for her business, and she mentioned several times that she would like to hire me to do some work. I found it odd, the way she talked of our potential future. After several weeks of euphoric interaction, I was already leaping ahead to us having far more than a business relationship. I didn't quite know what to make of this, but I let it slide. She talked about a few clients she was trying to land, and she sought my advice on various aspects of getting her business launched. This was just the beginning for her, and I had been in business on a full-time basis for nearly ten years.

Dinner was absolutely wonderful. She prepared a delicious salmon, and the wine was a perfect complement. The little dining area was gently illuminated by candles. We didn't talk about work at all. We talked about dreams and aspirations. She described her desire to have a family of her own and even said she'd already picked out a name for her first child. When I probed a little further, she refused to share the name with me. I found that a little peculiar, in light of her general openness, but I respected her right to withhold anything that personal. We finished the meal, and I helped her do the dishes while coffee was brewing. When we took our coffee cups into the living room and sat in facing overstuffed chairs, I asked her something that had been on my mind for the past few weeks. I asked, "Do you understand how I really feel about you?" She replied, "Yes, I think I get it," and she smiled warmly. I then asked, "Do you think you could ever have the same feelings for me?" Annie set her cup down on a saucer and looked at me with a puzzled expression. She said, "I think I *do* feel the same way about you already." I was very pleased at her response. "So, you mean you feel love for me, just as I do for you?" She claimed she did. Maybe I'm dense, but I had to press for more information.

Continuing the interrogation, I asked her if she meant "romantic love or brotherly love." She barely missed a beat and said, "I have to honestly say that I feel love for you in the same way you say you feel for me: romantic love, I guess you call it. It's more than just friendship, but I'm not ready to change this relationship into something other than what it is." That confused me. I confessed that I was in love with her and wanted to spend my future with her. I was unafraid to admit it, since I knew she felt it all along. I asked, "Why don't you want to move this further if you say you have the same feelings? If you're telling the truth, I don't understand why you wouldn't be as excited and willing as I am to take it to the next level." She looked hurt, and I quickly apologized for my words. She assured me it was alright, that she understood my frustration. But she added, "It's complicated. There are some reasons why it's difficult to move forward right now, even if I want to. I need to work some things out in my mind first." It all seemed mysterious to me, but I tried hard to imagine that there were some extenuating circumstances, perhaps remnants of a previous relationship.

A few things went through my mind. Maybe her former boyfriend had helped her fund all this new equipment I saw surrounding me. Or maybe there was still some lingering bond between them that she wasn't ready to sever. I decided that, although I didn't like it and it made me uneasy, I was willing to wait and see if it could eventually be worked out between them. We changed the direction of the conversation and talked about the coming spring. I told her about Michael's upcoming season of Little League, and she expressed interest in coming to watch a game. She asked questions about both children and was fascinated by stories of our exploits over the years. I was anxious for the kids to meet her, too.

We talked and talked as usual, and the time raced by. I worked up the courage to tell her a little about my long history with Minus. She listened intently and didn't seem to think I was crazy. Instead, she said my theory about Minus' origin made sense to her and she could accept the possibility that it was feasible. I was afraid she was just trying to make me feel good, but then she shared some personal experiences that were also of the metaphysical variety. She said she believed that some people have heightened senses, and they feel and hear things in such a way that it seems supernatural to others. She told me about some of her own experiences with reading thoughts her brother had. Another story involved her and her brother visiting a place in Arizona where a group of people demonstrated an ability to punch holes in clouds using their combined, focused mind power.

That story left me scratching my head in disbelief, but Annie said she saw them demonstrate it with her own eyes. I was starting to feel that my stories about Minus weren't all that crazy. Annie said she could accept the possibility that electrical energy from one's brain could conceivably be visible outside the body. The notion of Minus being a tangible manifestation of the human soul also made some sense to her. She expressed how excited she was to tell her brother about all of this, and she asked my permission to talk to him about it. I said it was fine with me because I had nothing to hide. My only concern was that he wouldn't quite understand it, but she told me he had become a doctor of holistic medicine. She was sure he would be fascinated by my stories, and he had already been planning to visit in May.

When I got up to leave, we hugged each other as we had become accustomed to doing when parting. This time I held her tighter than usual and whispered in her ear that I wanted to kiss her goodnight. Her reaction was not a complete surprise, but it stung nonetheless. She said, "No, Robby. We can't." When I asked why not, she said, "Because one kiss will lead to another, and then that will lead to something else, and this is not the right time." I was puzzled and disappointed but could only hug her for another minute before reluctantly heading out to my car.

We had more days and evenings similar to this one over the next several weeks. Even as we came to know each other better and almost instinctively knew we'd see each other on a semi-regular basis, each time we got together I felt ecstatic. I kept expecting that feeling to dull or go away, but it never did and that surprised me. Annie's brother, Daniel, came up to visit on a Friday in May. He was, according to Annie, interested in reacquainting with me, so we planned a lunch at the Pittsford Pub, within walking distance of my office building. I secured a booth and waited for them inside. I had alerted the hostess, who knew me well, to look out for my guests. She brought them over to join me, and I finally got to meet the present-day version of Daniel. He'd grown to nearly six feet tall and seemed so much more civilized than the somewhat manic kid I remembered from back home. He had hazel eyes and sandy-colored short hair and bore very little resemblance to Annie. Daniel gave me a firm handshake and seemed genuinely happy to see me again, after so many years. Annie had given me some background information, so we had an easy time carrying on a conversation. Annie seemed content to listen as she deferred to her brother rather than jumping in. I kept looking across the booth at her and

221

noticed she was obviously enjoying seeing the two of us getting reacquainted. My imagination led me to think she saw us having a future together, and that was why she so wanted us to get along.

Dan, as he asked to be called, steered the conversation to a discussion about my history with Minus. He said he worked as a holistic physician, which I didn't fully understand. He tried to describe what he did, and I did my best to understand. As a holistic physician with extensive training in physical medicine, he utilized many non-traditional therapies to aid patients in his practice in North Carolina. He had gone to medical school in Syracuse as part of his long educational process, so he felt at home here in Upstate New York, he claimed. He wanted me to talk about some of the experiences I'd told Annie about concerning Minus. He seemed to have a very genuine curiosity on two levels.

I think he was intrigued by stories passed along to him through his sister, and he wanted to know who this person was who had re-entered her life. On another level, he was curious from a purely scientific viewpoint, too. A thoughtful, gentle man, he very politely quizzed me about some of the more dramatic episodes I had described to Annie. While I had not yet imparted everything to her, she knew some of the stories and had done a very accurate job of recounting them to her brother. Dan was intently focused on all that I had to say. It made me feel a bit like a specimen under a microscope, but it was a great relief to be able to speak freely. He specifically wanted to hear about any physical sensations I felt during moments when Minus made appearances. I tried to describe it as best I could, but it was difficult. The best I could do was to liken it to a feverish feeling that started behind my eyes and then took courses that varied from one incident to the next. He nodded as though it made some sense to him. Then, he asked me to try to describe the physical appearance of Minus down to the most minute detail. Once again, I had to preface it by saying there was a range of different looks, and then I did my very best to describe some of the manifestations indelibly etched into my memory. It made me tremble visibly to recount these moments. Annie reached over and put her hand atop mine as it rested on the table. She looked concerned and told me I should stop if it was upsetting me. I took a few deep breaths and continued to tell Dan as much as I could remember about some of the episodes. He asked me if I had ever experienced physical pain when it happened. I replied that I had not, but countered that there was sometimes emotional pain associated with those moments.

Dan was very intrigued, even more so after hearing the details. I realized that I wasn't eating the meal in front of me, but I wasn't interested in food. It felt good to be talking with someone who was obviously genuinely interested, someone who took me at my word and was trying to understand what I had been through. Dan had hardly eaten any of his meal either but just kept posing more questions. I stopped him to ask him to tell me what he thought about the stories I had shared. He thought for a long while and then sat back in the booth and said, "I believe you. At first I was very skeptical and wanted to poke holes in your stories. It's a very unique history, but I don't for one minute think you've made any of this up. Nor do I believe you imagined it, at least not all of this." I thanked him for listening to my lengthy descriptions, but then he stopped me to say it was he who was grateful that I was willing to answer his questions. He suggested I come visit him sometime at his Hillsborough, North Carolina practice. He said he would like to hear more about Minus and conduct a few simple tests if I was willing. I said I would consider cooperating with the tests and would be more than happy to visit him. In my mind I figured Annie and I would go together to further cement our relationship in the near future.

He added, "I'm definitely convinced there could be a unique situation here, and there's a real possibility it can be traced all the way back to your childhood accident. This would likely be an unprecedented case, but that doesn't mean it's impossible. Do you still have occasional episodes? When was the last time you saw evidence of the phenomenon?" I had to really think hard. "It has been quite a few years, I guess. Yeah, it might be that this is all part of the past now," I speculated. What I didn't get into was that I had developed the ability to quell the emotions that seemed to lead to the emergence of Minus. During my married years and beyond, I had learned to recognize the patterns that served as internal warning signals, and had developed an internal mechanism that successfully kept Minus at bay. It had become almost instinctive, a second nature that automatically kicked in when the time was right. But I didn't know for sure if I had outgrown Minus or not.

Annie rejoined our conversation and added that I had done some cartoon sketches of Minus. She said she thought they were really great, and she wanted me to show them to Dan. We agreed to drive over to my office and show Dan where I worked, as a nice way to end our visit. We paid our bill and drove around the block to my office building. The place was certainly a low-budget, no-frills structure, but it had a certain charm. Dan made some generous comments about the place as we traversed the creaky floors and made our way to the small elevator in the middle of the building.

In my office we all huddled around the drafting table and I let Annie show her brother my work. He seemed impressed with many pieces, but then he remembered that Annie mentioned some cartoon sketches. Tucked into a folder in the back pocket of my portfolio were some of my pencil sketches of Minus. Some were very rough and unfinished while others were much more detailed and reflective of how he appeared to me on various occasions. Dan seemed to warm up when he held a few of the pencil renderings up so the light hit them. He said, "You ought to do something with this. I think these are really great!" I wasn't sure why he reacted so enthusiastically to the simple little sketches. Maybe he sensed the authenticity and honesty behind them, or maybe he had tried to visualize Minus from the verbal descriptions I had provided earlier. Perhaps he just liked cartoons. Whatever his reasons, Annie enthusiastically agreed. I had kicked around ideas about using the character in some commercial vein but had been too busy to do anything about it.

We had talked ourselves to exhaustion, and Annie finally announced it was time to call it a night. She and Dan thanked me for dinner, and I walked them out to the parking lot, where we headed our separate ways. Daniel pressed his business card into my hand as we said our goodbyes, and I promised to be in touch to discuss a future trip to North Carolina. He expressed a desire to talk to me more about my experiences with Minus.

I assumed we would have endless opportunities to talk when we became members of the same family.

19

Now That I've Lost Everything to You

Dan's expression stuck with me over the next several days. The smile on his face was only part of it. There was a look of wonderment in his eyes as he held those partially developed sketches of Minus up under the light on my drafting table. I took them out and carefully reviewed them one morning during the following week, and decided to try to do something to further develop the character. I figured that I could conceivably turn years of frustration into something positive, by using the character inspired by my unique experiences for a good purpose.

I scheduled some time over the next few days to refine my rough sketches into a more finished rendering of the little character. It dawned on me that maybe there was some way to reach children with this character. Instead of the character being a manifestation of a person's inner energy, as I had originally planned, I thought it might be interesting to establish him as an imaginary friend; maybe Minus could act as the voice of a child who was facing personal struggles. I worked out an outline of an "origins" script for a comic book geared toward a young adult audience. It was a rough first draft, but I felt this was an idea that was worth developing. I read the highlights to my children that weekend, and they liked the idea. My daughter, Violet, suggested that I should create a sample chapter or two of a comic and send it to some publishers. My son said he thought Minus was like a kid's personal superhero. I liked that idea, so I incorporated it into my drafted outline. "Minus the Imple: Every Kid's Personal Superhero" was the title I applied to my drafted manuscript.

I showed the mock-ups to Annie one evening at her place. She liked what she saw and encouraged me to send the proposal to a friend of hers, who worked as an editor at a New York publishing firm called SolCor. I agreed and mailed everything off to Dominique at the end of the week.

That afternoon, in anticipation of our planned Chinese stir-fry dinner, I prepared a little surprise for Annie. We had discussed plans that morning, and I offered to bring wine and dessert. Always willing to stick my neck out, I decided to put my cards on the table again. In my office that afternoon, I went to some creative lengths to ensure a romantic mood later. I had purchased a box of fortune cookies and carefully opened it at the bottom. After sliding the plastic bag of cookies out, I used an X-acto knife to cut a neat slit in the bottom. Then, I carefully used a pair of tweezers to remove the paper slips from each fortune cookie. Using my computer and laser printer, I created 30 new "fortunes" with my own original messages. The replacement fortunes were all unique, ranging from "I think you're beautiful" to "Will you marry me?" After carefully inserting a personalized message into each cookie, I returned them to the plastic bag, sealed it with invisible tape, and reinserted it into the box, upside down. Once I glued the box together again, you couldn't tell it had ever been tampered with. It was no small feat to painstakingly feed the folded slips of paper into the cookies, but I managed to pull it off. No cookies were destroyed during this exercise in romanticism.

That evening, after our meal, I couldn't wait for her to open the box. Annie served green tea, and then she opened the box, removed a few cookies and placed them on a small plate. It was difficult to not smile as she offered them to me and then took two cookies for herself. She broke one open and removed the tiny slip of white paper and held it up so she could read it. Her expression was priceless. She didn't react initially, but suddenly she looked dumbfounded. "What the heck?" she muttered. "Annie, please be mine," she read aloud. "How...?"

Then, she hurried to open the next cookie. She blushed and whispered, "Oooh, I can't read *this* one out loud!" Obviously, she started to catch on that this was no standard, factory-produced box of cookies, and she was still blushing while she kept shaking her head. As she said, "You're unbelievable," she pulled two more cookies from the box, quickly opened them and read the fortunes. "Oh my God! This is incredible. You never cease to amaze me." You'll forgive me for assuming I had made an impression, but I didn't know if it would do anything to change her feelings about our relationship. I was just following my usual pattern of being expressive. We had a good laugh as she continued to ask how I managed to replace the fortunes so deftly. It was a memorable evening, and I'll always cherish that image of the expression on her face when she first realized that the fortunes had all been created especially for her.

The weeks rolled on, and Annie secured a new client and had finally acquired some interesting projects worthy of her time and talents. We were still inseparable, and it was going on three months when the opportunity finally arose for her to meet the kids. She said she was nervous when I called her the afternoon of a Little League practice in early May. I told her she could wait for another opportunity, but then she insisted on meeting us at the practice field. I was very anxious and excited for her to meet them and for them to finally know the Annie I had described to them. Usually on practice days, Violet chose to join us just to spend time with me while Michael took place in the drills. Annie was right on time, around 5:30, on a gloriously warm afternoon. It was a magical experience for me. I think it was undoubtedly a very pleasant time for all of us, actually. Annie emerged from her car in the parking lot, and Violet and Michael immediately tugged at me to go over to intercept her. They were not putting on an act of any kind, but it might have appeared as though I had coached them. Sometimes a bit shy around new people, they both approached her and allowed her to hug them individually.

I was impressed at the almost immediate bond between them. Maybe I was seeing something that wasn't really there, but it felt like they belonged together, as strange as that sounds. I admit I was madly in love with them all and wanted so much for them to love each other. And the way it worked out, it appeared we were off to a great start. At one point I had to help Michael tie his cleats, and when I looked up I saw Annie and Violet sitting across from each other in the grass, and they were picking daisies and putting them in each other's hair. Violet was giggling and saying something about me and pointing. They both fell over, laughing and giggling. Michael, feeling left out, ran over to them and sat right next to Annie. He leaned his head against her shoulder as if he had known her for years. I had never before seen him react to someone like that.

I reminded the kids of the history between Annie and me, of the old days of Star Glider and Amazing Boy. They said it was so cool that we knew each other all those years ago. Annie put her arm around Michael, and I fell to my knees. Honestly, looking at this scene was incredibly moving for me. It was like a dream come true. Violet looked over at me and asked me what was wrong. I quickly reassured her that it was quite the opposite. "No, no," I said, "Nothing's wrong." "Then, why are you crying?" my daughter asked. I was unaware that tears had begun to well up in my eyes. "I'm not crying!" I insisted. "I'm just so happy because I finally have my three favorite people together for the very first time."

That memory still stands out as one of the truly happiest moments of my life. The births of my children are all that stand above this moment. I can't properly describe my feelings of joy and hope, so I won't even try. Michael wanted to stay with our little crew, but he finally joined the rest of the team, and we watched them go through their exercises and drills while continuing to talk. I looked at my precious daughter talking with my one true love and felt as though they were already building a connection. They seemed similar to each other in many ways, and I decided it was our destiny to all be brought together.

The next Saturday, when I picked the kids up from their mom's house, they both immediately asked if Annie would be able to come over. I said she couldn't because she had gone out of town. That was a lie. The baseball practice had taken place on a Thursday evening. On Friday Annie called and asked me to meet her at a hotel to discuss something important. When I asked why we were meeting in a hotel, she said she just wanted to have a change of scenery. The hotel was only a mile or so from her apartment, and I agreed to meet her there. She said she had a business proposal to discuss, and that we could decide if we wanted to go to dinner afterwards. I was intrigued, albeit a little curious about her choice of venue.

When I entered the lobby, I spotted Annie sitting at the bar inside the huge open atrium at the center of the hotel. This was a fairly new structure, and I had no idea how beautiful the inner courtyard was. The bar at which she was seated was one of two working bars in the sprawling area. There was an indoor pond stocked with goldfish, and the entire area was landscaped with lush plants and flowers. The atrium was equipped with a high glass ceiling, and natural light spilled onto the center section of the garden.

Annie waved me over and flashed that priceless smile. I hugged her with my free arm and placed my briefcase on the floor against the base of the bar. She had obviously been there for a while, pouring over a stack of notes as she sipped a diet soda. The bartender took my order and brought me a soft drink and then told us that service was ending at this bar, but that the bar on the opposite side was open all night. She told us we could stay seated where we were, which suited me fine because it meant we'd have more privacy. Annie said she had really enjoyed the kids the night before, and then she started to tell me a little about the project she'd been reviewing. Her new client wanted her to create a new identity piece, some sort of capabilities brochure. Annie said she had budgeted some money for me in her estimate and wanted me to help with the layout work so she could concentrate on the copy writing. It sounded like a great plan to me, and I eagerly agreed. I told her I would play any part that she wanted me to. It struck me as odd how she replied to that. She said, "I really think this will serve as a good test for the way we can work together in the future." I pushed myself away from the bar and looked at her, head askew. "Really?" I asked, rhetorically. "That's a strange way to describe it." She really didn't know to what I was referring, so I had to explain. "Annie," I said calmly, "I've been assuming we'd someday become partners, yet you talk as though I'll be one of your employees." She stunned me by replying, "Maybe you will be."

I was crushed. "Employee? Really? Is that how you envision our future together?" She put her hand on mine and said, "Don't overreact. That's not what I meant, but we don't know how this relationship will eventually develop. I see you as part of the business, but in what role, we don't know yet. Let's see how things work out with this project." For the only time in our entire relationship, I felt angry and hurt. It was unbelievable to me, the way she was talking about us. "Annie!" I exclaimed. "This is not about projects and employees or business arrangements! I thought we had something far more than any of that! You always say you love me, and now you talk about me as a potential employee?"

I felt the tension percolating under my skin. That old familiar feeling was growing inside my head and I could feel the first wave coursing through the arteries in my neck and behind my eyes. But I had learned to control it, and my inner voice was shouting "Back it down! Cool off now, cool off!" I looked at where Annie's hand was resting atop mine on the surface of the bar. My fingertips were glowing blue, enveloped in a white-blue aura. "Back down, back down!" my inner voice ordered. Annie looked at my hand and quickly pulled hers away from me. She pulled her hands up against her chest and stared in disbelief at the glow now emanating from both my hands. I quickly shoved my hands in my jacket pockets, closed my eyes tightly and took a deep breath. I had worked out a way to breathe a series of long, deep breaths and focus my thoughts in an effort to dissipate the excess energy until it disappeared. It slowly started to work and I felt the cooling-down process slowly taking over throughout my upper body. When I opened my eyes, I saw a horrified expression on Annie's face. She was speechless. I did most of the talking anyway.

I finally confronted all the frustration that had been building over the past three months or so. We had spent many wonderful moments together during the time we had together. We spoke in loving terms about one another, yet she never kissed me. She claimed to have a "complicated situation" involving some mystery man, yet she never elaborated and I never saw any sign of him. She never offered any information about him or what his role in her life was. I had asked her on multiple occasions if she felt love for me, the type of romantic love that could lead to a true partnership or marriage. She always said she did feel those feelings for me but was just not able or ready to move our relationship further. We would linger every time we hugged each other goodnight, but she never allowed me to even kiss her cheek. It was maddening because it never added up for me. She had gone out of her way to spend so much time with me for three straight months that there was not much time left for any rendezvous with anyone else, if they were even happening. She met my children, made it a point to have me meet her brother and called me at all hours just to chat.

I had always been completely honest with her about my affection and desire for her, and she always told me she appreciated my openness. She had said she was incredibly flattered that I was so devoted to her because, in her words, I was "one of a kind" and "any woman would be lucky to have you love her." So what was the problem? I begged her one last time to please tell me if she felt this was a one-sided infatuation. She refused to say that was true. I finally said, "You feel it too; I know you do. You couldn't have fooled me all this time. If you actually think you can have something more wonderful than the euphoria we both seem to feel whenever we are together, then tell me now and I'll remove myself from your life. I want to meet this other person if that's the case, because he must be incredible!"

It actually made the situation worse when she replied, "I honestly can't imagine anything more joyful or special than what I feel for you, Robby." I nearly exploded. Instead, tears began to flow, and I just put my head down in my folded arms atop the bar. I was glad no one else was in the vicinity because it was quite a scene. I was exhausted from the three months of unrequited emotions. Annie and I had so much fun together, and she had reassured me on several occasions that she was attracted to me physically. I kept adding the pieces of our relationship together, and they should have added up to be the love of the century, in my opinion. Instead, the madness of it all had culminated in her referring to me as some potential future employee. I had experienced enough emotional pain for one lifetime, I figured, and I didn't want to go through yet more heartache.

As much as it hurt to part ways, it was ultimately what I felt I had to do. I almost couldn't believe it when the words came out of my mouth. I raised my head and wiped my tears away with a napkin. Then I coldly said, "I can't do this anymore, Annie. I just can't take it. I care about myself too much to punish myself like this. I love you, and you say you love me back, yet we can't be together the way I feel we should be. This is not a threat. I love you and respect you too much to play games. Unless you want me completely, I don't want to go through this anymore. I can't continue to see you. It hurts way too much."

233

She said something about me being tired and emotional and suggested that I'd feel different in the morning. I just gazed into her beautiful green eyes one last time, collected my belongings and then headed out the door. I was already embarrassed that some people might have witnessed the whole scene, so I made haste as I went to my car and sped down the road toward home. I just shook my head in disbelief as I drove on. I took a detour and drove for a while in an effort to settle myself. I knew I'd have to see the kids the next morning, only a few hours away, and I didn't know what I would tell them about Annie.

The next couple of days came and went, and I resisted the urge to call Annie. It had become second nature to want to reach out to her. She had become vitally important to me in such a short time, inhabiting my dreams both at night and during the day. In my mind, there were going to be many years devoted to building our future together. Annie was going to marry me and we would have a couple of children together. I wanted to find out what our union would produce. There had been little doubt in my mind that we were destined to be together and that she was my true 'soul mate.' She was going to be a wonderfully positive influence on Michael and Violet as time went by. So many dreams would never come true now that I finally realized it was not going to happen for us. Our separation hurt more than any emotional pain I'd ever experienced, and that was saying a lot.

My overall mood had abruptly changed from euphoric and giddy to sullen and depressed. The kids picked up on it over the weekend, but I never said anything about Annie being the reason. Early on Monday morning there was a phone machine message awaiting me at my office. Annie had called to say she was sorry for causing me so much obvious pain. She said I should call her if I felt differently about things, and while it was tempting, I didn't honestly believe anything had changed. I still felt the same. I valued self-preservation over all else, so I never called her. While it was extremely difficult to resist reaching out to her, I felt I had to protect myself from more pain. Instead, I mailed her a poem I had written the night before:

I Can Dream Sweet Dreams

No answers for my questions.
No comfort for my pain.
No freedom from this heartache,
Which has come for me again.

Did I ask too much?
You are the miracle I prayed for.
To be denied your touch
Is so much more than cruel.

But in my dreams I hold you,
And our souls are intertwined.
The joy comes pouring through us
As if by right divine.

Our children laugh and take our hands
In journeys off to magic lands,
And peace has made a home in me
Where once was only sorrow.

You see, I've won... in my own way
I have you with me every day.
We are "as one" as it should be
In my dreams and fantasies.

Here, lost in my dream,
Our love is so complete.
Here, lost in my dream,
Your kisses taste so sweet.

I never did experience the pleasure of kissing Annie. After all the laughter and tears, all I have are memories from different decades and a very special emptiness that will never be filled. A few more days passed, and a letter was left pinched inside the screen door of my house. It was from Annie, of course. She had written a long letter explaining that she understood my feelings of frustration. In the letter she restated her love for me and, once again, clarified that she felt we did share the same type of feelings for each other. She went on to mention how much she enjoyed the kids and that she thought I was a good father to them. She spoke of the many memorable moments we had crammed into such a short period of time, and lamented my decision to stay away from her but promised to honor my wishes by not forcing her way into my life. She still didn't explain her mysterious arrangement with the "other man," but it was apparent she had some things to reconcile with that relationship.

My heart was broken. For the second time in my life, I felt like all of the energy had been completely drained from me. This time actually hurt worse than the other because I had never before felt so incredibly happy in the company of another person. To have it end up so disappointing was nothing short of devastating. There were no words that could console me and there was nothing I could do to change the inevitable. I carefully folded the letter and saved it in an envelope in my bedroom dresser. A few more cards and letters arrived over the next few weeks, and they generally were friendly hellos and questions about the children and me. I realized that Annie wasn't trying to hurt me. She was being honest about her emotions, and I believed she truly cared about me and about the kids. But the incomplete portions of the story were troubling, and I had no idea why this never added up to be the relationship we both seemed destined for.

Months passed and the letters and cards eventually stopped coming. I spotted Annie in her car once during that summer, driving on a cross street right in front of me. The temptation to follow her was powerful, but I resisted the urge.

Goodbye, again, Annie. I'll love you forever.

20

To the Vector Go the Spoils

Time has a way of healing even the deepest wounds, and today I can look back on my relationship with Annie as a great blessing. It has now been well over a decade since Minus the Imple was first introduced to the world as a fictional character. In October of 1994, I had finally received a favorable response from the publisher in New York. Annie's friend Dominique Serrano called me on my birthday, of all days. She told me that her team decided they really liked the potential of the character I had created, and they were interested in publishing a book. They were debating the optimal format and wanted me to consider changing the vehicle from comic book to traditional novel. I agreed to consider their ideas, and we had a meeting in the Manhattan Office of SolCor Publishing.

Dominique supported the concept of transforming the original version into a novel that used the character of Minus to help young adults deal with real-world issues such as domestic violence, drug addiction and abandonment issues. Their ideas appealed to me, and I admitted that I had wanted to see if there was a way to help people through use of the character. It seemed like a perfect fit, and the publishing house offered me a generous advance to produce the first two books within a sixteen-month window. It allowed me to maintain my design business while I worked on the books at the same time.

The first *Minus the Imple* book was published in July of 1995. The staff at SolCor Publishing was great to work with, and they did a great job getting exposure for the book. Due to opportune timing and a solid marketing campaign, the first book was popular almost immediately.

Sales picked up dramatically after the book was featured during a nationally televised interview of a New York children's psychiatrist who claimed she had prescribed the book to several young clients. She was a very popular public figure in New York, so her endorsement significantly boosted sales. She even held a copy of the book up to the camera during her interview on a talk show. Once that first book hit so big, people started hounding the publisher for a sequel. SolCor delayed the release of the next book for strategic purposes, and when it debuted the following winter, it sold in huge numbers. Schools purchased copies for their libraries, and it did well with therapists and other mental health professionals. Kids liked it because the character of Minus was depicted as a reflection of their inner strength, and it enabled them to realize they had more power than they may have otherwise realized.

Financially, the books did better than I imagined they would. SolCor flew me in to discuss a long-term agreement, and I carefully weighed all factors before deciding to stick with them. They had treated me with respect from the very beginning, so I felt a sense of loyalty and appreciation. We agreed to a three-book deal, and I signed the contracts in early 1996. The schedule we agreed upon was very reasonable, and in the contract we built in a provision for me to retain the rights to the character in future applications. The publisher was also interested in trying to utilize the character in other types of media, graphic novels in particular. Not interested in taking on more than I could handle, I interviewed several well-recommended young illustrators, and we agreed to collaborate on the new side project, with the blessing of SolCor.

The first Minus graphic novel turned out far better than I had dreamed, with fantastic illustrations created by my new friend Dean Cameron. A recent graduate of the Art Institute of

Pittsburgh, Dean and I had first been introduced at a local art gallery in Rochester, *Gallery r*. Dean was part of a very memorable show called Comic Geniuses, in which six young illustrators displayed their unique styles of comic-book–style art. Some of the participants had already published graphic novels and comic books, but Dean had not yet been published when we met. I liked his strong, confident style of pen and ink renderings better than the other artists, and when I spoke to him, I just felt we connected. He was young, only 22 when we met, but he was very mature for his age and quite articulate. He recognized my name from having read the second book in the Minus series. It was very rewarding to know that one of my books had made a positive impact on such a fine person. He jumped at the idea of collaborating on a graphic novel, and we made plans to create some samples and discuss the particulars with the publisher. Once again, the people at SolCor trusted my judgment and green-lighted the new project.

After the graphic novel hit the market, things really changed. I was suddenly thrust into the spotlight, a bit more than I felt comfortable with. But the runaway success of the new book led to more exposure, more interviews and a somewhat "hipper" image for the franchise. SolCor worked with their European outlet to translate all of the Minus books as well as the new graphic novel into several languages for distribution throughout Europe and Asia. For some reason, the Japanese market absolutely loved the character, and we received offers from two Japanese animation studios to transform Minus into a televised cartoon show geared for young children.

My agent, who I had hired prior to signing my second contract, convinced me to hold off on allowing Minus to become an animated cartoon. He expressed some concern that the property could become regarded as overly commercial if we weren't careful which projects we approved. After reviewing demo tapes from the Japanese studios and pondering for a while, I came to the same conclusion and we declined both offers. We were all making enough income off the property, and we agreed that we should be careful to protect its integrity for the long haul.

About three years ago, I was at a convention for writers and publishers in San Diego, and I saw the work of a Canadian artist named Ian Trent. He only had one arm, but he was an amazingly talented animator. Using both traditional techniques and computers, he had developed a beautiful watercolor-style animation that was refreshingly fluid and alive. It struck me as possibly the perfect look for an animated version of the Minus character. Through his agent, who was at the convention, I arranged a meeting with him.

I traveled to his home/studio in Toronto to discuss some ideas. He was a bit of an eccentric character, but in a good way. He seemed distant and suspicious of me at first, but after a few hours, he came out of his shell and we did some great brainstorming together. He was apparently quite wealthy, thanks to a hefty inheritance, but he was also an exceptionally talented artist who sculpted, painted and created his own computer animations. He was already deeply involved in producing a short animated feature of his own creation, but he said he would consider developing a Minus the Imple animated short if I could allow him three months to finish his current project.

I was in no hurry whatsoever, so I told him I would contact him four months later. I funded the project myself after establishing a new corporation called sIMPLE Tales, Inc. The new corporation was created, in part, to produce the new animated short feature I was now determined to make with the help of Ian Trent. It was also intended to help young writers and artists get their work published. We hired Dominique away from SolCor to head up the internal production staff after receiving the blessing of their board, who knew that Dominique was looking to join forces with me. I still had contractual ties to SolCor and had no intention of breaking from them as long as they still wanted me to author additional projects. That business relationship is what all of my recent success was built upon, and I remained loyal to them.

We established our headquarters in Manhattan, where I now live. Violet had been studying Creative Writing at a college in Boston from 2003 through 2006, and she has been invaluable as an advisor on some of the recent Minus the Imple projects. She's developed into a very compelling writer and was eager to help me further develop the Minus character and his stories. Violet moved to the city last year, and sIMPLE Tales hired her as Editor and Creative Director. She interviews artists and writers who come to us for help and she makes recommendations to the rest of the production team. In a few years, we plan on having Violet take over my position as CEO. Due to her numerous contributions and charming diplomatic style, she's already won the enthusiastic support of the rest of our staff.

One day not long ago, Violet called me while I was en route to the office. It was early morning rush hour, and I was stuck in Manhattan traffic, so I was grateful for the call. Before I could ask how her morning was going, she blurted out, "Epitheliums." I asked what she was talking about, and she explained, "Dad, are you familiar with the term epitheliums?" I said I had no idea what it meant but that it sounded like a medical term to me. She replied, "Well, yeah, it is a medical term. My medical dictionary describes *epithelium* as follows: *'In humans, epithelium is classified as a primary body tissue, the other ones being connective tissue, muscle tissue and nervous tissue. In biology and medicine, epithelium is a tissue composed of a layer of cells. Epithelium lines both the outside (skin) and the inside cavities and lumen of bodies'....*"

I said, "Yeah, so what is this about, honey?" She responded, "Hold on, Dad. There's more. *'Epithelium functions include secretion, absorption, protection, transcellular transport, sensation detection, and selective permeability.'* Dad, when I typed the words 'Minus the Imple' into an online word descrambler, the top result it produced was the word *epitheliums*. It was the only word that used eleven of the thirteen letters, and it was alone atop the list of words that use the most letters from the name. I had to call you right away! Don't you think it's weird? I mean, the one word that pops to the top of the list is a word that basically refers to the tissue that permeates the human body. Of all things!"

It was strangely coincidental, at the very least. How is it that the one word produced by the online program is a word that has so much to do with the inner workings of the human body? I had grown to believe that the phenomenon of Minus has something to do with the human soul, and the one word that uses nearly every letter in the nickname is *epitheliums*. If the descrambler had produced a word that related to a mechanical device or a mineral, for example, it wouldn't have made the same impact. Violet went on to explain that she had just been messing around with the online descrambling program and was entering various words in an effort to test it out. She had entered 'Minus the Imple' at random. She had no real reason for doing it, but when the result was a word she didn't recognize, she looked it up.

There have been numerous coincidences like this throughout my life. I've given up trying to figure out what it all means or why things keep falling together. Maybe someone smarter than me will one day put all the clues together. For now, I just roll with it and marvel at the way Minus keeps entertaining me. Minus still exists somewhere deep within me, and I'm aware of him beneath the surface now and then, but I've mastered the subliminal ability to control him, and he has not made an appearance in many years. It's best this way since I'm getting too old to be chasing shadows. This past fall, we established a fund at Golisano Children's Hospital in Rochester. It's called *The Minus Fund for Children*, and we raise money to support research of many types of childhood illnesses. So much good has ultimately come from a story that accidentally sprang from the mind and soul of a simple man.

I still think of Annie quite often, even after the passage of so much time. For years I dated other women and never found anyone to make me forget her. There have even been a couple of lengthy relationships, but they never developed into what I hoped. That magical feeling I once felt with Annie could never be duplicated. So, at some point, I stopped trying.

I did locate Annie a few years ago, after some fruitless attempts to find her. Through the Internet I found a record of her and learned that she's living in North Carolina and has joined Dan's practice. She obviously switched careers at some point and is now also practicing holistic medicine at their successful and very impressive facility in North Carolina. Shortly after locating her, I sent her a letter via snail mail. I never received a response, so I tried reaching her via e-mail but was just as unsuccessful. Finally, a few months later, I mailed a brief letter to her brother. He didn't reply either. It's difficult for me to understand why neither will respond to me, but I have since given up any hope of reconnecting.

"It is what it is," as my father used to say.

Imple-logue: Mind the Gaps

The doctors tell me I have a brain deformity. About two months ago, I started to experience severe headaches, almost migraine intensity. For days on end I took painkillers and nothing helped. My doctor prescribed something stronger for me, but it didn't make a dent either. I finally scheduled an MRI on my head, and my son, Michael, drove me to the lab for the examination. My doctor scared the hell out of me by mentioning the word *tumor*. He kept saying he wanted to rule it out, but I wasn't very happy that the word came up at all. Maybe he just wanted to scare me into agreeing to show up for the test. If so, it worked. The headaches persisted and I had been losing a lot of sleep, so I went along with the test, hoping we could identify the problem.

The test itself was painless, of course, and I actually enjoyed being slowly inserted into the cylindrical device. The oddest thing was the sudden and startling reaction of the attendant during the exam. I was relaxing as best I could with the headache pounding away when, all of a sudden, he exclaimed "Wow!" Of course that was a bit alarming to me as I lay on my back inside the oversize metal drum. "Huh? What's that?!" I shouted over the strange knocking noises of the machine. The young man operating the apparatus told me, "Hang on a second. Just relax and hold still, please."

Once he reversed the mechanism and I re-emerged he turned the machine off. I asked him again, "What was that you said? Why did you say 'Wow!'?" He fumbled a sincere apology, saying he shouldn't have blurted anything out. He was "not supposed to do that." Still flat on my back upon the metal platform, I asked again, "What was it you saw?" He replied, "It's probably nothing, and you should talk to your doctor about it, but the gaps between the lobes of your brain are so unusually wide. It's just something I've never seen before, that's all."

245

Obviously he could see the images the MRI produced while the test was being conducted. Maybe because my head was throbbing so much I didn't have the strength to chew him out, but his reaction was very disconcerting. I knew he didn't intend to upset me, but I had to ask, "What does *that* mean?" His reply was, "You really need to talk to the doctors about it. I'm not authorized to evaluate the tests."

The doctors have not been much clearer about the details of my condition. They keep telling me they want to do more tests, but I doubt I'm going to oblige them. At this stage of my life, I'm not willing to undergo any more tests unless they're absolutely necessary. In recent days, the headaches have lessened, and I feel I'm on the way to recovery. Over the years, there have been very few clues as to what might have brought about the phenomenon of Minus. My childhood head trauma may possibly have triggered everything, but perhaps I've had a physiological abnormality since birth. My mother most likely drank alcohol throughout her pregnancy and there's also the history of mental illness in the family. My best guess is that these factors have somehow added up to create the phenomenon.

There will probably never be a definitive answer, but Minus is part of me, and I've grown to accept it. The other morning, sitting out on the balcony of my Manhattan apartment, I was enjoying my vanilla-flavored coffee, reading the newspaper and passing time by doing a word scramble puzzle. Just for laughs, I jotted the words *Minus the Imple* along the top of the page. Curious as to what words I might be able to make from them, I stumbled onto something peculiar. When I reshuffled all of the letters in the three words, they formed four different complete words: *I must help mine.* It caused me to pause and look back upon the difficulty of my divorce. Back in 1988, it was the realization that I was not just living for myself that finally brought me clarity and bolstered my resolve. The image of my young daughter had appeared at a critical time to save me from

246

myself. *I must help mine* are words that will carry special meaning for the rest of my days.

The mysterious concept of the human soul may never be fully understood. After many years of introspection and discovery, I'm convinced that our individual souls are a combination of what we are given at birth along with elements of other people's souls. We leave a permanent impression of who we are and what we believe with every person we encounter. And, likewise, they return the favor. The deeper we touch another's soul, the more lasting influence we leave with them.

My wonderful grandmother passed on to me her peaceful humility and unwavering faith. My mother gave me an appreciation of unconditional love. From my father, I learned the power of self-confidence and the value of being in the moment. My children awakened my understanding of selflessness and nurturing. Father Gil demonstrated the incredibly powerful value of friendship and trust. Annie brought me an awareness of what true love can really feel like. And so many others have left me with an endless string of priceless life lessons. My soul may have been primarily established at birth, a combination of the codes of my ancestors, but it has been shaped and modified by interactions and experiences throughout the course of my life. I am who I am because of the influences of all who have touched my soul and left their indelible imprints upon me.

We are part of the greater combined soul of all humanity. We awaken various elements of understanding and illumination only when we open ourselves to other people. The key is to participate, to risk, to integrate and to truly live. The collective soul is all-powerful, and that is what I believe to be the true "higher power." We each represent just one cell of that greater entity. Good or evil, living or dead, the energy is very real and alive, and you and I are part of it whether we want to be or not. All those who have come before are still part of it because they live on in some form or another within our memories. Their influence contributes to our actions, so they are still participants in the very real world in which we live. Each one of us is powerful in our own right, and we have an obligation to learn, share, grow and love. Striving to unlock our potential makes us stronger, richer and wiser. We grow by risking, by giving and by demonstrating faith. Only by trusting and believing can we truly become enlightened and nurture our souls. We are all just works in progress, from the day we're born until the end of time. I often say things like, "I'm just a nobody," but I don't really mean that in a literal sense. Just as you are, I am somebody special. I am strong and unbreakable because I decided long ago that I was worth fighting for. It's my duty to defend my right to exist and thrive, and I consider it my obligation to continue improving myself until I reach the highest ground.

Minus is not only a reflection of my soul but also a messenger. At one time I feared for my mental health, but it was Minus who helped bring clarity and resolve back to my life. The desire and determination to trust in myself and find the inner strength needed to rebuild my life ultimately paid off for my entire family. Instead of selfishly destroying myself, I embraced my responsibility and made something good from a seemingly desperate situation. Anything worthwhile is difficult in some sense, and I simply decided that my children and I were worthwhile.

It was love, after all, that brought me back from the brink.

My son and daughter are presently healthy and thriving, and that's all that really matters to me. They have also grown to accept Minus as part of our lives because I've shared all the stories with them over the years. My life's journey hasn't always been pleasant or easy, but I honestly wouldn't change a thing. Some things never add up, and other things that seem impossible sometimes work out better than you ever dreamed. In many ways I feel I've lived a semi-charmed life. To celebrate my appreciation for all my blessings, I recently went and got my first tattoo: a single word spelled out along the inside of my left forearm.

It simply reads "P R I V I L E G E D."

The End

UNUSUAL EFFUSION